ACKNOWLEDGEMENTS

I am eternally grateful to the wonderful people who helped me through this journey.

To the lovely Janet Dulan-Jones for mentoring me at the beginning and giving me the confidence to start it. To Rebecca Rennie for dragging me along editing, formatting and giving me the discipline to finish it. To Alex Welch for his help and enthusiasm in pushing it along. To James Anderson for his insight and imagination which made it readable and finally to my wife, Sandi for having the patience to read it over and over again.

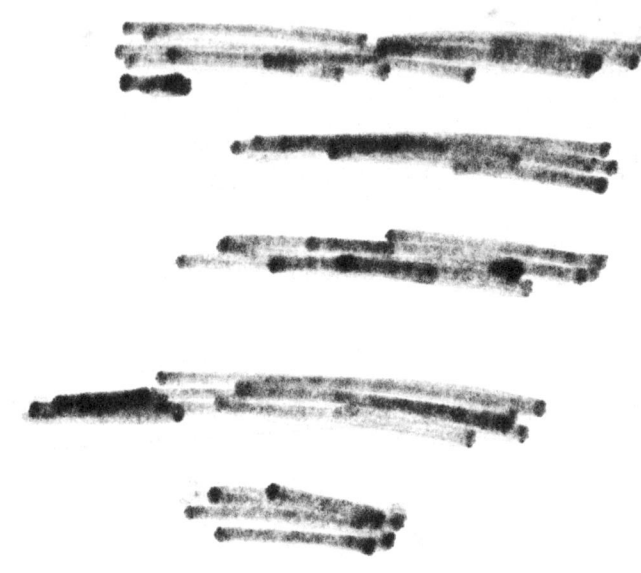

WHATEVER HAPPENED TO OLIVER TWIST?

Chapter 1

The night of my wife's funeral was eventful to say the least. The wake, as poorly attended as it was, had finished and the mourners had retired for the night, but I was agitated. I decided to go for a walk to clear my head but was all too easily drawn to a drinking den I knew.

I entered the noisy, smoke-filled public house. It was rowdy and filled with all manner of life's flotsam and jetsam revelling in the prospect of a New Year. I pushed through the throng and went to fill a gap vacated by the previous customer just as a stocky lad wedged himself betwixt myself and the bar. I looked around to see if anyone else had witnessed his rudeness. In the corner, I noticed a well-dressed couple. They looked as out of place as a fox in a hen house but vaguely familiar to me. The stout fellow was shouting to this group behind him about the storm in the Black Sea and how the rations and clothing had been sunk. "Our boys are going to struggle this winter," he shouted. I became impatient. The stocky oik was searching his pocket for some pennies to pay for his ale. And then I bristled as he turned to his friends and said:

"I see the bloody Russians got a pasting last week."

"The only good Russian is a dead Russian," came the comment from the back.

"Get out of the way you miserable oaf!" I ordered, and the scruffy lad turned to face me:

"Who're you are calling a' oaf, pretty boy!" he slurred and swung at me with his right fist. I stepped back as he swung again with his left. "I've spilt my beer you toe-rag," he bellowed, as he threw another punch. I swung back crashing my fist into his jaw. This seemed to generate more energy from my foe, who immediately sent out a flurry of punches the like of which I had not received since my days fagging for the Harrow school bully, Welch, each punch precisely landing on various parts of my face. My lip was split, my left eye swollen and blood dripping from

3

my nose. Stars were circling in my vision. Surprised by my assailant's aggression, I grabbed a pewter pot from the bar and swung wildly. Another flurry of punches were returned, and I began to sink to the floor. I held up my hand in surrender. "I yield!" I implored as my pot was now spinning on the floor.

"Yield my arse, you're not at school now!" and he landed another precisely aimed punch to my windpipe. I was poleaxed and dropped to my knees, clutching at my throat gasping for air. I saw my adversary pull back his filthy worn hobnail boot and crash it into my unprotected gut. My assailant then turned and nonchalantly ordered another beer while two burly onlookers rushed to my aid by unceremoniously tossing me into the filthy street outside. I recovered after a few horse-drawn cabs had trotted past splashing me with urine and horse-arse water. While still on my hands and knees, I looked up as the well-dressed couple I had noticed before walked past rm and tutted as they looked down at me wallowing in the filthy mire, I stumbled to the river to contemplate my position. Oh! The misery—the misery of life. I am a surgeon for God's sake. Of all people, I should have been able to save her. How could I, with my medical skillset, using every tool at my disposal—leeches, poultices, lotions and liquor and every concoction of herbs I knew—still find myself utterly helpless in the face of Anna's sickness?

I felt myself travelling back through the fields of my memories especially the weeks after the tragedy, to a time when guilt festered in my heart and slithered down into my gut to roll over and over on the seasick waves of time.

The decaying leaves crunched under my boots crisp now with hoar frost. The New Year revellers were making their way home, steam on their breath as they slurred their farewells "Happy New Year! Happy 1855!" and I was at the end of a long binge. The city was only just stirring itself from slumber. The sun was rising over St Paul's Cathedral to the east. A dog barked and barked.

The inebriated voice of a singer, accompanied by an equally intoxicated accordionist, waded through the putrid air, over the surface of the river and onto the north bank. Somewhere in the distance, a cockney fishwife scolded her drunken, lazy, good-for-nothing bastard of a bloody 'usband. I looked up toward the hazy yellow sun, where a passing cloud caught my eye. It looks like Anna, I thought. Is she beckoning me to join her? Or signalling me to stay? High above Anna's drifting apparition, wisps of feathered cloud floated by, foreshadowing the storm due later in the day.

My tears burned. The end of my nose was swollen, ripe and red as a plum. Spittle threads crisscrossed my mouth and in one uncontrollable spasm I lurched forward to dry retch. It may have been the stench—or a cocktail of grief, or gin withdrawal.

After some reflection, my diagnosis grew more certain. I was suffering from an acute human sickness, exacerbated by chronic bouts of self-loathing, which had been forced upon a lifelong weak constitution. I had never known, or experienced since, such emptiness, such a gut-wrenching twist of sorrow. My beautiful wife was gone, taken only weeks before she was due to deliver our baby girl.

Unlike me, Anna was always kind to the poor. In those days, however, I loathed and abhorred every little grubby flea upon the impoverished, and odorous shanty homes, filthy habits and pitiful hygiene. I knew, better than most, how dirty and small those urchins' lives were, for I myself had been raised amongst them, and my disdain for all things squalid had spread within me like a fungus.

How had Anna's gentle compassion been rewarded? With the gift of morbid death, drowning in her own lung fluid, that's how. Such was the immensity of the prize she contracted from the very peasants she had worked so hard to help. Tears of doom welled up from deep within the pit of my stomach, heaving with them a pain so acute that, as I sobbed into my handkerchief, I barely knew whether the snot I blew out was made of salty tears or bile. How gut-wrenching my despair was.

5

I crossed the path from the bench to the riverbank and looked down into the broth of raw sewage which bobbed back and forth upon the surface of the river. I watched in disgust as the nearby barges

vomited their waste into the water. A noxious vapour rose from the organic filth, rotting all beauty from its core. The pungency of that stench was too much to bear. I could hardly take a breath without the miasma causing me to gag. Had I fallen so low? Was this cesspit my final destiny?

As the sun continued to rise, it gave the Thames an appearance of a golden ribbon slowly flowing to the estuary, which belied its filthy and dangerous contents. I recalled Vladimir, my best friend and a brilliant Russian student, who had introduced me to his sister at School Founders' Day, which was the day Vladimir received his prize for science. His father, Professor Georgie Sawinov, and Anna had only recently moved to London when the professor took up his position as Lead Surgeon at St Bartholomew's Hospital. Anna was an elegant, beautiful and sophisticated young woman.

Later that week, Anna and I had wandered around the Royal Metropolitan Museum, and she enlightened me on several Russian exhibits. Her tone took on an unusual blend of formal professionalism whilst remaining friendly. "Now, this is a classic example of the kind of uniform worn by a Russian soldier of low rank," she informed me.

"The fabric is of such inferior quality. Doesn't look to me like he would run too far in that," I quipped. She crinkled her nose up and giggled at my half-cocked seduction.

"Someone of your physique would manage," she said. I did my best to disguise my blush. Was she flirting with me?

"Ah, now, this is more like it," she continued. "The uniform of a Captain would look dashing upon the likes of you."

Yes, she most certainly was.

My head was in a swirl; I didn't know quite how to respond.

"The uniform of an enemy? I think not," I winked.

She laughed, but only a little, for the joke was a pathetic attempt at disguising my awkward attraction to her and not so funny; we both knew it. I was positively swooning—in quite a muddle. So mesmerised was I by her easy manner and seductive accent, that I barely listened to a word she said. At one stage, she scolded me for my inattention and took my hand in hers. My palm instantly softened around her tiny fingers. I never wanted to let it go.

Soon enough, our innocent handholding evolved until we found ourselves arm in arm. That very night, we kissed the first of many long kisses and later that same year, I mustered up the courage to ask Anna's father for her hand in marriage. I was terrified but Anna's father was as kindly as his daughter. Of course, Vladimir, was best man at our wedding.

Now Anna was gone and, like a thread of memories swirling around the spindle of a spinning-wheel, I relived those tragic, final days spent accompanying her on her charitable sojourns. I had watched her hand out parcels of food and clothing to the street urchins who thronged around her. Both my protective instinct and my disgust kicked in when they'd hover too close, and I'd swipe at them with my stick or lash out with a boot. She would admonish me and then forgive me, for she knew my own roots were the same as the urchins that I now abhorred.

As I reminisced by the misty river with my cut lip, swollen eye, aching throat and covered in filth, I shuffled closer to the edge, summoning up the courage to end it all. Inch by miserable inch, I was going to do it. I really was about to take the last step. One last breath and I'd plunge myself into the freezing mire.

At that moment I heard a jingle to my left, and I became aware of a cloaked woman on the shoreline a mere thirty yards downstream. She glanced around before walking slowly away from me. It was the same woman I had seen in the bar and who had tutted as I lay in the gutter.

I was distracted and walked towards her, but my dizziness and the shale underfoot hindered my progress. There was something glinting in the early light, scintillating as it twizzled and swung in her hand and then she dropped it.

"Hold on, you've dropped something."

She stiffened at the sound of my hailing and hastened her pace, clutching the collar of her hooded cloak, and walked briskly towards a waiting carriage. The carman in the black Hansom cab shook his head of strewn, wiry hair and blew into the cup of his frozen hands. A bellow of vapour shrouded the rugged features of his well-worn face, one which had clearly been battered by a lifetime exposed to rough gales and fierce sunshine. "It's done," she said, climbing into the cab.

The driver flicked the reins and startled the piebald horse into a trot with a sharp click of his tongue. Another face appeared at the cab window. I fancied that I saw none other than the ghost of Fagin looking back at me! Was I glaring at a mirage from the past? Was I really in such a deluded state? Fagin! The man who took me in and then ran me in his gang of nippers stealing from the rich and fencing our ill-gotten gains. I shook my head to clear it.

The instant he saw me; he sat back out of view and banged on the cab ceiling. Another flick of the reins and the horse broke into a canter, vanishing into a swirl of mist. I was dumbfounded. After all, Fagin had been hanged at Tyburn gallows some eighteen years earlier. Surely I had imagined him?

I was staring, aghast and vacant, trying to take it all in when I caught a glint in the very spot where the woman had walked a moment before. She had dropped a gold-coloured chain on the gritty foreshore. I drew closer. This was very curious. My suicidal thoughts were put to one side; the river could wait. Despite the mist and my teared-up eyes, I was able to make out the object.

It was an ornate, gold-linked chain I would say about eight inches long with a button stop on one end and a silver pendant on the other. On the pendant was the masonic emblem but the eye in the centre had been replaced by an emerald stone about the size of my thumb! That will be worth a pretty penny, I thought. I could buy a few more drinks with that. My suicide bid to join my beloved would have to wait another day.

Ten minutes later I was on my way home, walking in a daze through St James Park and inspecting my newfound treasure. As I entered the Bayswater Road and spotted my less than welcoming grey house, I noticed that someone had perched a lost glove upon my beautiful newly painted railings. I was utterly disgusted. I pinched the glove by the end of its grubby finger and tossed the thing back into the gutter where it belonged and mounted the steps to my home

After Mrs Bedwin had retired a few years before, the new housekeeper was promoted in the Brownlow house. Mrs McNeil was short and corpulent—strong as an ox but always loving. Her soft Edinburgh accent lilted when she spoke, and she sang as sweetly as a ptarmigan. She had a naturally quiet and caring countenance. Her demonstrative affection for me was always warm, and she tended to my various minor wounds with some cotton and dabbed my cuts with iodine. It hurt her deeply to see how far I had recently fallen. Nonetheless, she didn't hesitate to tick me off when she felt I was out of line. Having devoted her entire life in service to my benefactor, she had never had children herself. Mrs McNeil had travelled from Edinburgh's slums at the age of fifteen and arrived in London on the back of a slow, horse-drawn hay wain. London's streets were filled with people cheering and dancing that day, for news had come in from Flanders about the success of Arthur Wellesley and the British and Prussians over Boney. Mrs McNeil started work as a scullery maid in the Brownlow house and steadily worked her way through the household as each position became vacant. Due to an ever-decreasing budget and spiralling costs, the Brownlow household was made up of only three staff: Mrs McNeil, Mrs Simpson (the cook) and my valet and footman, Mango Claggage.

I examined my new prize, a mysterious item indeed. The back of the pendant was decorated in the eastern fashion. The button stopper was also decorated which I thought unusual for such a practical piece. But the gemstone was the main source of my joy as it was a beautifully cut emerald, unbelievably valuable indeed. It practically glimmered with life, as if the entire season of spring had nestled inside it to wait for its rescue from winter. I placed the chain upon the sideboard.

"Master," she paused, "err, where exactly did you get this?"

Missing out the less flattering morsels of my story thus far I elaborated on a chance discovery whilst taking a healthy morning stroll. I'm not sure she really believed most of what I had related, especially as my eye had swollen considerable and there was blood all over my shirt, but after the last few weeks she was used to my appearance and merely let out a sigh. She placed it delicately back on the sideboard. Mango, my footman, came in and stood by the sideboard. He had overheard the conversation. I paid him no heed. But I despaired at his scruffy appearance, even in his fine household livery he looked a mess.

I poured myself a whisky from the lead-cut glass decanter on my little oak table, mixing it with a drop of water to stretch out the flavour. A haunting backdraft from the storm outside moaned through the chimney. It was so powerful that it sent the flames blue and almost extinguished the fire. The hearth crackled and brightened yellow regaining enough vigour to spit out the embers onto the fireguard.

Some hours earlier, Professor Sawinov had sent a message to me telling me he might visit today. He was one of the foremost doctors from St Petersburg and had been my medical mentor. There was much commotion in the hallway when he arrived because Mango attempted to take his hat and coat but failed as the professor refused to hand over the items to my incompetent employee. After all, my father-in-law had visited many times and knew the items would be lost, misplaced or even borrowed by Mango.

We stood and discussed my future. "It was a fitting service," he started as he inspected my superficial cuts and bruises. "Vladimir would approve I suppose," I replied.

"I am sure he would, but I'm not sure he even knows Anna and your baby have died," he said. I looked at him and realised that he was in even more despair than myself. "Forgive me, but I don't understand why he could not refuse the order to go to the Crimea."

The professor had ambled over to the mantlepiece and was now inspecting my newly found trinket. "If I taught him anything it was his duty to his country. Of course he would never refuse. I too would go, but these old bones in that winter would be the death of me. But your behaviour this evening concerns me. Brawling in public! You should be ashamed of yourself, and your drinking is getting out of hand." I felt aggrieved to be admonished in my own house, so I impudently retorted, "You are only here because of your friends in the masons who persuaded the home office to give you a visa."

"I am here, Oliver, because Mr Brownlow was my friend and asked me to watch over you after his passing, you will need to buck up. This house needs strong leadership, not the antics of a drunk!"

I hadn't seen my mentor so agitated in many a year. He slammed the pendant back on the mantlepiece and turned. "Please Oliver you have to straighten yourself out. It's getting late and we've all had an arduous day. I will return this evening to check for infection. I bid you farewell." And Professor Sawnov left. I called out "See the professor out, Claggage." But Mango was nowhere to be seen. With a sigh at his dereliction, I led the Professor to the front door. Now I could hear the clumsy oaf in the next room. "Claggage!" I shouted, "clear the glasses from the drawing room."

I decided to inspect my new acquisition again. However, when I went to the mantlepiece, the chain and pendant were gone!

11

I was too overwhelmed to sleep that evening.

I lay in bed staring at the ornate ceiling. Who was that woman by the shore? Had I really seen Fagin eighteen years after his hanging? As I pondered the ramifications of this most peculiar unravelling of circumstances, I wondered about the pendant. I was certain I had left it on the sideboard. Where was it now? I jumped out of bed and went to the drawing room. Perhaps Mrs McNeil had placed it in Anna's now nearly empty jewellery box (for I had pawned many of the more exclusive items to pay for my drinking and gambling and her funeral). I searched the floor behind the curtain and beneath the chair in the corner of the room, but it was gone. I suspected Mango may have borrowed it to add to his glittering collection of studs, buttons, pins and rings that he had in his secret stash that he didn't know I knew about. I would retrieve it in the morning.

Chapter 2

Three days had passed since that fateful morning by the river. Yet another miserable, windy night in January. The clock on the mantlepiece chimed seven—time for a drink. The rain pounded down on my slate roof with a ferocity that amplified my grief despite all efforts to assuage such pathos with gin.

The tat-tat of our front door's brass-knocker startled me out of my reverie. I ignored the sound as best I could, perhaps Mango would see to it. Another knock, perhaps Mango would do what I paid him to do in any way and returned to the job at hand of reading *The Times*.

I reminisced about my youth before I was taken in. Perhaps, since I was feeling sorry for myself, I could take it out on the useless footman I was saddled with. It's all bloody Mango's fault, I thought randomly. Or Fagin's. Yes, it was Fagin, he is the architect of my downward spiral. I remembered the streets at Seven Dials stealing 'kerchiefs and purses for my gang leader.

Mrs McNeil popped her head around the door.

"Is anything wrong?" she asked with just a hint of compassion.

"No, no, everything is fine, thank you Mrs McNeil." She knew that I would never admit to possessing such shortcomings.

A barrage of hard knocks followed. This was no tree branch. This was a deliberate attempt to irritate me. "Where the bloody hell is Claggage?"

"Get the bloody door, Mango!" I shouted, but he had already headed for the servant's entrance and started calling out to no-one through the streaming rain.

I slammed the glass down and grabbed a smoking oil lamp from the sideboard. I stumbled along the cold, clay tiles in my bare feet, cursing Mango's ineptitude as I went.

The lamp gave off a yellow aura which cast an ever-changing silhouette against the hallway walls, making me appear like a looming phantom. The irony of this was not lost on me—if I were indeed a demon, I was haunting none other than myself.

I often studied Mr Brownlow's portrait on my way to the front door. My late benefactor had been so dear to me, so generous. I paused and nodded to him. He had given me every opportunity to succeed, and yet here was I, shamelessly wasting the lot of it. Failing him and myself. Despite his stern demeanour, it depicted him as a jolly man with a twinkle in his eye. The portrait was rather flattering, I must say—no disrespect intended. He carried a book, of course—literature being his greatest passion—called *Universal Rictual*. It was the very same book he had given me after my investiture as a Freemason.

And then I noticed the watch chain on his waistcoat had an almost imperceptible gold set-square at the end of it. Its appendages crossed the open arms of a drawing-compass to form a hollow square. The entire figure sat within one single staring eye, which resided within the hinge at the bend of a drawing compass. It was remarkably similar to the one I had found, lost and found again in Mango's stash.

As was always my reflex when I passed this painting, I extracted my watch chain from my pocket and twirled the family heirloom between my fingers mirroring him, as if in homage to my two greatest influences. I call it a family heirloom but, in truth, I had lost the original piece in a card game some weeks before and been forced to purchase a new one (when my fortunes temporarily improved) from the nearest Masonic lodge shop on Queen Street.

The door knocker clanged again, even louder this time.

"Who's there?" Mango yelled from the far side of the house. "Who's there?"

I sighed at his daftness, drew the bolt across and opened the front door to a bedraggled boy.

He was barely ten years old and soaked from head to foot. His torn clothing was soddening through, reminding me of my own shabby rags when I first arrived in London all those years ago.

"Yes?" I said.

"Begging your pardon, sir, but I have a message for a Dr Twist."

"I am Dr Twist," I replied curtly.

"My master asked that you join him in the Fortune of War tavern. Do you know it?"

"Of course, I know it. I trained at Bart's. And who might your master be? Certainly, no gentlemen, to send a young lad out on such a night."

"My master is no gent, sir, but he's insisting you see him. He says you'd be more likely to turn up if I mention the name Fagin."

The hair prickled upon my neck. "Fagin," I whispered, blanching. A swamp of forgotten horrors flooded through me. "Fagin, you say?" Now I really was intrigued. "What do you know of Fagin?" I came in close to the boy's face. "That man is long dead. He was hanged these eighteen years since. What's your name, boy?"

"Rocco, sir. My master told me that's what you'd say, sir, and so he bids me tell you that Fagin lives, sure as eggs is eggs. You're to meet my master at the Fortune of War tavern, soon as you get this 'ere message." The boy stepped forward, pushed a folded piece of paper into my hand, tugged his cap and ran off towards Bond Street. He ran to a cab parked next to a dimly lit gas lamp. The wind wailed and the rain fell in sheets. A shadowy, moustached face emerged from the cab's window and tossed the boy a coin.

"'Fanks' mister," the boy shouted before darting around the corner in the direction of Lancaster Gate. I shut the door in a bewildered stupor and headed for the drawing-room.

I placed the lamp back on the sideboard, raised my whiskey glass, tossed back a slug and unfolded the note.

It read:

To: Detective J Dawkins.

From: Captain Arthur Connelly.
Scotland Yard.
Intelligence Officer.
London
6th Bengal Cavalry.
British East Indian Company
15 May 1854

Re your enquiry to wit one QMC Fagin

Sir,

I can confirm an arrest warrant is still outstanding on Quartermaster Corporal Major Fagin about the theft of great personal wealth and importance from Her Highness Maharani of Jammu.

Additionally, between 1810 and 1823, Fagin acted as clerk to the Quartermaster of The Leicestershire Regiment. During this time, he was responsible for the accounting of a vast fortune in gold, silver and precious stones liberated from the many moguls throughout the Punjab, Jammu, and Kashmir regions. Given the information you gave me, it is not beyond the realms of fantasy that Fagin had amassed an absolute fortune.

He was last seen escaping from Jammu on an elephant in May 1823. There are several reports of sightings of him in Tehran and, Sevastopol .

Yours aye

Fagin amassed a fortune. How could it possibly be true? He is living. And the fortune? Would it still be there? Why would someone try to involve me in this most unlikely plot? What could I possibly have to offer? Is this some elaborate confidence trick? Perhaps linked to the elaborate pendant, was it from the treasures? It definitely looked Indian

Curiosity had me by the collar. I prepared myself at once to cross London, donning my green tweed cloak, taking my sword-cane in hand and throwing on my Brown Derby hat. I tapped my wallet and flipped open my Hunter. Twenty past seven. I tucked the watch back into my waistcoat pocket, ensuring the note was secured in my inside pocket.

"I'm going out, Mrs McNeil," I called up the vast Georgian stairs. "Do not wait up."

Mango emerged from the scullery covered from head to toe in silver polish chalk. His hands and face were black as the silver cloth he carried.

"Oh dear," I said, shaking my head. There was not enough time to wait for him to clean himself up and saddle my horse. And in any case, looking thus, Mango would have spooked the poor beast. "You stay here, Mango," I told him.

He mumbled something-or-other back at me, but I had neither the time nor the patience to decipher it. I stepped out into the winter gale. A woollen scarf had been knotted around the top my railings this time.

"Will these people never stop?" I cursed, as I dragged the wet clump off the spike and chucked it into the road. A blanket of cloud disgorged its cargo upon London and especially me. I pulled my hat down about my ears, drew the cloak up over my neck and held my collar to my throat as I dragged myself along the Bayswater Road towards the city.

I hailed a cab. And a little later, we pulled up outside the tavern. Here, drunk abattoir workers and cattle drovers, loud and raucous countryfolk, milled around in the street. It was a foul place, full of

London's riffraff. The stench of beer and livestock manure permeated the air.

No matter how tentatively I trod, there was no way of avoiding the faeces, but I soon found myself a tiny sterile island. I turned and flipped a silver shilling to the cabman. He caught it and studied it for a moment before slipping it into his sock and clicking his tongue for his horse to move on.

I hopped from one raised cobble to the next to avoid soiling my shoes. Two unfortunate inebriates were asleep, propped up against the wall on their backsides, with their legs in the mire. A wall of sound hit me as I entered the Fortune of War—endless cursing, toothless women, cackling hags turning tricks for a tanner at every turn. The smoke of cheap tobacco-pipes clogged the air. Beer swilled and spilled. A punch was thrown here, another there. An empty seat with a sign reading Reserved for E. Barthelemy took pride of place at the end of a particularly rowdy table where a singer, accompanied by a dismally played harmonica, was so discordant and drunk that he forgot the words to his song and was promptly booed off the table. I hadn't entered such premises in many years; it was a familiar world from a lifetime ago.

I had the vague sense that I was being watched and as I turned around, a man emerged through the haze of smoke. He wore an ill-fitting brown suit over an off-white shirt. He reached out to pinch my upper arm, and I stiffened.

"Relax, Dr Twist," the man said, "we're all friends here." He leant in closer, baring his black, tobacco-stained teeth. His breath reeked of cheroot, forcing me to lean away. "Go through that door and up the staircase," he instructed. "I will secure the foot of the stairs to stop anyone entering. You're safe here."

Safe? I wholeheartedly doubted it. How foolish to have left Mango behind.

As my unwilling feet carried me up the stairs, each step sang a

18

signature note—one bellowed low, like the drawn-out groan of a creaking ship; another rang high-pitched and shrill like a fish crow. That stairwell could have woken the devil himself from slumber.

There was no harmony in it, and my skin crawled to imagine what or who awaited me on the first floor. The place stank of stale urine, and the banister was sticky with crud. My eye-line met with the base of a door. A yellow candle flickered through the gap and the shadow of two feet shifted on the floor behind it.

I lifted the latch and pushed the old, oak door open. The smell of tallow-fat candles and black-spot mould were first to invade my nostrils, triggering flashbacks of my desperate childhood. The worst of it, however, was the leaden weight of dread which loomed as the all-too-familiar mixture of dry rot and lilies hit the back of my nose. Lilies were the smell of death to me. The room was so gloomy, its furnishings so cracked and chipped, that I couldn't help envisioning the objects as ghosts themselves; like strewn bodies of brothers in arms and all that remained of their dashed dreams on Wellington's battlefields. The mild trembling which rippled through my core caught me quite off-guard.

Chapter 3

I estimated the room to be fifteen feet across and about twenty feet in length. A threadbare rug lay in the centre, beneath the table, covering about half the room and leaving wooden floorboards around the perimeter. The window opposite the table was shut. A set of tattered, red curtains flanked the misted-up glass. A small fire crackled, offering up ample warmth for such a room.

A dresser with one missing drawer stood by the nearest wall and beside it, a single wardrobe with a broken door. A small mirror stood on the mantel and a portrait of a racehorse hung on the wall by the door. The mildewy wallpaper was peeling and the architrave, which was once (undoubtedly) white, had turned brown over the years.

A crash from the tavern below broke the eerie stillness, making me jump a foot deeper into the room. It was then that I noticed the rickety metal-framed bed, covered in a garish-coloured bedspread and roughly folded patchwork quilts, with a bedraggled old man in a grey nightshirt on the edges of it. The figure was hunched over a spittoon which placed between his naked legs. He hacked a phlegm ball up and spat it out, making the candle on the table by the bed flutter. The spittoon sounded a ping.

The fierce rain battered down upon the skylight. A porcelain bowl sat aside a chipped water jug near a washstand. Both the bowl and jug were decorated with painted meadow flowers. It seemed a strange place to keep such delicate washing accoutrements, but the plink, plink, plink which echoed across the room indicated that they had been placed there strategically to catch drops from an evidently long-established roof-leak. The water had sat there for so long that it was green with algae. Another leak was collected in a stained chamber pot near the end of the bed.

The old man struggled up off the bed and teetered over to me. "Welcome, Oliver," he said. I recognised Fagin's voice and thick Yiddish accent at once. "Fagin," I gasped, "as I live and breathe!"

"Yes, the old Fagin also lives and breathes," he smirked. "I haven't done the dance of the gibbet yet, my boy." He hawked up another phlegm ball. "Come in. Come in." He wiped his lips and shuffled closer. Towering over me in that small room, he stretched his long arm around my shoulder and guided me to a stool by the table in the centre of the room. With a wide, sweeping gesture, he directed me to sit. "How are you, Oliver?"

Fagin bent in toward me. I had no choice but to look directly into his face and was shocked by the state of it. The half-light cast an unforgiving shadow to be sure, but the last eighteen years had certainly taken a heavy toll. He was a caricature of himself, with a sallow face and deep black eye-sockets framed by unwieldy, overgrown brows. Deep crevices were gouged into his former laughter lines. Fagin had lost a great deal of hair, though large clumps were sprouting from both his ears and his familiar hooked nose, which had grown even longer than I remembered it. His cheeks were sunken in, and his blackened teeth resembled a witch-doctor's necklace. Those old, needle-like fingers were now capped with sharp, discoloured nails, under which months, perhaps years, of grime had collected.

"What do you want with me, Fagin?" I asked, in no mood for Fagin's games.

"Doctor Twist, isn't it? The surgeon now, I am told. But why so cold, Oliver, why so untrusting? Didn't I always do right by you?"

"Do right by me? Really? You think so?" I could barely look at him and dared not hold his gaze for longer than I needed.

"Of course, lad, of course. How is your family?"

I winced. "Get to the point, Fagin. You don't care one jot about my family. Why am I here?"

"Remember, Oliver, when you were in the Jago, and I' gather you boys around to share tales of riches I had collected on my travels?"

21

"Yes, yes, I recall your fairy tales," I scoffed. "What is it you want me to do for you?"

"It's not what you can do for me; it is what I can do for you."

I laughed. "What can you do for me?"

He began to unbend and, much to my horror, started scratching and picking at his temples, peeling the flaky flesh away before plucking the hair around his unkempt brows. I sat in stunned amazement as he removed a set of false teeth, shook off a straggly bald wig and ripped a wispy beard from his chin. I watched transfixed as he wiped a layer of stage makeup from his face with an alcohol-doused rag and revealed a man in his mid-thirties. The man began to unwind, blossoming from that hunched-over creature into a strapping fellow some six foot two inches in height.

"Hello, Oliver, me ol' pal," he said. He had discarded the Yiddish brogue and adopted a cockney accent, in no way proper nor educated. Knock me down with a feather! Was it Jack Dawkins himself, or yet another manifestation by this cruel trickster?

My jaw must have dropped a foot before I got a grip on myself. "Jack Dawkins! It's you? Were…were you…?" I already knew the answer. "You were Fagin the other morning too!" I exclaimed. "Dawkins indeed, to this very day, what a talented fellow you are!" He stood, crossed to me and embraced me like a long-lost brother. Then he stood back, smiled and nodded in affirmation.

I reached into my pocket for the note, but it was gone. I checked for my wallet in my other pocket. Gone. It wasn't until I felt around for my Hunter watch and chain that I noticed Jack's fingers, which were twizzling the items between them. It seemed he'd lost none of his guile.

"Little has changed then, Jack," I laughed. In honesty, I was ashamed he had fooled me so easily. The disguise had been good, but it was by no means fool-proof. How had I missed it?

I blamed the low light, Jack's expertly applied makeup and his equally expert impression of Fagin's accent. In a way, I missed Fagin, the old crook. My gin-soaked logic had added to the confusion, no doubt, but overall, Jack Dawkins had made a very plausible Fagin indeed.

"On the contrary, everything changes. What's more, everything is about to change for you," Dawkins said, a cheeky glint in his eye. He sat down opposite me and handed the stolen articles back. Something was missing.

"What about the note?" I asked.

"Ah, the note was simply my insurance to get you here. It's government property, you see. Listen, Oliver, do you remember sitting around and listening to Fagin after supper when he used to talk about that buried treasure and how one day, we'd all end up rich?"

"Yes, of course I do. All tales, with not a pennyweight of truth in 'em," I replied.

"No, no. Quite the contrary. They're true and this note proves it," Dawkins continued. "It turned out that Fagin was an accountant for the East India Company. Whilst he was there, he seems to have siphoned a little here, a little there, from each account he was in charge of." Dawkins relaunched into his (very passable) impression of Fagin as he recounted the story.

"There was so much loot. Whenever Fagin was preparing to scarper, the company would move on, only to gain yet one more new account somewhere else—each one more valuable than the last.

"Fagin gathered enough on which to retire and was about to flee when his office received orders to move to the newly conquered provincial capital of Kashmir.

So, Fagin buried his fortune in the caves of Jammu and prepared to go with his company to Kashmir. Unfortunately for Fagin, he became somewhat distracted by the Maharani in Jammu and they embarked on a steamy affair.

They eventually conceived and she was forced to have the baby in secret." He then surprised me by adding, "You know that girl, Oliver."

"Hello, Oliver," a woman's voice said, and I turned around. Unbeknownst to me a lady had silently entered the room without my noticing and stealthily positioned herself on a seat in a recess behind the door. She wore a smart beige day dress made of high-quality striped silk. It had puff-ball sleeves and a collar which covered her throat. There was something familiar about her. I couldn't place why, at first, but then the cloaked silhouette lunged out of the recesses of my mind—it was the lady by the shore who had dropped the pendant and fled.

"Fagin seized me when he fled India—"

"—with Thuggees and half the East India Company chasing him," Dawkins added.

"Remember me? We ran together in the Seven Dials gang. Back then I was half your age."

"My God, Pia! Pia how are you?"

"I'm surprised you remember me, Oliver. I was so small, and you were so"

She held her hand out and I stood to walk over and shake it. She had grown into a beguiling young woman, taller than average and probably around twenty-eight years old. Her mane of black hair glimmered in the candlelight as it tumbled halfway down her back. "We went to Kabul first, then on to Sevastopol, where we holed up until I was six. Then the money ran out."

"My father thought the St Giles might welcome a good Jewish boy like him, so he sold me off to a small travelling circus in Bratislava and he came to London. Over the years I caught up with him. The point is every penny he earned from the spoils of our crimes was collected in a fund for the ultimate expedition back to Jammu on which he intended to collect his booty." She leaned in closer and whispered, "Oliver, we're going to India."

24

Pia had a somewhat Roman nose, and her columella drooped slightly below her nostrils. Her coffee skin tone reminded me of the Creole girls I had met in New Orleans. Her round, dusky eyes sparkled in the glimmer and her full eyebrows wriggled with excitement as she spoke. Several facial scars indicated that life on the lam had taken its toll, but they did not detract one iota from her dark beauty. "We have to go to Sevastopol on our way to India."

"Why Sevastopol?" I asked. "What's so important that you have to go there?"

"We, Oliver. We! You are coming with us."

"Oh," I replied, barely taking this all in before she continued.

"Fagin hid an important book in Sevastopol, you see. The caves in Jammu are extremely complex, and Fagin had rigged up deadly traps to catch any curious adventurers. The instructions to thwart those traps are in a book Fagin had hollowed out, on a secret shelf, beneath the floorboards in our old house in Sevastopol."

"Sevastopol is in Russian hands," Jack added, struggling to climb into his breeches, "and under siege by the British and French armies. You speak passable Russian right?" I nodded. "And you being a surgeon an' all that," Jack said, "means you could navigate your way around the barracks unimpeded. I will be your orderly." He buttoned up his shirt and sat back down.

"And I shall play the role of your nurse," Pia said. Her volcanic-red lips formed the shape of a kiss when she finished her sentences, like a personal punctuation mark, which I found extremely distracting.

"I can't drop everything in my life here and take off just like that," I said.

"Codswallop! Everything like what exactly? What do you mean?" asked Pia earnestly.

"My surgery for a start," I replied, indignantly.

25

They both laughed. "Balderdash You've been skipping your practice for weeks!" Dawkins said. "I'm sure Mrs Featherstone-Shaw will find some other doctor to lance her bloomin' boils."

"Fanshaw," I corrected.

"What?" he asked.

"Fanshaw," I said. "It is pronounced Fanshaw. What about the house?" I offered hopefully.

"Don't be ridiculous. From what we gather, you cost your house more than you put in. If you keep going the way you are, with the gambling and drinking, you'll all be out on the streets in a matter of months." The edges of Pia's chiselled cheekbones were covered in fine, black downy hair.

I wanted nothing to do with this project and made every excuse I could. I rambled on about Mango, Mrs McNeil—even my horse made a fleeting appearance in my monologue. Though I was obviously too proud to admit it, they had correctly analysed my situation. I threw in a few final protests, told them I needed time to think and pointed to the candle, which was on its last inch. In truth, I had developed quite a thirst after all this extraordinary news and needed a drink. I bid them farewell and promised them my answer by morning.

As Jack guided me to the door, I peered over his shoulder to catch one more glance of the gorgeous Pia, but she had turned away to attend to the leaks.

Down in the tavern, I spotted the man with the black teeth, whom I had met earlier, standing by the entrance.

He edged out the door and slipped away into the dark, wet night A nearby clip-clop indicated that a cab was leaving the vicinity, and with that man aboard no doubt.

I walked up towards Smithfield's, intending to cut across to Whitechapel to an all-night drinking den. Mr Pun's,

I was about to hail a cab when a drunk driver brushed against me. I recognised this modus operandi from my previous life as a pickpocket! He had attempted to relieve me of my goods, with a clumsy mucher's attack. When I turned to confront my assailant, this area was frequented by farmers and their cowhands, so he seemed particularly out of place.

I caught his hand and twisted his thumb back, causing the man to reel away. The sharp edge of the silver knob on my cane sliced through his left cheek and tore a jagged, two-inch gash. Another man punched me from behind, whilst a third went to grab the cane I had raised to strike again. The injured man got up, drew his skull back and head-butted me on the bridge of my nose. Stars exploded in my head and another fist landed in the centre of my gut.

I had just started to buckle and go down when a voice shouted out, "Hold there!"

The stranger brought a large sword down, flat on the injured man's head, sending him staggering before falling into a horse drinking-trough. He gathered himself together quick-smart and shlip-shlopped off into the night, clutching his head.

The man who'd grabbed my cane could see the game was up and dropped it before disappearing into the crowd of drunks, along with the man who'd punched me from behind.

I wheeled about blindly, flailing, and lashing out at every sound. I felt blood pouring from my nose.

"Hold, sir!" my saviour shouted once again. As my head cleared, I made out three officers' uniforms from the Royal Fusiliers who were standing over me. One held a handkerchief out in offering.

Bit by bit, my surroundings grew more vivid, I noticed the older of the officers held the rank of Captain. He had a fine set of sideburns, as was the fashion set by Prince Albert.

"Thank you," I croaked.

"That is alright, old man," the captain said. "I would not usually get involved in such a fracas, but Merrick-Jones here could tell that you were a 'gent.' Allow me to introduce myself, Martin Morgan, Captain Royal Fusiliers. This is Merrick-Jones. His father is the Colonel, and this tyke is Lieutenant Ward. He's from Essex but you can't blame him for that." At which point, he let out an enormous guffaw.

Upon each introduction, the man in question stiffened, court-bowed and said, "Your service, sir!" By the sound of their slurring, they were a tad inebriated.

"We're off to the mess for a night-cap. Care to join us? We'll get that cut sorted out while we're at it."

I hadn't noticed until now that someone had managed to nick me on the neck during the fight with what I assumed to be a cut-throat razor. I agreed. I needed to get away from there. London's Tower seemed the safest place for now.

A group of inebriated officers greeted us with convivial (albeit slurred) welcomes in the officers' mess. From what I recall, I attempted to buy a round of drinks at some point, but I was soon put in my place by an old major.

"No, no! Young snotty here," he said, wildly gesticulating toward a man by his side, "he's the Orderly Officer. It is his duty to pay for all guests' mess bills." He turned toward the mess waiter, jiggled his glass and slumped into a large leather chair.

I left the mess at midnight. It had been a lovely end to a very strange evening. When I arrived home, I found yet another glove perched upon my railing. I tossed it over my shoulder with such enthusiastic vigour that it landed across the road on fresh pile of steaming horse dung; a moment which gave rise to my final chuckle for the night.

When I woke up on Wednesday morning, my hangover was at its zenith. The sun streamed in through a split in my brocade, stabbing at my eyes.

The glare was so strong and my vision so blurry that for a moment I thought it was Mango plumping up my cushions. The confusion was not particularly surprising, in fact. It wasn't the first time I had noticed how similar he and Mrs McNeil were in stature, not only in the width and height of their bodies, but their awkward, bustling gait.

Seeing I was awake, Mrs McNeil poured my usual cup of tea (and most welcome it was too) and I took a long, lingering slurp—Assam, my favourite.

"Have you cleared up the Master's sick from the floor, Mango?" Mrs McNeil enquired.

"Yes'm,'' he replied.

My lord, they even sound the same! I thought.

"Good boy," she matronised "on with your chores then."

"Yes'm''

As reluctant as I was to partake in this dangerous voyage to Sevastopol and the caves of Jammu, one must never underestimate the persuasiveness of an opportunity to procure unimaginable wealth. The fact is, I was far too extravagant after my benefactor died, attracting so many outstanding accounts that I could barely keep up. The debts incurred from our wedding and Anna's subsequent funeral were substantial enough. My inheritance, however, had also been spent on bribes (to keep me out of gaol), and then there was the cost of my gambling and drinking habits.

On top of all this, a ream of monthly household bills remained unpaid, the details of which I won't go into here but suffice to say, that creditors had begun harassing poor Mrs McNeil in our own home. What's worse is that I essentially ignored the day-to-day running of my practice as well, so incomings had completely dried up. I was in no clear-headed state of mind. One could go as far as to say, that I had grown entirely and utterly irresponsible.

29

I glanced over to the smaller charger plate where we kept incoming mail. There was a stained note lying upon it. It was folded and addressed to me in very neat hand-written script.

"I found it in a pocket when I was cleaning the sick from your jacket last night," Mrs McNeil whispered.

I examined the note with one hand whilst gnawing at my buttered toast in the other.

"That will be all, Mrs McNeil." I cringed as she left.

"No thanks, no nothin'," she muttered from the doorway. Under normal circumstances, with such a headache I would have devoured that toast in one mouthful, but the letter was from the Regimental Headquarters of the Royal it had me utterly bewildered. Someone must have slipped it into my pocket the previous night. The further down the page I read, the lower my hand dropped until, finally, my hand fell, toast and all, back upon the crested plate. This was an invitation to join the army in the Crimea as a surgeon! There was a postscript which read.

I felt it important to inform you of the following news. It has been confirmed that the White Star liner, Carpathia, was sunk off the coast of the Crimea. Your good friend, Dr Vladimir Sawinov, was rescued by the Russians and is being held in Count Calkachov's summer palace in Sevastopol.

I rose at once and grabbed another slice of toast.

"Mrs McNeil?" I called. No answer. "Mrs McNeil?"

The door opened slowly, and Mrs McNeil entered, tentative and deliberate. "Sir?" she said, looking everywhere but at me.

"Fetch me a cab, would you?"

"And where shall I say, the master is going?" she asked.

"Tower of London," I replied, as I tussled to get my hand—still gripping the toast through the sleeve of my jacket.

"Will Mango be accompanying you, sir?"

"No. The horse is beginning to look like a musk ox. He should be mucked out and brushed down."

"Who? The horse or Mango?"

"Both," I giggled.

I descended the white steps, checked my railings for any articles of knitwear and crossed to the waiting cab.

"You know where to go?" I asked the cabbie.

"Yes sir," he replied.

After an hour I'd arrived at the Bulwark Gates at the west side of the Tower of London where I was met by a corporal. I showed him my letter, and he sprang to attention at once.

"Take this gentleman to RHQ," he barked to a private.

"Yes Corporal, Follow me, sir." Said the soldier

At the centre of the Waterloo block were two large black doors. We were met by a young officer holding his sheathed sword on his left side to stop it from tripping him up and hurried into the building.

It was warm and vibrant compared to its austere neighbouring towers. Soldiers scurried with purpose along the corridors. I saw Lieutenant Merrick-Jones carrying a reef of papers and nodded to him. He gave me a smile and nearly dropped a few and, whilst wrestling with the mutinous papers, his kepi hat fell to the floor, I bent and picked it up for him. He really was an awkward fellow. After gathering his dignity, Merrick-Jones knocked on an oak door.

"Come!" came a voice from behind the door.

"Doctor Twist, sir," the young officer said, by way of introduction.

"Thank you, Merrick-Jones. You are dismissed." The lieutenant gave me a short nod, swivelled on his heels and left, closing the door behind him.

"Major Andrew at your service. Thank you for coming, Dr Twist. Please take a seat," he said, indicating an immense, shiny, brown-leather chair by an occasional table. The major sat down behind his desk.

"Lieutenant Merrick-Jones tells me you wish to expand your surgical knowledge," he said. "I am informed that you are trained in surgery. Had any amputation experience?"

"I'm sorry to say that I have had the displeasure of such an experience, yes."

"Good, good. We need more men like you. What about blood-stemming. You manage that all right, do you? Tourniquets and the like?"

"Oh, yes," I sighed, "I can do that. Where are we going to be in the Crimea?"

"Well, that's top-secret, old boy, but I know it's near a place called Balaclava, so no surprises there.

You shall depart on the *Hollander* on Tuesday. We have a berth for you and your party. It'll be quite the adventure, what?"

I did not need to think on it a moment longer. After the assault on me and, armed as I now was with the knowledge of Fagin's treasure and Vladimir's dilemma, I realised that this might be my only chance to escape London.

"I'll need to take my orderly, Dawkins, Pia my nurse and Mango Claggage, my man," I said.

"Yes, yes, that is fine, take who you need. Just be at the St Katherine's dock at eight in the morning.

You'll be travelling on a steamer. Oh, and make sure you bring winter clothing. It's the worst winter in Crimea for twenty years!"

"Good." Then he shouted at the door, "Lieutenant!" Merrick-Jones marched in. "Arrange all necessary paperwork, tickets, and whatnot for Dr Twist, would you?" He turned to me and said, "As for you, we'll see you Kalamita Bay in just a few weeks." Merrick Jones said "Sir!", saluted and marched out. I followed with a spring in my step

Chapter 4

Mango Claggage struggled up the gangplank, laden with my valuable, studded-hide travelling trunks. They were particularly prone to cracking, especially around the intricately engraved letters O. TWIST. I rued the day I'd employed the clumsy fool as my valet.

"Be careful, you gigantic oaf!" I admonished. "They're made of the finest Italian leather." Mango already knew that, of course, as it had been his job to rub them down with dubbing wax in the first place.

Unperturbed by my scolding, he clunked my precious gentleman's cases up each wooden rung, carrying the heavier of the two in his right hand whilst scuffing the case in his left against the side-rods. A third, smaller case was clamped betwixt his breast and bicep of his right arm. My canvas duffel bag swung this way and that at the end of the noose around his neck. Argh!

"Let me give you a hand," I sighed. I slid down the plank and propped the duffel upon his back where it belonged. "There you are." I patted his sweaty cheek (a tad harder than I should have perhaps) and climbed back up the gangplank as Mango griped behind me under his breath.

"You're welcome, I'm sure," I said, doing my best to maintain some semblance of composure as I negotiated the frosty ice which coated both the wooden boards beneath my feet and the handrails. In the name of efficiency, I thought, perhaps I'd lend Mango an old pairs of gloves next time.

The *Hollander*'s master was Captain Trowse, who was a genial old man hailing from Liverpool. He was typically cheery, and weather worn. He puffed night and day upon his decorative meerschaum pipe, whose Syrian Latakian tobacco blend gave off the delightfully sweet fragrance of oak. Even when his pipe was unlit, he used the stem as a prop to point out potential danger up ahead on the nautical charts, or to pinpoint the ship's position on the globe which stood in the corner of the bridge. He was utterly unflappable and ran a smooth, relaxed ship. His men reacted promptly to any order, no matter how laconically it was given. He was an amiable chap; we got on very well.

The *Hollander* set out from London on January 29th, 1855. According to the ship's manifesto, she had a cargo of one thousand four hundred tons of salted pig meat. The weight of her cargo sat her low in the water. Aboard were twenty passengers of various ranks, including Mango, Dawkins, Pia and myself, all of whom were served by a sixteen-strong crew.

It was a calm crossing. I spent three comfortable weeks, both within my cabin and, on pleasant days, walking upon the promenade deck, simply staring out to sea.

I spent many hours in the company of one delightful West Indian lady by the name of Mary Seacole. Her friend (and business partner) was Thomas Day. Mary was full of fun and laughter. They were on their way to open an Officers Rest and Recuperation Hostel in the Crimea. She told me about some of her previous adventures abroad. I found her animated story-telling entrancing and enjoyed her company very much. We were all passable bridge players, and we whiled away the hours playing cards, punctuating the creeping hours with bawdy tales whilst sharing the occasional cheroot upon the quarterdeck. It was at our first dinner together that Mary asked, "So how did you all meet?"

An innocent enough question and one which, under normal circumstances, would have elicited an equally simple story, but it took the rest of the journey to tell our tale. Pia and Jack weighed in with some exciting details where they could, but we remained vigilant—obliged to hide the real reason for our trip—aware giving up too much information might well unravel the adventure ahead of us. The better side of discretion is imperative when one's life depends upon it. In such cases, one must remain suitably vague no matter how charming or trustworthy the listener. Thomas loved snuff and often passed his ornate snuff box around our circle. The florin-shaped lid and base were soldered with tubing between them.

The lid flipped open via a hinge, revealing a small basin brimming with finely-ground tobacco. He showed me how to take it correctly, extracting one pinch twixt thumb and forefinger, before gently sniffing.

"As if smelling a summer flower," he instructed. "Those who snort violently and to the back of the nose," he explained, "run the danger of generating mucus in the form of brown slime, which carries with it the most bitter taste of tobacco. Given half a chance, such goop will drip down the back of your throat all the night long. The experience is not in the least bit palatable to my mind! Not in the least." Any sneezing (and this was his rule-of-thumb) and you'd be forced to down whatever drink before you in one gulp.

Of course, such nights always ended in drunken antics, with bodies strewn about the ship, shaking in fits of laughter—often at Dawkins' expense. Dawkins had not been fortunate enough to learn bridge or whist, nor how to take snuff with some dignity. Though we had both been raised in the slums of London, he hadn't been as blessed as I, nor saved by a rich benefactor, as I had.

Mary had imported a small travelling piano and ordered Thomas to play it. To my astonishment, Pia rose to stand by him and, poised as any professional, she sang. Pia had a beautiful, contralto voice. the magnificence of it! We gawped at the majesty of her birdsong, until the moment we realised that, beneath her lilting heavenly sound, were the bawdiest lyrics we had ever heard. I swear, even the sailors blushed upon hearing those rude words. I shan't repeat a single one of them here.

We congregated several times over the following evenings and took turns performing our individual party pieces. Mary sang in her rich Jamaican accent, whilst Pia and I composed several indecorous songs which kept us mightily entertained. Dawkins, however, was gracious enough to step aside, and fortunate for us, as he had a voice which could curdle milk (though no one ever told him so). The few times Mango was present during the entertainment, he would stand with that huge grin of his, clapping out of time until the moment I shooed him back below decks where he belonged.

36

Despite being prone to aberrations of worthiness, Mango carried out his duties to his master with vim and vigour, but he did more than that. He also took the initiative to search the ship for whatever brass he could buff up. This made him incredibly popular with the busy crew who rewarded him in kind with trinkets. At first, I left him to it, but I soon grew suspicious. He seemed to collect an astonishingly rich array of shiny objects which I was to learn, had not been gifted to him at all, but merely purloined by the fool! In due course, I repatriated the trinkets to their rightful owners with an embarrassing apology on Mango's behalf.

All in all, from what I remember through my gin-addled haze, it was a pleasant enough trip. Already a world away from the horrid, life-changing series of events which had taken place by the cold, unwelcoming River Thames only a few weeks before. I stared out into the distance upon the port side of the quarterdeck one tranquil evening, and my mind was dragged back as I spotted the lights of Cadiz harbour a few miles off to the east. I shuddered. It had been but a few short weeks since I was stood battered and bleeding by the Thames with suicidal thoughts and no hope, Now I was standing on the quarterdeck on the cusp of a life-changing journey. I was full of energy and revitalised. I was actually happy.

The boat berthed in Kalamita Bay on the 3rd of March. Although the sun blazed down, the light breeze which blew off the Serbian Carpathians caused icicles to clink from the rigging lines of the *Hollander* as she trembled in the water.

Our first impression of Kalamita Bay, or "Calamity Cove" (as the soldiers had christened it) was an absurd scene to say the least. A dozen naked soldiers stood shivering up to their thighs in water, washing themselves. They were about two hundred yards from the shoreline and wore only one item—a shako—which I can only assume they kept on in the unlikely event that should a senior officer pass by on a boat, they could maintain some semblance of dignity while saluting him. That was not in itself the strangest aspect of the tableau. They were divided into pairs and bent over; they inspected one another's pubic hair.

Occasionally, a soldier would holler to his comrade before moving in closer and picking out what I assumed was a louse. There was much hilarity amidst the interactions.

A distinct line of flotsam driftwood and discarded fishing nets trailed along the beach, delineating the low and high tidemark. Evidently, this part of the sea was not particularly tidal. There was no dock, just a few jetties jutting out from the beach which were served by rafts built from expertly lashed together logs.

Three sweating soldiers (stripped to the waist) punted out to the Hollander in the raft. Two of them stood at the bow plunging ash-poles into the water and walking backwards to the stern before sprinting forward and repeating the dance, whilst the third soldier steered, orientating the balance of the vessel with a long paddle. The thick rope which trailed through the water behind the raft, remained attached to our assigned jetty. This raft would usually have been assigned to load ammunition, black powder, horse meat, untamed horses, canvas and all manner of weaponry. On this occasion, however, it was to carry passengers, personal baggage and the salt pork cargo of the *Hollander*. It was an awkward process, to say the least, even for the deft amongst us. I winced watching Mango, the clumsy oaf, struggle with the weight of my luggage and bash yet another of my fine leather cases against the frosty, gangplank rails on his way to the raft which bobbed on the water below.

I could no longer hold my peace. "Careful there, you clot!" I shouted. He threw me his usual anguished look and carried on. Twenty minutes passed before we had all managed to disembark the *Hollander* and climb aboard the raft. Captain Trowse waved his pipe to bid us farewell.

One of the haughtier passengers in our midst asked, "What regiment are you from?" and flicked an accusing finger toward one of the soldiers.

"The Corps of Engineers, ma'am," replied the soldier.

She looked him up and down, curling her bottom lip down in disgust. "And the Corps permits you to wander around half-dressed like this?"

38

In that moment, the steering soldier shouted, "Hold tight!" Another soldier held up a red flag which he waved to six similarly semi-attired sailors who'd lined up on the jetty. On receiving the signal, the leading hand ordered the line to gather the rope till it was taut and on the count of "Two, six, heave!" they leant back and pulled, jerking the raft beneath us forward. Those of us who had heeded the warning to hold tight managed to grab the nearest wooden handrail. The hoity-toity woman, however, was sent reeling to the stern of the raft where she landed flat on her backside in that middle of a pile of food supply sacks the hem of her skirt up around her chin, revealing layer upon layer of petticoats and a flouncy pair of pink silk bloomers to boot. It was hard to contain a snigger as she complained on with indignant snorts and fumbled back to her feet.

The sailors on the jetty sang "Bound for South Australia" to keep their rhythm up, and the raft glided gracefully through the shallow water until it reached the jetty where they helped us climb out and unloaded our gear onto it.

"I'm going up the beach to find some transport," Dawkins said.

I ordered Mango to guard the baggage whilst Pia and I promenaded along the shoreline to take in the epic visage over the Black Sea and survey the tall cliffs which surrounded this vast and calamitous bay. Another ship arrived in the bay and dropped anchor whilst we were disembarking. A huge French tricolour flag splayed out from her stern and a crew busied themselves upon the deck. A company of soldiers paraded to the port side deck to greet the three rafts which punted out to the boat from the shore.

I turned to Pia. "They are surely not going to try to fit all those men upon three small rafts?" I said.

"No, not three, one!" she replied. "Look over there."

She was right. Incredibly, they were going to try to fit the lot of them onto one raft!

Perhaps this was a portent of the incredible ineptitude of their leaders in the battles to come! The other two rafts had headed off in another direction.

The beach was as busy as any dockyard I had seen in London. Scores of sailors hauled leaden-weight boxes up to camp. Dockers stuck gaffer hooks into sacks to drag them off the pallets which had been unloaded from various rafts.

As the horses were being led in single file down the gangplank on the larger transport barge (which had berthed further out in the bay), a startled mare flared up and slipped off into the sea, dragging its poor minder into the water behind her. The other cavalrymen mocked the poor man like a mutiny of clowns, which utterly infuriated the Corporal of Horse who let loose a rhetorical tirade mixed with an onslaught of abusive expletives. The buffoons wilted into silence. The horse thrust its neck forward and strode through the choppy whitewash all the way into shore. She ambled up the gentle slope, shook herself dry and walked nonchalantly off up the beach. Her dripping minder did not handle his own beach landing with as much dignity as his horse. Filled with self-pity, he dragged his feet toward the track at the top of the beach where the rest of his troop had planned to rendezvous.

Local vagrants mud-larked along the shoreline, picking through washed-up refuse, just as I had seen the bone-grubbers do back in St Giles Rookery. The beach road was jammed as tight as any day on the Strand and the drivers' language was equal in its ferocity. Officers rode back and forth on their mounts, beating at the drivers with their crops, trying to shuffle their way forward, but the further forward they moved the more crammed the road grew.

Our allies the French and the Turks were also using the same disembarkation port. A French Cuirassier Lieutenant swiped at one stubborn driver with the side of his sword. In a swift manoeuvre, the British driver turned and grabbed his opponent, dismounting the Frenchman at once—an action which was greeted with jeers from the watching soldiers. They had never taken to the idea of being allied with the French. The log jam gradually eased, and we were relieved to see Dawkins Stroll back down the beach accompanied by a Turkish guide and a nursing orderly who was introduced to us as Osman.

The Surgeon General had already informed Osman of our arrival and assigned him to lead us to our billet—such were the wonders of the new telegraph system.

We marched towards a waiting cart where Mango fussed over the luggage for so long that Pia took it upon herself to unburden him by taking one of the smaller Valais off his hands. I helped balance a large kitbag on his back, yet another simple task he couldn't seem to manage on his own. I had interrupted my smoke to offer this immense act of generosity, and the blackguard never even thanked me.

We loaded up the rest of our baggage and supplies and climbed onto the back of the primitive looking cart. Osman clicked his tongue and ruffled the reins, spurring the bedraggled horse into action. I made a note to myself to instruct Mango to give the pathetic beast a jolly good brushing once we had arrived at our billet, or we might be taken for ne'er-do-well paupers. It took a mere twenty minutes to reach the narrow path which led up to the small village. We made our way through crowded, cobbled streets to the main square where harlots spent time shouting from the windows, beckoning off-duty soldiers who streamed in and out of bars in pristine uniforms, their waiting tethered horses lathering white with sweat, blowing steam-puffs from their nostrils. The smell of burnt gunpowder pervaded the air, and the odd bugle call punctuated the rumbling battery of cannons off to the south. We turned into an alley before turning into a small courtyard which reminded me of the Straw Quarter in the notorious Rookery. The cottage was basic but preferable to the tented encampments we had passed.

Dawkins helped Mango lug our cases up a small flight of stairs, where Mango clunked them down on the wooden floor with an ill-tempered thud.

Dawkins then lit a fire and carefully unwrapped a small, brown parcel from which he produced eight thick sausages which Mango had pilfered from the galley of the *Hollander*.

Dawkins and I would have to purchase more substantial victuals from the market before the spring offensive.

It was obvious that we couldn't depend on the British Army to keep us fed, since it was in a terrible state. We both agreed that an even worse decline might be inevitable if they didn't address their current level of morale by changing the prevalent attitude the soldiers seemed to have of every man for himself.

I cooked the sausages in a cast-iron skillet using their fat as a cooking agent. Mango inspected the black-iron kettle, turning it this way and that, as if he had never seen one before, let alone operated one. If the look on Pia's face as she swiped it from his hands was anything to go by, even she was losing patience with his lubberliness. She fixed up a jerry-rig to hang over the fire and had it bubbling and whistling as quick as you could say Jack Robinson.

We settled in for the evening, exhausted and slightly on edge, when Dawkins opened the very discussion I had suspected was on its way.

"We need to consider how to get inside Sevastopol," he offered as his opening gambit.

"Do you have the address?" was my noncommittal reply.

"Yes, I remember it," said Pia.

We stared into the hypnotic flames. I pondered the future and the danger we were about to be embroiled in when I decided to break the silence.

"Dawkins, how do you propose we get past the fortifications?"

"I'm relying on you and your fluency in Russian," he replied. "We should prepare for any eventuality. Perhaps we will get lucky and secure some Russian uniforms. There will be some lying around after the big push." I looked over at Mango and Pia.

"Well, they can't dress as Russians, they look nothing like a Slav! Besides the British, French and Turks have been trying to get in there for two years,"

I added. "I'm not quite sure how you think we are going to manage it when they couldn't."

"Let's see what the next few weeks bring. I'm sure an opportunity will present itself," Dawkins said. "Do you want that last sausage?" He stabbed the remaining sausage with his knife before any of us had a chance to reply, then reached into his jacket and brought out a sheaf of papers from which he drew a large silken handkerchief which seemed to have some kind of map embroidered on it. Dawkins smoothed it out on the table, and we all stood up to gather around it.

"First chance we get," Dawkins said, brandishing the sausage around the map as if it were a pointer, "we'll hire some horses and skirt around the encampments. Let's go north here," he indicated an escarpment before biting off one end of his pointer, "then head west to this redoubt. We're an innovative bunch, we'll think of something once we know more about the obstacles, we're likely to face." Dawkins was well within his element, that's for sure. I sat and took yet another gulp from my whisky flask. and as the heat from the fire, the whisky and the lecture combined, I dozed.

When I next opened my eyes, they were sitting by the fire again. I noticed Pia nudge Dawkins and he glanced my way; they were surely whispering about how appalled they were. Yes, of course, in some hidden vestibule of my mind I was most likely appalled myself, but I couldn't have cared less—of either my own opinion or theirs—not right now, in any case. I shut my eyes again and vanished to the land of wherever.

43

It was on the *Hollander* that they had first started lecturing me.

"You realise how fierce your drinking is, don't you, old friend?" Dawkins had said.

"I'm not a drunk, you know. I could let it go tomorrow if I liked. Leave a man what little joys he has in life. I'm in mourning," I replied.

"It might be time you ease up a bit, Oliver," Pia said.

And it almost mattered what Pia thought of me, but not quite. I was weary of the truth; life had dosed me enough of that. Let a man drift in splendid slumber when he needs it. Allow me my rightful dues. I don't think I said it aloud, but I may have done.

The unquestioning trust which I had placed in them was partly due to this inexplicably quiet confidence Dawkins seemed to have developed over the years. And as for Pia, well, I had grown to appreciate her remarkably cultivated air of integrity since our reunion in the Fortune of War tavern. They left me with a strange and unfamiliar sense of security, something akin to what I imagined siblings might feel.

I awoke in the morning with a fresh appetite for adventure. Much to my surprise, I found Pia stirring a bubbling pot of porridge. Perhaps it was because of her poise, something in the way she held herself, but she hadn't struck me as the domestic type. Dawkins shook me and said our horses had arrived and I should go downstairs and haggle with the sutler. I peered through the window. Down in the courtyard were four horses tethered to the bar. Next to them was a swarthy looking Crimean

When I came back up I was in a foul mood.

"That scruffy local!" I declared. "He is as untrustworthy an individual as any I ever met in London. Where did you find him?"

"He was hanging around by the beach. He captures loose horses—

the ones who've bolted after being unloaded. He has too many to feed. Their army numbers are stamped into the top of their hooves, fer gawd's sake, so obviously they're not his to sell, but he does it anyway."

"I'm sorry, but why do they stamp them?" I asked.

"So that the quartermaster can account for the animal's feed. If the beast dies, the farriers hack off the stamped hoof with an axe and present the hoof to him," Dawkins explained.

"You seem to know an awful lot about this area, Dawkins," I said, curious to know how on earth this could be.

"It's because of me," Pia said. "I lived here as a child. I told him about this gypsy family who lived north of Sevastopol. They have been horse-trading since Genghis Khan invaded." She was quite the specimen, this woman. The more I got to know her, the more she mystified me.

"We need to wolf this down and pack up," Dawkins said, gulping a dollop of porridge from the end of Pia's stirring spoon without so much as a by your leave and licking it clean before dipping it back into the pot. Disgusting, I thought. It took me back to our days in the Jago. Despite my bewilderment at how he had retained his urchin streak, after all these years, I didn't say a word. I simply handed him his tin cup of steaming tea.

Mango went downstairs to answer a knock on the front door and returned with a note; a movement order from Major Kemp, telling me that my party were to report to the Royal Fusiliers Field Hospital, located on an escarpment near the front line north of Sevastopol.

Chapter 5

Our new camp was perched at the top of the southern escarpment. It consisted of row upon row of white hospital marquees,

Our hospital only had three surgeons, and I was the most junior of them all. Like the other two surgeons (Doctor Wombwell and Doctor Duffy), I was always in a drunken haze and, in honesty, rarely fit to operate but we still did. We performed operations in pus-stained coats smothered in bloody handprints we left as we wiped the blood from our hands. Our instruments were never sterilised. They were kept in velvet-lined cases. It seems unimaginable now, of course, but when a sponge (although we rarely had sponges) or an instrument fell to the floor, we simply dried them off with an old rag and kept on using it. Bandages were barely rinsed out, let alone washed. They were reapplied over and over again.

The duties required of me were beyond challenging and undertaken in a frantic rush whilst surrounded by chaos and cries. The horror of a battle's fallout peals with hellish screams and it is not a nightmare one wakes from easily. Dawkins and Pia assisted by managing to keep our orderlies in check as best they could, but I am sorry to say that many ran amok. Pia withstood it all, drawing on some inner fortitude.

Although still in its infancy, I was aware of the existence of anaesthetic science. Neither gas nor pain-relieving drugs, however, were made available to us as the dockyard was simply too busy (or preoccupied with what they considered higher priority stores like silk petticoats for the Generals' ladies, no doubt, or silver for the 11th Hussars Officers' Mess Ball) to acquire them. We were forced to resort to other methods with which to hold down the victims. One orderly would place a towel above the wounded limb and pull it down from beneath the table with all his might, whilst a second orderly would pull on another towel below the wound. Dawkins used a stick, wrapped in leather, which he pressed into the victim's mouth before the tourniquet was applied above the wound. That was the moment I entered with my surgeon's knife.

I'd sweep it around the top of the wound to remove any destroyed tissue and dig all the way to the bone. Then came my surgeon's saw, which I sank through the bone as quickly as possible. It wasn't a pretty scene, and the horrific pain those patients suffered during this traumatic operation caused many a poor soul to pass out. As soon as the limb had been amputated, Osman used the tarbrush to apply the boiling tar to the wound in order to both cauterise it and (hopefully) stem any potential infection.

Day in day out, we toiled away. Most of our work was made up of frost bite, typhoid, cholera and shrapnel gashes. We did our utmost to stem bleeding lesions. We cleaned pus-filled wounds to prevent infection. We conducted amputation after amputation. My fingers prodded around the innards of abdomens, seeking out lead balls, the silent screams and pleading eyes pricking me down to my very soul, all the while. I removed all manner of horror which had exploded into these bodies via grenades—shards of wood, bone, shrapnel, and stone. I berated orderly after orderly. Nurses and aides were so frantic that they even started hauling in limp bodies of soldiers they hadn't noticed were long dead.

It was near impossible to keep up this pace for so many hours, day after day. I knew I was only human, but I still berated myself for not working fast enough. It was no wonder that after one extremely busy day, I fell into an exhausted funk unable to think or talk. Dawkins put me to bed that night and I slept without stirring for eighteen solid hours.

When it was available, I took opium every day, and every day the horrors worsened. Bit by bit, day by day, I increased my dose, until I had stooped to as many as four injections per day. Those shots were interspersed with four hours of sobriety, during which I worked. The few times I happened to fall asleep without opium, I was awoken by nightmares and swimming in a sweat-soaked state of panic.

A few days later, a dispatch rider came down from General Raglan's headquarters to announce that the army was advancing, and he had orders to pack up the hospital.

Both Duffy and Wombwell were indisposed and, since I was next in charge, it became my duty to oversee the orderlies' move to the hospital.

Dawkins was on-hand to sort out the details and luckily for all of us, he had befriended a large bully of an orderly—a Turk—who, despite his size and aggressive demeanour, grew surprisingly compliant and caring under these stressful circumstances. Dawkins planned the move, and the Turk undertook both his and the general's orders to the letter.

Despite their obvious disapproval of my addiction, Dawkins and Pia were vociferous in their praise of my work as a surgeon. They had done their best to protect me from myself, particularly when I worked through my fatigue, and were as aware as I was that the relocation would offer me the opportunity to take a few days off, so the decision to slip away was an easy one to take.

The next day, we arose with the sun and conducted our usual ablutions, then Dawkins and Pia busied themselves by the fire preparing breakfast. I was standing by the bed, practically naked, with my trousers unbelted and my white shirt unbuttoned. I held out my arms and waited for Mango to spot my drooping cuffs. He stood a foot in front of me, mirroring my stance as if it were some game.

"My cuffs…" I said, nodding at my wrists.

"Cuffs?" Mango queried, nodding toward his own wrists just as I had.

Pia looked up. "Jesus, Oliver, can't you do anything for yourself?"

"You don't need to bark for yourself when you have a dog to do it," I replied, winking at Mango, but he simply looked at me blankly, with no idea of what I was hinting at nor indeed any comprehension of what we were talking about, and I had to fasten my own bloody cufflinks!

Dawkins prepared the horses and the three of us headed south. We rode four miles, following the route Dawkins had traced on the map. I noticed the lamentable condition of the soldiers' as we rode past.

Whilst their lords and masters lounged around on yachts moored offshore, their emaciated military wards were sprawled out in the dirt like nothing more than the beggars back in the Rookery or the Tyndale slums of London. Their filthy uniforms were in tatters and most of them were barefoot, despite the freezing cold.

Much to my disbelief, several soldiers stood to attention upon seeing us. One particular soldier, who was clearly in shock, saluted me with such stoic exuberance, it was almost comical. I am sure he thought it was the correct thing to do, poor man, but there was something so pathetic about the gesture that I couldn't even respond. In the meantime, the lords—Raglan, Lucan and Cardigan—were rocking on the bay, sipping their Madeira and devouring canapés with their wives. I looked away, too ashamed to admit we cared.

We soon arrived at the redoubt, where we dismounted and tied the horses to a wooden tethering post. A group of senior officers had arrived before us. They stood in the cannonade with their wives and glanced up our way. One young officer was peacocking in front of the senior officer's eligible daughters. Back and forth he paraded, swinging his swagger stick before them with his chin in the air. I recognised him as Lieutenant Merrick-Jones, whom I had met in London, and waved. He was surprised to see me and offered up a congenial smile and a wave.

A sergeant major from the Regiment of Royal Artillery organised the cannon point. We could see all the way across Sevastopol from this vantage point. From time to time, a series of large mortars exchanged twenty-five-pound shells across the mile expanse.

Sevastopol was once the pride of Crimea. It was now a broken city

49

in a devastated position. Smoke billowed up from where the last shell had landed in the city centre.

The civil population had been forced to live like rats. They scurried between the artillery barrages and dug themselves into the soft sandstone walls. They busied themselves extinguishing fires, knocking down any building which appeared unstable (making them dangerous enough to topple over) and foraging for food in the burnt-out shops.

The Russian Army seemed to have retreated in great haste, leaving behind makeshift barricades they had constructed using scattered debris from the modern city walls when the original walls had breached, along with the stone, gravel and wooden beams brought from destroyed buildings.

Dawkins scanned the view with his small telescope. A flash lit up the horizon and was swiftly followed by a plume of smoke behind the city battlements yonder. A black dot appeared. It seemed to grow bigger and bigger and—

"Get down!" Pia shouted.

It all happened so fast. A fizzing ball landed in the gun emplacement some thirty feet below us, rolling at great speed before exploding and instantly amputating the legs of three artillerymen in one fell swoop. It carried on thundering through the ammunition powder bags at the back of the cannonade. The first explosion went off beneath us. The secondary reaction blew up the entire magazine of ammunition and a shock of heat passed through me like a wave. A screech pierced my ears as if a spear had lanced my head. The blast's tremor rocked me utterly to the core, knocking me off my feet. The wind was whacked out of me as I hit the hard earth and I staggered about whilst struggling to regain my breath, searching for something stable to grab hold of. The dust settled and I took a moment to look around for the others. Miraculously, we were all there and in one piece. We eventually pulled ourselves up and regained our feet only to look over toward the cannonade where there was... well... nought but devastation… The place was destroyed. As the ringing in my ears began to fade it was replaced with the screams and groans of the injured.

The air had that rusty, iron-filled smell about it, like the taste of blood. Naked women, many of them limbless, were sprawled out like shattered China, and their severed, bare legs, some with shoes still attached, lay strewn across the road. A young soldier, no older than seventeen, had a barrel-mop sticking out from his chest.

He stared down at himself, mouthing inaudibly, trying to make sense of this ravaged, scarlet-drenched body, his eyes wild and large as dinner plates. Women without hands gaped at their own bloodied stumps; blinded men lurched, so numbed they were oblivious to the fact that their bodies had gone up in flames. Legs, arms and heads were scattered everywhere. Life had been utterly mauled in a split second.

Aside from a few bruises and scratches, the three of us were largely unscathed. It truly was as if we had some angel wings wrapped around our circle. None of us spoke a word. As the smoke cleared, we hobbled down to join some other unharmed soldiers in the pit. A corporal had already started to order the survivors to treat the maimed. We joined in and followed the whimpers and cries emerging from the nightmare scene. We scraped and pawed our way through to any wailing survivor we could find.

A young gunner lay on the ground screaming. He appeared to have missed the worst of the blast, but his face and hands were covered in flash burns, and his hair was smoking. I held the boy's head, for that is what he was, face down in the snow to stop his skin and hair from smouldering any further and calmed him with a dose of brandy.

A woman meandered through the scene pointing at body parts. Dawkins and Pia reached out to help her. The lady's face was cut up and pouring with blood, and her tousled hair poked out from a skew-whiff bonnet tied to around her chin. She was drawn to a swagger stick which stood vertically from the mud and blood-drenched snow. It was then that I realised; this was one of the young ladies we'd seen earlier who had been so impressed by Lieutenant Merrick-Jones's strut down centre-stage. The only sign left of Merrick-Jones was his swagger stick.

After all the dead were separated from the living, the first aid party carried the patients down the hill towards a building we had passed on the way up. Upon entering the oddly named British Hotel, we were greeted by the unmistakable Jamaican accent of Mary Seacole.

"Bring them in, set them down," she said. "Sarah, bring some water. Sarah! Hurry up."

The young lady she beckoned seemed no older than twenty. She looked up like a frightened mouse and carried the bucket and suture equipment to where Pia had begun cleaning the wound. I watched Pia's long; nimble fingers deftly manipulate the cat gut and needle. Her stitching was impeccable. Mary wiped down the artillery corporal's hands with great care and rubbed rum into his burns. He winced.

"Don't move, child," she said. "You'll thank me in the long run. You may think I am clumsy here, but I'm touching you as delicate as a feather. I only do my best for you, child. There, there, not long now. Say a little prayer, that's right." Mary's running monologue was as loquacious as it had been on our trip from England. I smiled to myself, for it was one of the few sounds I found comforting that day.

We headed back to the cannonade to see if there were any other wounded blast victims we could help. Neighbouring soldiers had started organising the disaster area as well as they could. It seemed the generals could not imagine lightning striking the same place twice, for a new cannon had already been put in place in the same spot, ammunition boxes had replaced those that had been destroyed, and fresh sandbags were installed at the front, patching up the gap left by the explosion. We surveyed the new cannonade and wished the occupants luck, before trekking back down the hill to our casualties at the British Hotel.

Pia led the way, looking magnificent in her riding breeches with her loose shirt flapping in the breeze. Her cascade of black hair glimmered against dawn's red sun, and a Javee harmonica-pistol swung from her hand. What a spirit this woman had; what a sight for poor eyes!

We returned to the cottage where Mango had prepared a pot of stew, and we settled in for the evening. After supper, I sat back on the bed, smoked a pipe and promptly fell asleep, only to be woken by Dawkins pulling at my sleeve.

"Follow me," he whispered, urgently.

It took me a while to wake up but as I did, I saw that the room had been cleaned, the hearth extinguished, the pots put away, and the knapsacks packed. Dawkins had been keeping busy whilst I slept.

"What is happening?" I asked, as we headed briskly down to the harbour.

"I hired a small fishing boat," he said.

When we arrived at the beach there was a line of fishing boats tied to a row of large boulders which were dotted along the shoreline. They were all alike, roughly sixteen feet in length and eight foot wide at their widest part. They were built of rough wooden planks, and each had two rowing wells upon which to sit. The bow was higher than the gunnels, and the stern was cut square. The boats had a large keel but no tiller, which meant that we would have to steer using the oar-stokes. The boats were entirely purpose-made, with no aesthetic detailing, coloured paint or any other decorative adornments.

We climbed aboard the one Dawkins had hired. The four oars were stored beneath the seat-planks. The gunnels had rowlock holes, and the rowlocks were stored up in the bow inside a locker, which was covered with a small triangle of tarpaulin.

Mango fitted them. They resembled catapults which had lost their slings.

"You and Mango take the ropes at the bow and pull," Dawkins

instructed, "while Pia and I will push from the stern."

We did as commanded until the boat finally shifted, arguing its way reluctantly out toward the waiting sea, scraping along the pebbles as if in protest. The whiff of spoiled fish drifted through the salty air and cries from black-headed gulls filled the skies.

Once the bow had reached deeper water the boat began to float freely. We splashed our way back to the stern, took a small run-up and pushed the boat in fully. Then, Dawkins helped us as we jumped up over the stern..

Mango and I pulled on his arms until we were thrust back into a pile, up-ended and tangled in the rolled-up fishing net in the bottom of the boat. None of us laughed at the absurdity of it all. The sun had set, and it had suddenly grown cold. We were wet through, which made matters worse of course, and the night was as black as it could be for there was no moon lighting up the harbour town. Thankfully, there was no wind either and so the waters were still and silent.

This was the beginning of what I can only describe as the most miserable journey of my life so far. I was not to know it at the time, but this would only be the first of many a miserable journey. In hindsight, it was not world-class "miserality", but it was bad.

We rowed away from Kalamita Bay, heading south towards our destination, a small cove just south of Sevastopol. It was back-breaking work and made only worse by Mango. He was the strongest amongst us and I was the most technically adept, so it made sense for us to sit together. But Mango is so simple in character—he is either on or off—and because of his freakish strength, one single oar-stroke from him was worth two from me, which meant we constantly ran the risk of spinning in a never-ending circle.

Every now and then I had to whisper, "Easy, easy, boy," to remind him to bring it in some. In his enthusiasm—which was perhaps exaggerated because he felt like an equal in our team, for the first time—Mango rowed too shallowly on the water's surface and occasionally showered Pia with freezing seawater, making her yelp and scowl.

We had barely rowed fifty yards before Dawkins stopped us.

"We're making too much noise. We're splashing too much." He produced four small hemp sacks which we wrapped around our oar blades to muffle the sound. It certainly helped us row more quietly but now we became aware of a robust, percussive squeak, the kind of sound which would give us away in its regularity.

"Squeak! Squeak! Squeak!"

Again, we stopped. Oars up, we bobbed in the calm water.

"Look for some tar or grease," Dawkins hissed.

He passed between each rowlock, twisting it to evaluate its squeakiness. The problem lay with Pia's rowlock. It practically squealed in comparison to the others. We paused whilst pondering on the conundrum. What to do? Hmmm what to do?

Mango took this opportunity for a picnic break and produced a fat piece of bread, smothered in lashings of lard, from his knapsack. He was just about to take an enormous bite when Dawkins snatched the bread from out of his hand, pulled the rowlock from its hole and rubbed the bread inside the gritty shaft. He replaced the rowlock, turned it around and re-evaluated the noise. Silence. Hoorah! He handed Mango back his dinner, who completed his bite without a pause, as if the interruption had never occurred, and sat there, staring ahead, chewing slowly on the greasy bread like a cow chewing cud.

And so, we set off once again with me reminding Mango time and time again to ease it up a bit and Mango inadvertently splashing Pia.

Eventually, she had had enough, and we all changed places.

I spotted several well-lit yachts moored a hundred yards offshore and rowed silently past them all. The sound of clinking crystal tinkled across the water, along with the guffaw of entitled brutes, the tittering of swooning ladies and even a string ensemble playing Mozart.

Considering where we had come from that morning, and what we had seen, all this was bizarre in the extreme.

After about an hour, the classical ensemble was replaced by the familiar lilt of a fiddle playing something like a hornpipe, and as we approached the stern of a frigate with *Intrepid* inscribed on its nameplate, we noticed an impressively large, Union flag. It hung limply on that windless night and even though partially obscured, it was unmistakable. We rowed close enough to be able to touch the ship's starboard side and passed without incident, but after only a few more strokes we passed another frigate, this one called *Invincible*, and then another named *Indefatigable*. Their lookouts were, no doubt, looking towards Sevastopol and we were passing directly under their bulbous hulls, the bulge of which seemed to have kept us out of sight from above.

Through the gaps in the line of frigates we spotted a squadron of smaller ships. As we rowed past another bunch of frigates the atmosphere changed. These ships had equally impressively large flags wilting from their sterns but this time they were Tricolours! We rowed beneath the guns of *L' Cigne, Achilles* and *Ville de Paris* undetected by their notoriously sharp-eyed lookouts. A squeeze box played, accompanied by a raucous array of French voices.

A small splash sounded off just to the left of us, and I looked up to disappearing. Fortunately, the last thing they'd be looking for was a small, local skiff on their starboard side and, in any case, their crew were likely to have been scoffing enough wine to miss us completely, it was a moonless night, and our black cloaks served to further hide our form. It wasn't until we rounded a spur in the cliffs that we were detected. A voice rang out through the dark from the pier on the shore. It was Russian!

I froze but Dawkins nudged me with his oar. "Answer him, Oliver," he ordered.

The voice in the dark repeated his question. "Who are you and what are you doing?"

For some reason, Mango started repeating it perfect Russian under his breath. This took me by surprise his pronunciation was perfect. Even Pia looked quizzically at him. It took a moment for my mind to switch from its mother tongue, but my survival instinct kicked in soon enough.

"We are fishermen looking for sea bass."

Mango muttered the same phrase, again in perfect Russian. The voice muttered something to his colleague.

"This is a military area. Fish somewhere else," he replied.

"We are trying our best," I said, "but we've broken an oar." I stared at Dawkins, but he simply shrugged and wrinkled up his nose.

"You don't sound like you are from round here," the voice said.

"We are from here. I have a cold," I replied, though I felt completely stupid.

The guard seemed to take a moment. I could hear him repeating the word Seer—Russian for Sir. "This is an odd time to be fishing," he said, "but wait there, we have a spare. I'll bring it over." At that the Russian turned and said something to his men, and they began to untie their launch.

"Row faster," I whispered to Dawkins. "I have to pretend we have a broken oar." He just glared at me quizzically. "Just do it!" I insisted. Mango looked at me and far too loudly said "We haven't got a broken oar!"

"Just row, you oaf," I hissed

"I can't, we have a broken oar you said," was Mango's impertinent reply. Pia put her hand on Mangos shoulder. "Just row," She whispered.

"Halt where you are!" The Russian sounded furious.

An enormous boat loomed up to us.

Three Russian soldiers stood upon the prow, their rifles ready and levelled at us. An ominous click sounded from the barrel of one of the guns. The soldier-in-charge had engaged his hammer, and he was aiming directly at me.

"Stop what you are doing," he said in perfect English!

Chapter 6

At that precise moment, a large cannon ball whistled overhead. A fountain of water bloomed to his left, soaking him and the other soldiers to the bone and knocking them all off their feet. They tumbled backwards into the boat like a strike of skittles.

A moment later, we heard a roaring cannon bellow from the *Ville de Paris*. They must have been alerted by Mango's oar protestations.

"Row!" Dawkins shouted. "Row as fast as you can."

We only just managed to move our skiff out of the path of the French cannon ball before it smashed into the Russian launch, utterly destroying it. A short rally of fire between the French frigate and onshore cannons followed.

We rowed and rowed for all we were worth.

Once the booming barrage had petered out, we drooped over our oars, panting with exhaustion, but we didn't rest for long. We picked up our oars and headed toward a crest of waves—a possible shoreline break—in a small cove.

As we approached the beach Mango and I climbed to the prow, readying ourselves to jump overboard. On the count of three, I sprang out over the edge, landing perfectly with my legs astride and feet firmly planted in the sand. I steadied the boat and took hold of the line. Mango, of course, floundered like a startled heifer, snorting, huffing, puffing and splashing about in chaotic panic.

We led the boat up towards a trough in the dunes via an inlet. As fortune would have it, the tide was at its zenith, so we didn't have to pull too far. Dawkins and Pia found an old, discarded fishing net which they dragged over the sand to sweep our footprints away and we camouflaged the boat with branches, driftwood and sand. The dunes were dense with marram grass, and groups of Russian soldiers were encamped amongst them on the slopes at the top of the beach. We kept low and out of sight.

Just as we were about to break cover, a platoon of mounted Russian military police appeared, scattering the deserters like cockroaches. A chase followed and, eventually, the police scooped up several of the absconders and marched them back to where they would, no doubt, face trial and the inevitable disciplinary sentence.

Once the danger had passed, we headed towards the city. Our black suits were smeared with salt and filth from the old fishing boat. They stank of sweat and rotting seaweed. Fragments of debris and driftwood protruded from the weave where we had caught ourselves on flotsam, but we were well within the defensive line of the city now and didn't bother tidying ourselves up, knowing our dishevelled appearance would raise less suspicion as we'd look like everyone else in Sevastopol.

We were walking towards the outer perimeter of the picket line when Dawkins suddenly stopped and held up his hand, and then silently ushered us into a nearby hedge.

Dawkins looked worried. "I've seen a guard post up ahead; they're going to call out a password."

Mango repeated "They're going to call out a password."

"What shall we do?" whispered Pia.

"What shall we do?" Mango repeated in exactly the same way.

"What?" asked Pia. Even she (by her tone) was becoming annoyed.

"What?" Mango repeated.

"Thats it, When I tell you, Mango, walk towards the guard post and stop still when they call to you, they're going to shout 'Halt!' and then 'Who comes there?' in Russian. It'll sound like this," and I whispered the Russian sentence into his ear. "You just shout what you hear back at them. They'll say something like 'What's the password?' You repeat back to them what they say, they'll get confused and shout something to you and then you shout it back.

If they raise their rifles you better scarper into the nearest ditch. We'll wait for the guards to change and then we'll give it a go.

Pia said "Why don't you do it? Your Russian is good enough."

"What? I might get shot, let Mango do it. So, it's agreed then," and I pushed Mango out on to the track. While we waited in the ditch Mango tentatively set off. Within a few steps we heard "Halt!" Mango halted.

"Who comes there?" the guard shouted.

"Who comes there?" Mango repeated.

I couldn't help myself. "Very good!" I whispered in English, and Mango bellowed "Very good!"

"What?" said the Russian in his own language… we were doomed.

"What?" mimicked Mango.

"Who are you?" We were back on track

"Who are you?" Mango replied.

"What's the password?"

"What's the password?" The guard looked confused and turned to his accomplice.

"TRUNK!" shouted the second soldier.

Mango shouted "Trunk" and turned and walked calmly back a few steps and slipped into our ditch with a smug look on his face.

We waited and watched as the two guards paced back and forth. I could tell by their demeanour they were conscripted peasants and not used to sentry duty. They were sloppy and drank from their canteens a lot, they had lent their weapons against the gate and urinated in full public view. Surely they would report such an odd occurrence to their superior officer, but they just carried on.

Pacing back and forth. Perhaps, an hour and a half passed, when we could hear the guards' relief marching towards them from the town. There was a brief conversation, and the guards changed over. We waited a few minutes until the new guard had started their routine. "We go now!" ordered Dawkins.

Dawkins strode ahead and when we heard the expected "Halt!" halted.

"Who comes there?" shouted the guard.

"Friend," I replied.

"What's the password?"

"Trunk," I replied.

"Pass friend!" and that was that. Once again one of Mango's many pointless talents had accidently rescued us, and we strode through the picket without a care in the world. The guards were just as sloppy as their previous comrades and barely glanced at us.

Now Pia was in familiar territory, she strode ahead, while I marched purposely behind her. At first, I orientated the map on the ground, fumbling around and lining up my tiny compass at every turn, but it wasn't long before I abandoned my clumsy charade and decided to trust in Pia's intuition, shamefully falling back to join Dawkins and Mango in the rear.

"Come on, hero," he said, throwing an arm around my shoulders. We walked into the city centre just as it was starting to stir for the day.

"We're here!" Pia said over her shoulder as she turned into an alley.

We followed her around the bend into the ginnel, where we found ourselves facing three surly-looking Russian soldiers. They were bedraggled, unwashed and, from the way they slurred their words, drunk.

One was slouched against the wall smoking a pipe as he listened to the other two squabbling over where to hide next. The smoking soldier straightened up as soon as he saw us, the others stiffened.

They were terrified they'd been caught by a superior officer.

"Bluff it out," Dawkins whispered out of the corner of his mouth. "Act as if you're in charge." The soldiers picked up their muskets and pointed them at us.

Pia gathered her wits quick smart and called back up the alley in Russian, spurring the soldiers to gather their chattels and run off as fast as you could say: "Boo!"

Dawkins was aghast. "What on earth did she shout?" he asked.

"She simply alerted an imaginary Captain of the Guard behind us that she had found the three deserters he was looking for," I laughed, both proud to have understood what she had said, and impressed by the degree of Pia's fluency. My Russian was good but if put to the test I would never have managed to react quickly in a foreign tongue without any hint of an accent the way she had.

We came upon a large, boarded-up terrace house with half its roof missing. I smirked and pulled a lock-pick from my pocket.

"Breaking into a Black Sea merchant's house should be a doddle after all our years in the business," I bragged, sticking the pick between my teeth and crouching onto my knees.

I fiddled around, swearing here and there, before swaying back onto my haunches in frustration. No matter how hard I tried, I'd never be as good as Dawkins was at this.

"Leave it to the real expert," he said, shoving me aside. Of course, he had the door open within seconds. I told Mango to stand guard, and we entered the house. The hall was dark and dusty. It seemed to have been hit some time ago by a large shell.

"That's where the book is supposed to be," Pia said, indicating a battered rug beneath the rubble with a scraggly, purple butterfly-bush growing up through it.

I stumbled across the rubble to reach below the rug and found a loose floorboard. I lifted it and there beneath was Fagin's book.

I picked it up and opened it. Its pages had been hollowed out and replaced with a smaller notebook which I opened. I recognised the slant of his scrawl at once. This was it, Fagin's instructions!

"Oliver," Pia said, "I think I should be the one to carry it. Anyone who enters the deadly system of those caves without this book is truly doomed. Using this as a guide is the only way we'll get in and out of the place alive." A warm sensation rippled through me.

Pia's heart must surely have been broken to see her childhood in tatters beneath our feet. She stood on the spot and turned full circle, gazing at the pile of detritus—her former home—before pausing to kneel down and examine a small shred of gingham. She pulled at the fabric until a raggedy doll's face peeped through the broken plaster and brick. I couldn't see her face but her barely audible gasp said it all. This doll must have been a favourite friend. She tucked it into her pinafore pocket and turned around. A tear streamed down her dusty cheek. It meandered all the way to the end of her pink nose before muzzling into the dust at her feet.

"Come on then," Dawkins said. "We had better get back to our boat."

Pia wiped her face and shook her head as if to toss all her woes to the wind.

"Yes, let's go," she said. "There's nothing else for us here." This scene of remembrance must have seemed like family skeletons lying in the ruins of an ancient graveyard to her,. She took one final look

And her eyes began to well up before purposely striding out through the front door and back into the alley. She never looked back.

We followed her in respectful silence and retraced our steps back to the dunes but, now forewarned, we avoided any more interactions with the Russian guards. Once back at our boat we huddled down in the sand, wrapped in our black cloaks, and we discussed our next move.

Gulls dove in and out of the waves, tussling over their catch; their distinctive screeches punctuated by the morning's first salvo exchange. The vague lemon scent which oozed out of the grass tufts blended with an all-too-familiar smell of cordite on salt spray, triggering my old urge. It was time to seek relief. I reached into my pocket for my preloaded opium pipe. It wasn't there. I patted myself down, in the past, I had slipped the implement down my socks,. I felt every inch of my body, but it was not to be found.

I glanced over to Dawkins. He knew what I was looking for, I was certain he did, and the way he avoided eye contact only confirmed this. I searched my coat again and ran a hand down my legs. I scoured the ground one last time but still found nothing.

"What have you done with it?" I asked, glaring at him point-blank.

"Done with what?" Dawkins replied.

"You know very well what—my pipe."

"No idea what you're talking about, my man."

"Liar!" I launched for his coat pocket, but his iron fist was swifter than I and knocked me senseless.

I felt the ache in my jaw as soon as I came to. Pia and Dawkins sat a meter away. Their mouths were moving—they were talking—but I couldn't hear a sound. The outline of their bodies was out of focus. Everything was slightly blurry, in fact, and they were rocking like a boat, swaying this way and that. Or was I the one moving? Dawkins' punch had certainly knocked me senseless, but these other sensations were a feature of my withdrawal. I simply had to have that fix! Now.

The cramps started clenching my abdomen. I trembled, I twitched, I rippled and itched.

I rocked forward and back, in an effort to ease the jitters and scratchy claws which scraped at my insides. I had to distract myself. Keep moving, I whispered. But there was no escaping the cavity within.

Then my ears popped, and I could hear my comrades' voices which, although hushed, seemed like a thunderous, booming chorus of claps to me.

"He has the opium cramps," Pia said.

"Yeah," Dawkins replied, "I know." He didn't care a one iota.

Dawkins hacked a morsel of cold meat from a sausage with a vicious-looking knife and tossed me a piece. Yes. Yes. Perhaps eating would help, I was determined to bite down into the pound of flesh, but my hand trembled on its way to my mouth, and the stench of dead pig overwhelmed me. —the stench of lilies in the market stalls next door to the butcher—lilies, slaughter, death. I tossed the morsel away as if it were a spider caught on my sleeve. I couldn't keep my head up, nor my stomach down. The last thing I recall is my face heading toward the ground to meet my own regurgitation and laying my cheek down onto a cushion of brush behind our camouflaged shelter.

Another blindingly sharp day arrived. We would be in full view of the Russians if we left now. Though I hadn't been conscious during the discussions overnight, I assumed Dawkins had decided we should stay hidden until the next nightfall due to a cloudless sky. Thank heavens, I thought. I was incapable of moving anywhere.

The next thing I knew Dawkins was kicking my feet.

"You're on lookout," he said. "Two hours. I've done mine; Pia has done hers. It's your turn. Don't you dare fall asleep this time."

I crawled out from our shelter and took up my position a few feet away, using the boat as cover, where I could look out without being seen.

We were supposed to take it in turns to keep watch but Pia, took over my watch, which allowed me to return to the makeshift camp. I tried to sleep but by now my nightmarish withdrawals had completely overwhelmed my efforts. Mango, on the other hand, was dreaming at full volume. He growled, and whimpered, and snorted like a carthorse.

His giant hands limply flopped about as if he were a dog chasing rabbits through meadows. He finally woke himself with a giant snort and I found the perfect opportunity to dump my mood upon him by shouting abuse for losing my pipe and opium. I worked myself up into an absolute frenzy, screaming and lashing out.

The next thing I knew, I was easing out of slumber, snugly tucked in a cushiony bed inside a large cabin. I remembered copping a sharp thwack on the back of my head and suffering a blinding flash before I passed out. The sun blazed through a porthole with glaring intensity, and the whiff of coffee pervaded the air. There was a hullabaloo from a market nearby, along with the unmistakable chatter of street hawkers. I blinked, then squinted, but could make little sense of where I was. I tried to get up, but my limbs had been bound with a course hawser—my wrists were securely anchored to brass rings on the cabin walls and my ankles were tethered to the bed posts.

I tried calling out, but my throat was so parched that little more than a shrill squeak fell mockingly from my mouth. There was a pile of sweat-stained bedding heaped on the floor by my bed and my pillow was covered in patches of blood stains where my injured head had lay.

Muffled voices filtered through from the other side of the door. The weight of strangers outside my room shifted on the boards. The creaking ominously loomed closer, and footsteps thumped louder as someone approached the door. The handle angled down, heralding the arrival of my unknown captors.

A blue fish jerked past the porthole, writhing as it rose and splattering blood on the glass as it vanished into the sky. What kind of hell was this?

Chapter 7

The handle clicked and the door swung open with a high-pitched creak, revealing Mango's portly frame. He was carrying a breakfast tray. Pia stood behind him smiling, Dawkins stood by her side with the sternest expression on his face.

"Feeling better are we?" Dawkins asked, as they marched into the room.

Pia lowered a side table from the wall and locked it into position with brass fixing rods. Mango placed the tray upon it before clearing the soiled bedding from the floor and stuffing it into a canvas sack in the corner. Dawkins whistled as he untied my wrists and ankles.

"Where on earth are we?"

"Constantinople," Pia replied.

"Constantinople? In heaven's name!"

"Dawkins clumped you good," Mango chuckled.

"He had to," Pia said. "Your cramps got so bad that you started screaming. We had to do something before you alerted the patrols."

"What the hell did you hit me with, a rock?" I asked.

"He knocked you out with his pistol butt!" Mango laughed. I shot him a threatening look.

I asked, "How did we end up here?"

"We launched the boat once the sun had set. We threw you in the bilge and rowed for a few hours. It was gruelling work, but, thanks to Mango's strength, we finally made it back to our billet in the village."

"You was hallucinating" Mango added. "We tied you down to a litter."

"I fetched the Surgeon General," Dawkins said. "The instant he saw what a state you were in, he declared you unfit for service, so you have been discharged from your duties."

"You've been a mess these last few days," Dawkins said. "We've taken turns looking after you."

It was hard to believe that I'd left Crimea without recalling a single thing about the journey. Dawkins had apparently procured berths on a Turkish freighter carrying stores to the Alma River front. It was set to return to Turkey with injured English, Turkish and Egyptian soldiers.

I ate my breakfast, dressed and headed to the sunshine on deck where a row of Turks lined a stone jetty fishing. Every couple of seconds, one of their rods would bend over into the water and drag along the surface before pinging an enormous, blue fish into the air. I smiled to myself. They hadn't been hallucinations at all; iridescent fish really had flown past my porthole fighting for their lives!

Pia was concerned that the force of Dawkins' clump may have fractured my skull, and the surgeon had only given me a cursory inspection, so when we disembarked onto the Constantinople docks we made our way to a field recovery hospital called Scutari Hospital. The conditions were far better there than they had been at the tented hospitals of Balaclava. The rooms were spacious and airy. Twenty wooden beds were neatly laid out in each ward, offering ample space for orderlies to move around. They almost looked inviting, what with their dazzling white sheets tightly tucked in and turned down, their feather pillows—of which there was one to each bed—and their coverings of grey blankets running down the centre. I spotted an orderly bouncing a coin off a bed to test that the nurses had tucked the covers in tightly enough.

The unoccupied beds, had their bedding piled into a rectangle about two feet long, which included a sheet, a blanket, another sheet, another blanket. The entire bundle was then wrapped in yet another tightly folded blanket. The orderly referred to these as bed blocks and woe betide the nurse whose bundle was left drooping or, even worse, smiling.

69

Light flooded in through a massive window. A small pot-bellied stove stood in the centre of the room and a stove pipe chimney towered up ten feet before angling horizontally across the ceiling and out the window.

The nurses and orderlies all appeared professional and caring. A Turkish doctor inspected me thoroughly. He suggested I stay for observation, and I spent an extremely comfortable night at Scutari Hospital. In the morning, when no one was around, I went through the cupboards in my ward and there to my delight, in a drawer amongst other surgical instruments, was a brand-new brass syringe accompanied by a set of needles!

Later that day, Dawkins collected me, and we rode back into Constantinople. The Turks hated the Russians as much as we did, so we felt safe in Constantinople. The Russians carried themselves with a certain arrogance and because they looked undeniably Slavic with their broad foreheads, strong jaw lines and blonde hair, they were easy to spot in a crowd.

We rested in a small, rented house across from the vast Blue Mosque in Constantinople's centre, which was not far from the bridge over the Bosporus. My shivers were still uncontrollable. I rocked back and forth, rubbing my arms to get myself up. Pia and Dawkins left me alone and headed off to spend the day in the Grand Bazaar where they'd collect provisions and arrange transportation for the long journey ahead. As soon as they left, I searched the room, again and again, turning out drawers and sweeping my hands over table surfaces in the hope of finding even the smallest remnant of opium.

I soon wearied of all the frenetic activity though, and carried my self-pity back to bed, but once I'd regained a little energy,

I turned the room upside-down again (having forgotten, in my delirium, how thoroughly I had already searched). My need to free myself of this destructive habit was outdone by my need for that one last fix.

None of my behaviour made sense, of course, but at the time, it didn't occur to me how pathetic and contradictory my desperation was. I eventually gave up my search and braced myself to face the world beyond those four walls. I headed to a local bazaar, where I knew I'd source copious supplies. I arrived at the cloistered market square and scanned the crowd. It didn't take long to spot a likely user. I approached the shady-looking fellow and opened my coat to show him my brass syringe. He nodded and beckoned for me to follow him into a side street, where I procured a large bottle of the yellowy-white thick liquid for an acceptable price (after a fair degree of miming and finger-gesturing). The enthusiastic salesman assured me the stuff was of the finest quality.

"Magnificent dream," he said. "Magnificent!" he repeated.

I raced back to the flat and purified the liquid over the fire. I filled my syringe, injected my forearm and I was gone, all my troubles dissolved into bliss. I sank back into my cushion and watched the world wander by. A British Grenadier skipped down the lane with a lion on a leash. A great fat ginger unicorn trotted passed the window in the opposite direction before doing a double take, stopping in his tracks and leaning in through my window.

"I like your hat," he said. "Can I have it? I am rather partial to the colour blue." He sounded like Mango.

"But I rather like my hat too," I replied.

"How dare you refuse a unicorn," he neighed. "No one refuses a unicorn!"

I couldn't muster the will to resist; I simply didn't have it in me. I handed the hat over and, as I did so, it turned the deepest shade of crimson.

A cockerel crowed. It had Dawkins' face announcing the entrance of a bear who came prancing through the door.

He headed straight for the turkey that had hidden its head beneath its wing in the corner of my room. (I sometimes wonder if the turkey was in fact me.) That's all I recall of my adventures. They were vivid, yes, and as magnificent as my friend had told me they would be.

"Oliver! Oliver!"

Had I told the turkey my name? I wondered. That wasn't very smart of me.

"Oliver, wake up." I opened my eyes to find Dawkins and Pia busying themselves around the room. "We have a wagon," Dawkins said, "and we've gathered all the stores we need for our pilgrimage to Fagin's cave. Dawkins gabbled on about the Grand Bazaar, the coloured fabrics in the stalls, the pushy hawkers, the vibrancy of life in the city centre...

"Did you find any opium?" I asked.

He ignored my question. "The scent of mocha was luscious; it pervaded every crevice of the place. And there were thousands of musical instruments, the likes of which I'd never seen or heard."

"Did you find me some opium?"

"Entire stalls were dedicated to frankincense burners, Oliver," Pia said. She went on to describe the exotic smoke which wafted through the alleys, permeating everything like layers of history. "There were stalls piled high with shelves of hooker pipes—"

"—the Grand Bazaar runs for half a mile," Dawkins continued. "It is the biggest market you have ever seen—the largest in the world—selling every kind of luxury.

'Best price here!' 'Special price, come, look.'" We laughed at Dawkin's impression.

Dawkins did his best to hide a smirk. He had something else to tell me. Opium, I was sure he'd found some opium.

The news he had stifled soon broke through the creases of his smug face and my hopes rose. It turned out that Dawkins had contacted Turkey's internal secret service via an operative with whom he had worked with previously.

"His name is Mehmet. Oliver, it's such good fortune. We have worked together many times; I trust this man with my life." His uncharacteristic excitement didn't lift my spirits one iota. I had only one thing on my mind. "He'll join us tomorrow as he has offered to guide us through Turkey into the next leg of our journey."

I rested well that night. Mehmet turned up at the break of dawn. He wasn't at all as old as I had expected him to be. He had the air of a thirty-year-old man. His black hair was thick and curly. He had brown eyes which were framed by deep eye sockets and a large, hooked nose underlined by a wide, neatly trimmed moustache. His tanned leathery skin was punctuated with scars. He was of average build and height and moved deftly, without fuss. His long, elegant fingers were immaculately manicured. They seemed incongruous at the end of such freakishly hairy forearms. His crimson fez had a golden tassel hanging from one side, which swished as he talked. Brown leather slip-on sandals poked out from his long, brown and white and beige striped dish-dash[i] which was woven out of coarse wool.

Whilst the others loaded the wagon and tacked up our horses, I returned to the market to acquire enough liquid fuel from my new friend to keep me going. I returned to tack up my own horse and help load before anyone noticed I'd even left.

The wooden yokes interspaced along the tongue hooked up four fine brown mares.

They were immaculately brushed and shod and stood about seventeen hands to the shoulder. Their manes and tails were cropped right back to avoid entanglement with all the leather and brass paraphernalia.

Pia decided that the horses' Turkish names were too difficult to pronounce so she renamed them after some of her friends Edit, Doris, Agatha and Vicky. Traces ran back to the wagon and the driver's bench-seat was positioned on top of two springs and topped by woolly sheepskin to help make it just that little bit more comfortable than the hard-oak block.

Despite having tried to assuage the withdrawals by lowering my dosage somewhat, I was still in a blur. I did my best to appear as if I were working but I don't know if I fooled anyone. I pretended to check and cast a cursory eye over the horses' withers to ensure their bridles and traces were fitted and comfortable for them. The ornate, polished brasses which adorned the tack were of remarkable workmanship; as I marvelled at them, I made sure they were clean and secure and that they swivelled correctly.

We had stocked the wagon with stores allowing for every possibly eventuality—picks and shovels, clothes, tents, sacks filled with coffee beans, pulses, salted meat, ammunition, blankets and bedrolls, flint, steels, kindling for fires, cooking pots, tin plates, cutlery, pails, buckets, mugs and cups, paraffin and lamps, wicks, candles and matches—all neatly stowed in chronological order of priority, so that the items we used least were stored in the deepest part of the wagon. In one underslung box lay an anvil, hammer and portable forge for metal work.

Dawkins and Mehmet mounted their horses and Pia climbed aboard the laden wagon. Mango's horsemanship was at best rudimentary, so he elected to travel in the wagon. I mounted a smaller pony whom I named Lester Bumble (he was a cantankerous beast, and I could beat him without a single pang of guilt), and we set off for India.

It didn't take long before the itching started, sinking me into my usual malaise. We pulled in off the road for our first rest, and I snuck off behind some boulders to administer a much-needed dose.

I wasn't the only sickly one amongst us.

Pia hadn't taken well to the constant rolling of the wagon and developed motion seasickness, which meant Mehmet had to tie his horse to the rear of the wagon and drive. It was no wonder his poor horse looked so unhappy given that its only view for the rest of the voyage was of the back of the wagon and Mango's ugly mug.

Pia recovered after a few days, but I didn't, and as we passed through several villages, I descended into an excruciating hallucinogenic stupor, sweating in the cold, trembling when it grew even a little bit warmer. I managed to find an opportunity to administer my dose at every stop. It became my raison d'être. I convinced myself that the dosage I had allowed myself was normal and that I had it all under control, though I'm not sure how I kept this self-delusion going. I wasn't consciously aware of how exaggerated reality had become but every sense became heightened. We even passed bright fields of poppies (ironically enough) which towered to impossible heights and whose colours were so bright they made me squint. It must have been my gaping awe which roused Mehmet and Dawkins' suspicions, prompting them to take turns to watch over me.

Another unfortunate side effect I suffered from was constipation. This problem was only exacerbated by my need to inject myself every time I excused myself to go to the toilet. I didn't pass a single stool on these trips, however, and a few hours later, I'd crave another rush and announce that I needed yet another toilet break, which became terribly tedious for everyone. I prayed for Anna between doses, and I prayed for death too, but the most constant prayer was for my next dose. The poison had consumed me in such a manipulative and pervasive way, that it convinced me.

We gathered quite a pace and were welcomed with open arms by the local chief in every village we passed through. Despite this being on the main trade route, very few travellers came through from outside the country, so white foreigners stood out.

Dawkins had bought them in Constantinople for this very purpose. They were delighted by us and so were their parents. It seemed we weren't the first Abyad adoo (white-eyed enemy) to have passed this way recently for it soon became obvious that some group of Russians who had passed through before us travelled in an awful hurry and, by all accounts, were rude and insulting. We always bid our hosts ma-is-salama and said shukri for their help which meant we were regarded as courteous and respectful.

We made about twenty miles per day. Each night, before sundown, we stopped at the most sheltered spot we could find, to set up a camp. It was February, so those Turkish mountains were freezing cold by night. We built our campfire within a stone perimeter, thus conserving enough heat to keep us warm, long after the fire had died down. Our fur bedrolls and blankets were cosy and served as ample cladding, even at the lowest of temperatures. Naturally, being the only female in our group, Pia slept in the wagon.

I was placed in charge of ensuring the horses were watered and tied to a tether-line. Despite the nightmares from my drug addiction, trauma, exhaustion and grief from losing dear Anna, looking after the horses offered me profound solace.

Mehmet shared warm stories around the fire about his family and friends, which made him terrific company. Once he had grown more at ease in our company, he prayed regularly alongside the wagon (giving me the perfect opportunity to sneak off). On one occasion, Mehmet treated us to his delicious recipe of Iskendher kebabs made with goat mince and spices. He served it in flatbread with salad bought from the market at Ercis.

That was the night that Mehmet announced it was time for him to return to Istanbul. Before he left, he presented Dawkins with a beautiful, highly polished, dark walnut box. It was about six inches deep, two foot in length and half a foot wide. An inch below the lid, in the centre of the front panel, was a brass keyhole. Mehmet passed Dawkins a cut key.

Dawkins inserted the key. He was just about to turn it when Mehmet grabbed his hand.

"Careful, my friend," he said. "There is a booby-trap device built into the lock. You have to turn it the opposite direction."

Dawkins looked confused. What kind of gift has a booby-trap built into it? he must have been thinking. But then it dawned on him, and his face lit up.

"This is specialist spy equipment, isn't it?" He was even more excited than before now.

"That is correct," Mehmet smiled. "And it was made specifically for you. So, here is the trick: if you turn that key the traditional way, you will release blue squid ink infused with skunk spray.

Which means you will certainly know if anyone has tampered with your box and what's more, you'll be able to easily identify them—if they are foolish enough to hang around, that is."

Dawkins' eyes widened, and he opened the lid with renewed reverence and curiosity, whilst we peered over his shoulder. A red velvet tray lay inside, with two brass thumb knobs, which Dawkins twisted in order to lift the tray out. He placed it carefully to one side to reveal a soft, satin-lined filling which had been cut and moulded into the shape of several articles it secured, thus ensuring the components did not rattle.

At top left, lay a tube, shaped like a cigar-holder but half the size. It tapered at both ends and could be unscrewed in the centre, perfect for concealing any item which might need to be secreted and was utterly watertight. For expediency (and to save space) the inventors had placed a cyanide pill, in the shape of a molar tooth, within it, which was secured (again to prevent rattling) by four richly detailed, silk maps.

Apparently, they were city maps of Tehran and Jammu, a topographical map of Kashmir and a map of the Middle East from Egypt to the Dutch East Indies.

Both their suppleness and lightness would make concealment, in the event of a strip-search, simple.

"The cyanide tooth is only to be put in the mouth as a last resort, of course. Crunch down and death will be at your door in seconds," Mehmet said.

Dawkins took out the pocket watch, which was cushioned-in next to the cavity tube. He held it up in his right palm and lifted it up and down as if estimating the weight of a plump apple at a market. It seemed extraordinarily heavy for a pocket watch.

"It is a watch," said Mehmet.

"Well, yes, I know," Dawkins said, "but what does it do?"

"It tells the time," Mehmet replied impertinently.

"And...?"

"And this." Mehmet flicked the outer ring off and pulled a yard-long tensile steel wire from the body of the watch. "Now we have a garrotte. You see how it is serrated—it also serves as a hacksaw." And with its sharp, razor-fine teeth, it looked to me like it could surely have cut through steel. It could also snare small animals. On the other side of the watch face was a tiny button compass and a detachable lens with which to read it.

"It's tricky to read the time when I'm riding. I always fumble to find my watch when handling reins. It would be better if the watch were strapped to my wrist with something strong like steel perhaps and encased in leather to prevent sweating."

"Let me talk to my contacts and see what we can do," the ever-helpful Mehmet replied.

His contacts? I wondered.

There was so much more to this man than I had fathomed.

A black fountain pen was cradled alongside the now-empty watch space.

"This pen will write approximately one hundred words before it runs out of ink, but if you twist the top this way, it transforms into a vial of sodium pentothal, a phenomenally potent truth serum. Once administered, the victim will first become drowsy and then answer any question as if they were drunk. If you click it again, the pen liquid changes. Push down here," he continued, pointing to the pocket slide, "and it will spray a mix of formic acid combined with concentrated pepper and chilli spray. It is for close-quarter fighting, effective up to about four feet, and will disarm whomever you spray, for thirty minutes. Turn it once again, and you'll be writing in invisible ink made of lemon juice. Alternatively, you could add the juice to your pancakes," he said, with a cheeky glint. "There are three of them in here." A small, ivory tube was stowed beside the pen.

"This contains kalium permanganate for rubbing on wounds. Dissolve it in water or alcohol to form a dye, eat it to settle your stomach, or use it for replacing important salts in the body. It can be used to start fires and even spontaneously explode if you mix it with commonly found chemicals, especially useful for blowing things up on a timed delay."

Within the lid of the box was another lens, covered by an ivory disc.

"Remove this disc and insert the watch's lens in this end. Then slide this tube away from that one, and you will have made yourself a powerful telescope."

Beneath the white container was a red candle.

"This is a special candle, indeed. The first inch will burn as normal, for precisely one hour, after which it will ignite a concentrated formula of a newly discovered high explosive named nitro-glycerine, which is mixed into the wax and extremely unstable. The British acquired the formula from a young inventor who was trying to patent a gas meter in London.

He wants to be famous, but I doubt if anyone will ever hear of Mr Alfred Nobel."

The next item in the box was a hatchet.

"The blade is cut from the finest steel money can buy," Mehmet said. "If you connect the 'tomahawk with the knob on its sheath—here let me show you—it becomes a pair of wire cutters, you see? On one side of the sheath there is a loadstone for honing the blade to a razor-sharp edge. Feel how heavy this is, and yet it is perfectly balanced—excellent design for throwing." He spun around and launched the tomahawk in between Pia and me. It flew behind us a good forty-five feet before striking a tree and wobbling into its resting place. Mehmet retrieved the tomahawk, unscrewed the metal cap at the hilt's top, then poured its contents onto the carpet we were sitting on.

"In here, you'll find everything you could possibly need: hooks for fishing, hunting snares, a flint and steel, a spare compass, some long-lasting waterproof matches, tweezers, some chalk for either messaging or for eating—it settles the stomach, you know." He rubbed his tummy and winked.

"The hilt is bound by a thread of steel-enforced silk one hundred feet in length which can be used to tie anything from a fishing line to a garrotte or even a rope. The tomahawk itself has been moulded from a single cast, making it an extremely sturdy piece of metal. You can use it as a door opener, It's as strong as any crowbar." Initially, I thought that a knife would be more useful but after Mehmet's extensive description I had to agree the tomahawk was a formidable item and I would not have swapped it for anything.

Next, came the most comprehensive brass picklock set I had ever seen, and laid out next to that was an unbreakable signalling mirror (constructed out of highly polished steel), three inches in diameter.

Once every item had been identified and explained, it was either stowed safely back in the box or tucked into Dawkins' pockets.

I didn't express my sentiments aloud, of course, but I admit that I felt slightly jealous. I realised, when Mehmet patted the hilt hanging from his belt, that his tomahawk was an exact copy of the single-cast one he'd just shown us.

"Incredibly strong," he beamed, noticing my gaze.

In the morning, Mehmet handed me a blank piece of paper.

"I have written down the recipe for my kebab dish, the one you liked so much," he said, "but now there's no invisible ink left in your pen. Sorry for that."

"Thank you, Mehmet," I replied, "for everything, and especially your recipe." He embraced me warmly and kissed me on both cheeks, then fare-ye-welled each man in the same manner. To Pia, he nodded respectfully with a meek smile. "By the way," he said in an incredibly clipped Etonian accent, "my real name is Antony Lambert." And at that, mounted his horse and he rode back towards Constantinople. I was flabbergasted.

It was mid-April by the time we entered Persia, and the temperate weather meant I was able to enjoy riding shirtless for the first time in my life. The sun danced over my skin like a thousand paintbrush tips dipped in a bronzing sheen of dew. Having realised how impractical her long flowing dresses were, Pia borrowed some trousers and a shirt from me. She tied her hair back and donned a large, brimmed hat to shield her from the Mesopotamian sun.

Bit by bit, the opiate's taut stranglehold loosened, and I started coming to my senses. I had lost a fair degree of weight and was constantly thirsty, but I was glad be alive and through the worst of the withdrawals. This relaxing part of the journey had eased my exhaustion somewhat. The glorious landscape, unusual smells, and colourful flora and fauna made for a much-needed distraction; not only from my grief for Anna, the acuteness of which softened with each passing day, but from the horrors of the Balaclava field hospital.

We arrived just north of the town gates of Tabriz within two weeks and set up camp. Dawkins went to the market to find someone who could speak Turkish and returned to tell us that he'd questioned a guide through an interpreter. The man informed him that there was a Russian group travelling to India on hired Bactrian camels. They were several days ahead of us. Apparently, a doctor in their midst had helped stitch a tribesman's severely cut hand while harvesting opium from the fields. The Doctor had a scar on his cheek. This doctor, they said, had bossed around his fellow travellers with brutish force.

Mango and I took a list to the stalls to buy enough stores to last two more weeks. We did our best to haggle prices down, but these traders were expert defrauders, and we were their prey. The game was in the haggling for them; they didn't care a jot if we walked away because they knew we needed provisions far more than they needed to sell them. We paid far too much for everything.

At daybreak, we cooked up some fresh eggs that Mango had purloined from one of the market stall. The way Mango saw it, his theft simply made up for the way they had defrauded us the night before. We packed up our camp and headed east, through the mountains near the Caspian Sea, before turning south.

As soon as we arrived in Tehran, we went straight to the main square. Dawkins, Mango and Pia went off to the market, leaving me to feed and water the horses, and watch the wagon. I was leading Doris to the trough when a tall Iranian man approached me.

"You are travelling a long way, yes?" he asked. His shifty manner made me nervous, and I instinctively reached for my 'special' pen.

"Yes, we are," I replied. "My friends are on their way back now."

"Where are you going with a large wagon as this?" the man enquired.

"Oh, we are trading furs in Afghanistan," I told him, switching the pen to the spray setting.

82

The man chuckled, "You think there is a lot of market for furs in our hot country?"

"Yes, there is, as it so happens, near the mountains," I stated indignantly.

He chuckled again. "I believe they have yaks for their own, don't you know? You think Afghans have much of money?"

I was just about to spray him when he started sidling around the wagon. I followed him cautiously, pen still secreted away, and my thumb on the pocket slide.

"You're not going to spray me with that, are you?" the man asked.

How many of these contraptions had Mehmet had made?

Chapter 8

"I am Mohammed," the man said. "I am a friend of Mehmet. He sent a message ahead via telegraph asking me to help you. I will be guiding you into India, Inshallah."

He handed me a telegram which confirmed all he had said. Mehmet had even asked after my horse, Lester, so the letter was certainly legitimate.

Mohammed was a tall, thin, muscular man. His skin was leathery, tanned and crevassed with crisscrossed wrinkles from his years scratching a living in the harshest environments of northern Afghanistan. His clothes were loose, functional for scorching days and freezing nights. His sand-coloured turban would have served to protect him from the infamous wind which blew morning, noon and night in those parts of the world. His lashes were black and thick as a camel's so even in the most impenetrable sandstorms (they churned up regularly in this truly godforsaken place) he would have the vision of a camel too. His hands were sinewy but firm and pocked with calluses from years tilling the field.

Even before he began quoting Plato and Socrates, I could tell he was an educated man. His English was faultless. He was familiar with modern poets like Byron and Shelley whom he recited by heart along the road as we went.

We stopped regularly to allow Mohammed his time for prayers, which he incanted even more earnestly than Mehmet. He quoted the Prophet Muhammed, and teachings from the Quran as well.

Initially, we were naive enough to imagine we could continue without his help, but we soon came to realise that the expedition would have been torture without him. The most invaluable guidance for me personally was when he showed me how to protect my all-too-English alabaster skin from the harsh Mesopotamian sun which meant that, thankfully, I was never unfortunate to extract water from camel dung.

As the sun began setting in the west, Mohammed navigated us with absolute precision to what turned out to be a hidden well. When Mohammed first instructed Mango to help him roll this large, flat stone aside we had no idea that he would reveal an Ashlar-lined well, a yard wide. It was connected to a brilliant system of engineering. A small trench bisected said hole, and an iron peg tethered one end of a long, neatly folded leather rope. Two straps at the other end were tied to the four legs of a mottled flap of brown and white goatskin. The hide had been tightly sewn up at the corners where the animal's hoofs had been axed off; its privy parts and butt were also sewn watertight, leaving a hole where the head and neck had once been. This deft bit of ingenuity allowed water egress and meant the fluid could be poured with little waste. Mohammed dropped the skin into the hole and waited. After half a minute or so, he began pulling the leather rope back up and, as the skin appeared at the top of the hole, it was filled to the brim with drinkable bore water.

We transferred the skin's contents to buckets and carried them to the wagon several times until the wagon's water butt was fully replenished. Only then did we take some for our own personal canteens and pause to drink the refreshing water, after which we returned the empty skin to its rightful place in the trench and placed the rope as neatly as we had found it, before pushing the stone lid back over the well. Our thirst slaked; we sat on the ground to rest for a while.

Our next task was to set up camp. It wasn't until we had carried out our habitual chores that we truly relaxed and found our first opportunity to really engage and chat with our new accomplice. His opening gambit made for quite an interesting start for Mohammed took us completely by surprise as he presented each of us with a uniquely novel invention. A watch, but altered to be worn on the wrist, just as Dawkins requested! Courtesy of none other than Mehmet.

Mohammed said, "Mehmet was the one who had observed Dawkins constantly fumbling with his watch whilst navigating and simultaneously trying to steer his horse, which he noticed became too vexing by half."

Mehmet had returned to his workshop and fashioned a way of fixing a fob to the top centre of his bangle—a slip-on brass bracelet secured with a strong clasp which he wore at all times. Once he had perfected his prototype, he sent details to Tehran via the telegraph system, and suggested Mohammed fabricate the gifts according to his instructions and descriptions.

Mohammed walked around our circle of comrades and presented each of us with a watch, including Mango. (I felt that Mango was unlikely to appreciate either the ingenuity or the value of such a device, so I confiscated his forthwith and determined to barter the timepiece in the next village.) Dawkins was as delighted as we all were with his watch. It seemed, however, Mohammed had even more delights in store.

"This bangle is very strong," Mohammed said. "It can be used as a hook with which to carry the weight of several bodies. And look!" he exclaimed; his eyes wide. "When the strap is fastened off the wrist, it also serves as a strong hook. It is a karabiner."

I had never heard of such a word. "What is a karabiner?" I asked.

"This device," Mohammed explained, "is used in abseiling. A climber employs it to fix their rope securely to the mountain face."

"Oh, how clever." I still had no clue as to what he was talking about but was too embarrassed to ask. Instead, I declared, "What will they think of next?!" I was neither over- nor underwhelmed, I was simply whelmed, which is why I continued, "But once secured to a mountain, the watch is lost forever. How very annoying, not to mention impractical." I looked around our group smugly, expecting a warm nod of agreement. None came.

Mohammed seemed peeved by my patronising tone (in retrospect, it was a tad rude of me). He pulled the watch from the bangle and held each piece in his hand. "This is iron," he said, pushing the bangle towards my face. He then retracted it and said, "This is magnetic." He pushed the watch toward me with his other hand before clicking them back together.

"Don't use this near a compass or you will go round and round in circles." His laughter bellowed through the camp.

We were soon to discover just how inspired Mehmet's recruitment of this character, Mohammed, had been. Mohammed knew the mountains by heart and spoke dozens of the local dialectics. Besides which, he was a highly respected imam, and a fine reputation preceded him. It wasn't until later that we discovered how well Mohammed knew Jammu and its surroundings. Mehmet had even told him the story of Fagin and Noor.

We all agreed to wait until morning before breaking camp and, whilst the others prepared supper, I snuck off into the souk to refill my opium jug. On my return, I presented the group with a cheap carpet I had purchased for us to sit upon together. This served to deter any questions regarding my absence and helped offer me the time I needed to smuggle my bottle back into its hiding place on the wagon.

Mohammed made us a delicious (though spicy) meat-filled stew called, Habsah.

"There was a prisoner amongst the Russians," Dawkins told me over dinner, "and by their description he sounded exactly like your friend Vladimir from school. They even described a scar on his cheek. They told me one of them was tied up and blindfolded. I can only assume that it was him."

Poor Vladimir. He'd been such an innocent back in our schooldays and continuously bullied about his mop of golden hair. He had a sallow complexion back then, and he matured late so was small for his age. Vladimir was forced to endure many a snide comment from the wealthy elite. He had shone at university, not only as a brilliant doctor but also as an athlete, especially in fencing and horsemanship, which I assumed he'd learned from his father. I once struck him, fairly clumsily, during a practice match, severely scarring his face. Over the years, that mark only added to his good looks, he grew into a ruggedly handsome man.

We were remarkably close friends back then, but as we neared the end of our training, something seemed to distract Vladimir. He became more and more aloof, and we started seeing less and less of one another, especially after I married Anna.

This routine—breaking camp, travelling, setting up camp—became the norm for the next few days. We passed through villages which skirted the mountains, where friendly Kurdish tribesmen told us the same story: a small group of Russian speakers were on camels, with a blindfolded man bound at the hands. Although he was said to be wearing the same civilian garb as the others, their brusque manner and efficiency was what gave them away as soldiers. Their leader had a scar on his face and blond hair. They were about two days ahead of us.

The closer we got to the Indian border, the more unfriendly and less welcoming the natives grew. We started ensuring our fires were smaller and we slept under the wagon at night. Thunderstorms were frequent in these parts at this time of the year, and the electric skies were hunting the earth for collections of lightning-rods such as us, so when they got really bad, we tended to leave our wagon and horses and head into the scree slopes to sit on our bedrolls for we had learned this lesson the hard way. On our first brush with a Himalayan thunderstorm. The night was oppressive, and the atmosphere had grown heavy with mugginess when, within minutes, we were forced to evacuate the wagon. I headed for a nearby cave.

"No!" Mohammed shouted. "Stop. All of you." Apparently, such caves and sheltered enclaves were frequented by deadly bears, snow leopards, snakes and even the occasional wayward tiger. But aside from the ferocious animals living there, we were likely to be fried alive in such a place should lightning strike, making the cave equally lethal, beast or no beast. So it was that Mohammed taught us that the best option was to sit on our roll-mats, despite the jaundice-tinted air—which is how mountainous thunderstorms appear in this region—tingling with sparks about us.

Rain pelted down, penetrating our clothes, and explosive thunderclaps startled us half out of our wits, but the lightning bolts went for the trees not us, splitting them in half, hurling a cacophony of creaks and groans, the likes of which I had never heard, into the echoey valleys and gorges.

Once the storm passed, we emerged all intact and slowly shuffled our way back to the wagon, shivering and soaked through to the bone but alive. A clothesline was erected for our sodden attire, and I checked on the horses.

By June, our party had turned south and into a deep ravine to follow a fast-flowing river of churning water topped with impenetrable foam and viciously perforated rocks. A deathly grumble, like some awakened giant, roared through the canyon. Rockfalls and mudslides, abbreviated with twinkling spots of rainbow whorls, menaced our trail at every turn. It was here we met our first ambush.

We had only just decamped. Dawkins sent out the alert after sensing a shuffling in the brush, but his short, high-pitched whistle was partially drowned out by the river's rumble. Once he captured our attention he pointed to a large bush, two hundred yards to our front, and signalled the presence of tribesmen with a closed fist, "Ambush!"

I stared at the spot he had indicated and caught the unmistakable glint of a long Afghan bonduque. As part of our preparation around the nightly campfire, we had discussed our anti-ambush drills and always travelled with our rifles semi-loaded and at-the-ready for exactly this kind of event. I placed a percussion-cap over the ignition tube. We crept towards our assailants, positioning ourselves into the predetermined tactical procedure, when some ill-disciplined assailant fired a shot. We retaliated at once with full force. Our group area was divided into quarters; each quarter controlled a zone. Mango was to stay underneath the wagon and attend to whoever needed help. Mohammed turned to scrutinise the rear, in case there was a cut-off group behind us.

Once he had ascertained that it was safe to do so, he took the quarter to his left whilst Pia backed into the wagon, protecting the rear to the right.

I dismounted and took the front-left quarter and Dawkins did the same to the front-right. Between the lot of us, we covered an arc of just over ninety degrees, ensuring every arc interlocked.

Dawkins shot first. A cry of anguish was followed by a tribal bandit, dressed in black, slumping over the bush he had imagined had been a safe haven for him. Pia fired at another to her right, where a man lurched back from a ditch, the force of her shot left him gurgling in his own death-rattle.

I was fumbling with my weapon when a bandit emerged from the side of a boulder just fifty yards from me. It should have been an easy shot, but my opium-induced shakes and sweats caused me to miss. Mango, who was lying prone beneath the wagon saw my predicament, took aim and shot the tribesman, who fell to the ground at once. I flashed a look at Mango for his impudence. He simply looked back and smiled, nodding with swelling pride in the direction of his stricken prey.

It seemed that despite my own personal failure, as a group we had repelled the chaotic bandits with ease thanks to Dawkins' training, Pia's years with the circus as a trick-shot artist, and myself for the summer holidays spent with my benefactor, Mr Brownlow, in Scotland stalking stags with our Gilly, Munroe. I conveniently overlooked Mango's part, pretending that he had served as an excellent reloader, for he had been deceptively agile when called upon. Of course, it also helped that we were organised, and that our assailants were slow to reload their ancient, inaccurate muskets. They were no match for our relatively modern percussion-cap firing rifles. Because we could load and fire so much faster; we were a force eight times our number. Top that with a precision (even from a great distance) unmatched by the enemy.

We stripped the dead Afghan bodies of useful powder and ammunition and returned to our wagon base. Dawkins was still uneasy.

I tried to lighten the mood by making some joke, but such humour was evidently ill-timed, because no one made eye contact with me all day. Dawkins simply tossed all the foraged booty into the wagon and mounted his horse and rode on without a word.

After a frosty supper that night, I slipped away for a small dose. When I returned, the others were sitting around the campfire whispering amongst themselves. The moment they realised I was in earshot they stopped, clearly embarrassed that I had stumbled into their conversation.

"What are you talking about?" I asked.

Dawkins sighed. "You. Your habit nearly got us all killed!"

"What are you talking about? What habit?" I replied, with the innocence all addicts feign. I was a qualified liar.

"Oliver, we know," Pia said, in a low monotone. "We know what you are up to when you slip away. I followed you a few days ago. We know about the opium. You're going to get us all killed. We can't depend on you."

"What? Of course, you can. I'm a better shot than any one of you!" I felt so indignant, so insulted, that in my delusion I pointed directly at Mohammed.

He simply looked up and waved a hand as if to say, "Don't involve me," and continued staring into the fire.

"Any one of you." I jaggedly pointed at Mango, desperate to target my scapegoat.

"Yes," she blurted, tears in her eyes, "when you are sober that's true, but you are completely doped up most of the time, we can see it and we need you, not the shell of the man into whom you are turning. You—"

Dawkins grabbed her arm, perhaps to stop her going too far, she shrugged him off but said no more.

"Balderdash! Codswallop! Really! is that what you think?" I was red with embarrassment, ashamed that my own friends believed I had endangered their lives.

"Yes! We are all agreed. You need to clean up," Dawkins said and then, to my despair, he held up my secret bottle of opium.

I anticipated what he was about to do. "Wait a minute," I pleaded. "Don't! I'll kill you! Please, God, no!" He unscrewed the cork and turned the bottle upside-down.

"Mango, stop him!" But no one moved and the precious contents were poured out into the dust. I was beside myself. My own team had ganged up on me, stolen my only succour. They thought I was the weak link. I'd show them! How infuriated I was. Me! regarded as the burden in their midst. The trouble was, I knew it was true.

Dawkins stood up and approached me with a fatherly arm. He turned me around and led me into the darkness away from the fire to the wagon. After several paces, he stopped and turned me to face him, gripping my shoulders as he stared squarely into my eyes. Tears were welling up.

"Oliver, we had all of us imagined this ambush and how it might unfold long before the first shot." He never broke his gaze—he was genuinely earnest. "I am relieved that we all came through unscathed, but such fortune cannot endure. We need to examine how this ambush unfolded and repel the likelihood of it reoccurring or we will stumble into real harm's way. We can't have twenty percent of our little army off their heads on drugs. We need to be able to fire at our enemy accurately from a lot further away, reload and fire again, do you think you could find a way to produce a solution?"

He was right and what's more, he had taken the right approach with me. By focusing my mind on the problem at hand, he had given me a possible chance to restore my reputation and make it up to my travelling companions. The Artful Dodger had certainly grown into a shrewd man.

Chapter 9

We traversed the passes of the Hindukush ravines, crossing roaring rivers and negotiating deadly rocky trails along the way. As I rode in silence upon Lester's back, I pondered all the possibilities should another ambush take place. I trotted up to Mohammed.

"Mohammed, do you know the sort of tactics used by the bandits in this area?"

Mohammed pointed to the area at our front and bit by bit, explained how the next ambush would play out.

"So, if I were to fire off a shot early and the bandits saw the devastation it caused, perhaps the rest of the bandits would be demoralised. If they then persisted, however, I would have to find some way of killing—or, at the very least, maiming—the lot of them from a distance. Then we'd be safe."

"What you need to do is to develop a rifle which could accurately fire five hundred yards. Gravity is stronger than a shot's momentum which in effect means that a projectile needs to be able to travel a lot further than its ultimate culminating point. Such a distance would therefore require an enormously powerful propellant indeed," said Mohammed.

Distance was not the only aspect which left us vulnerable, loading our rifles had been much too slow and laborious. I reflected on this issue for days, aware that I was unlikely to have the means to put a solution into action even if I did produce one.

In any case, I broke the procedure down step-by-step and concluded that we needed to be able to preload a tube with the lot—propellant, ball and percussion cap. Such a device would save us enormous time in the loading process. We are talking seconds, of course, which can be a matter of life of death in such a scenario. But how to make such a contraption?

Although the drug had shut down half my critical thinking skills, I began to regain clarity, thanks to my friends, who helped me as I emerged from my hallucinations and made the tedious journey towards sobriety more bearable. The drying-out period was horrific. I spent days in the wagon vomiting and fouling myself, screaming throughout my endless nightmares and sweating profusely. Pia and Mango nursed me, ensuring that I didn't dehydrate, and cleaning up after my disgusting movements until eventually, the cloud lifted from my mind.

When a chain connecting the swingle trees to the yolk snapped, Mohammed, in his usual efficient manner, unloaded the travelling blacksmith's kit (which we carried for such emergencies) containing an anvil, billows, pliers, snips and a hammer. We collected driftwood from the riverbank, then stoked and billowed the kindling until the flames were leaping high and the fire began to roar. Our guide placed the broken chain into the inferno and waited for the metal to grow red-hot enough to be worked upon. What an accomplished metalsmith Mohammed was! I parked the knowledge in the back of my mind and continued to watch him repair the chain. Once done, we carried on our way.

I let the wagon trundle on ahead so I could walk with Mohammed. He listened intently, staring at the ground beneath our feet and nodding sagely as I explained my conundrum. I could almost see his cogs turning, and the instant he lifted his head, I knew he had devised a plan.

His eyes lit up. He was clearly inspired by the challenge. "The tube should be made to be slightly smaller than the calibre of the rifle. If we seal one end with pliers, pre-pack the bullet tip with powder and crimp it into place, the long loading process will be negated."

"We can certainly make a tube long enough to hold an ounce of propellant," I said. "What if we seal the other end of the tube with wax and a percussion cap." I also explained my rear-loading breach idea.

Mohammed smiled. "If you ask me, converting this rifle is going to be easy."

We went to work on one of our spare rifles straight after supper. Mohammed removed the hammer and trigger mechanism before sawing through the butt. He spent hours whittling and chiselling until he was finally able to fit the hammer in such a way that it struck the centre of the barrel-opening, or chamber. He also inserted a flat piece of metal to act as an anvil on the breach so it resisted the cartridge's natural reaction to push back into the butt when initiated, ensuring that the maximum energy would be forced forward into the base of the bullet tip. He found a spare trunnion pin and filed it down until it formed a hinge for the butt to lock to the stock. We fixed a spring and lock at the top of the butt and screwed it tightly into place.

We then discussed the ammunition. The cartridge needed to be constructed from a metal which would heat so quickly that, when struck, the gas from the explosion would heat the shell case instantaneously and swell the seal with enough force to breach end of the barrel. Within milliseconds, the compressed gas would expand and heat the other end of the tube, which would also swell, thereby releasing the lead ball.

"And then we need the metal to cool and contract so we can easily extract it. What kind of metal does that?"

"Brass," Mohammed smiled. "It has particularly good qualities." He demonstrated by opening and closing his thumb and forefinger. "It obturates, you see," he added, much to my surprise.

But where could we find enough brass to make a substantial quantity of ammunition? I mused over the problem whilst feeding the horses and checking over the wagon, when I found the answer right under my nose. Middle Eastern traders take great trouble to adorn their horses' tack with flourishes of brass embellishment.

If we snipped off all that non-essential, decorative brass and melted it in the forge pot we'd have our casings. Mohammed was equally enthusiastic about my idea when I shared it with him the following day.

We were resting after a particularly gruelling traverse when Mohammed pointed into the sky at a harrier on the lookout for prey.

"Look at that harrier, Oliver," he said. It was awe-inspiring watching the way it hovered in the mountain's updraft, before—without warning—diving earthward at incredible speed to spear its victim with deadly talons. "Did you see? Did you see?" he asked.

"Yes, Mohammed, it was swift."

"Yes, but did you see the shape? A true sign from God," he enthused. "We should shape the bullets like a diving bird. If we make it hollow it will reduce the ball's weight and. being aerodynamic, it will travel further. I'll cut a deep cross into the tip, so it disintegrates on impact, thus causing more damage and losing even more weight."

"You know what I just realised? If we add sweat beads of nitro-glycerine from our exploding candles, using tallow wax to secure them to the bullet-head groves, then we'll increase their killing power ten-fold as it will prevent the nitro-glycerine from evaporating or dropping off."

Dawkins came over to the fire to see what Mohammed, and I were whispering about. Mohammed and I showed him how we were going to manufacture the ammunition. And that very night we all gathered, and I showed them. First I used blacksmith snips to clip the brass from the tack, while Pia and Dawkins tended the fire. I melted my offcuts in the forge pot and poured the molten metal onto an anvil. Once slightly cooled, Mohammed beat it out into small two-inch by three-inch ingots.

After two hours, we had twenty workable pieces. He heated them again and beat each one around the baker rifle's ramrod, ensuring the cartridge fit.

Once the edges met, he placed them in the fire and soldered them to form a round tube. Again, we waited for them to cool before filing off the rough edges to smooth the tubes. Mohammed tested each for size, filing where required until they slid into the chamber with ease.

We kept working until we had twenty completed tubes, after which we set about making the lead bullet head. We moulded a wax version of the appropriate bullet-head shape and let it cool. Mohammed made a clay mould, covered it with sand and clay and poked a hole through the bottom before cooking the entire mould in the fire.

Wax ran out from the hole within no time. As soon as it had stopped dripping, we rescued the hardened mould and poured molten lead through the hole. Mohammed cut the mould in half to reveal a perfectly formed bullet; sharp-pointed and, to our delight, it had a cross in the centre. We carried on all night, completing twenty bullet heads in total. Mango diligently filed a cross into each one.

The next day, Mohammed and I walked behind the wagon discussing ways to improve the sighting system. Dawkins rode ahead, scanning the horizon for signs of an ambush using his new telescope. Mohammed and I exchanged a glance and grinned, both thinking the same thing.

That night, we filled the tubes with black powder and sweat beads from our exploding candles and crimped the loaded bullet heads to the tubes with great care. Mohammed crimped the centre of the base of each round with a percussion cap. For added power, we placed a small sliver of a dynamite "candle" in each cap as well.

The following day was spent testing and practice-firing. It was my invention, so I was given the dubious honour of testing the first shot. I took up my strongest standing position. I broke the breach and nervously inserted my first of twenty rounds into the chamber. I locked the weapon and brought it up into the aim, levelled at a rock about one hundred yards away. I applied a light pressure to the trigger. Boom!

The rifle recoiled into my shoulder, knocking me onto my backside. Everyone ran towards me.

It took a few moments before I could make out what they were saying. "Oh, my days," Dawkins laughed, "Can you see? Look at that rock!" It had completely disintegrated, "Let me have a go."

He took the weapon and broke it, popping the spent cartridge out of the chamber.

My ears were still ringing. "We ought to stuff our ears with cloth for the next shot," I mumbled.

"I'm going to aim at that tree over there," Dawkins announced.

"But that must be three hundred yards away!" Pia exclaimed.

Boom! Dawkins flew back.

"Missed," I said. Seconds later, a branch exploded and dropped from the tree.

We took turns, firing further and further each time. Mohammed went over to find my first bullet I had fired into the rock, when he returned he showed me the remains it had splayed across his palm and was at least two inches across in every direction.

"You have devised a truly impressive weapon, Oliver," Mohammed told me. "It could kill a man from five hundred yards before he'd even heard the shot."

"Now, we have to work on the sighting system," I said.

I instructed Mohammed to fashion a cradle with his knife from some dried wood we had scavenged. He whittled it to fit both the rifle and the round telescope. I fixed it in place with some wax and unravelled the knife's silk and wire hilt until I had enough to wrap around both the telescope and the rifle's stock. I secured it with a small brass stud I had fashioned into the shape of a tack.

I then fitted a wooden wedge at the back of the telescope and carved graticules along the side with values at 200, 300, 400 and 500.

"Pia," I said, "I'm going to need some hair."

"Alright then," she said, but smiling all the same.

She winced as she pulled out a few strands of her raven black hair. I measured the lengths into sections and cut them at the correct length (approximately one inch) so that, once fixed, each would be exactly half the diameter of the optic end of the telescope. I cut a further two strands and set them all perpendicular to one another onto the glass (with candle wax) so they formed a cross at the front of the telescope, thus ensuring the firer taking aim would have precise centre of the scope in his sight. By mid-afternoon, we had recharged all our spent cases with powder, bullets and caps.

"Well done, Oliver," Pia said, as we laughed and chatted around the fire that evening, "it is a marvellous weapon."

"Who would have thought a guttersnipe from the Jago would come up with such a thing?" Dawkins teased. "Tell me, what you are going to call it?"

"Guttersnipe?" I retorted, in mock indignation.

"And so, I hereby name it the 'Snipe's Rifle'," Dawkins said.

We all fell about laughing for he had accidently stumbled on a pun. Dawkins didn't know that sniping had been in common usage since the English civil war.

Over the next three days, we worked on perfecting the weapon, adding a brass shoulder-stock for comfort and a spring into the butt to absorb some of the recoil. We adjusted the trigger to lessen its sensitivity and added belt loops so we could carry it in an adjustable leather sling. We also built a bipod for stability. Mohammed cut off superfluous wood to make it lighter, thus making the stock more comfortable.

When the ammunition supply allowed, I took every opportunity I could, to practise. After a few minor adjustments to my new weapon and applying the hunting knowledge which I had learned in the glens of Scotland, I began to bullseye small objects up to five hundred yards away. My ears rang constantly, and my shoulder ached.

We followed a rapid river on a well-worn track along a ravine. Once the terrain flattened out, we arrived on a luscious green plain, so green, in fact, that I had to squint to take in the vastness unveiling before us. The landscape was punctuated with white dots. This would be the sternest test of all for me, for the flowers in the fields were none other than poppies. Miles and miles of raw opium!

Everyone was aware of how easily I could relapse. Pia, Dawkins and now even Mohammed kept a close eye out. The thought of saving the lives of my new best friends, was enough to prevent me from delving into my selfish past, but he wasn't taking any chances on that promise and went as far as tying me up at night, which meant that we never did find out whether I could have resisted, through sheer willpower alone, the fix I so yearned for.

We were only a few hours behind our quarry by now and the atmosphere changed in our gang. I became aware that Mohammed was shuffling uneasily his saddle and Dawkins was peering through his telescope far more often. We jolted when we heard a boom in the far distance. A few miles on we came upon a landslip, but Mohammed pointed up to the cliff face. We could clearly see scorch marks. Someone had let off explosives. This was no natural occurrence. More obstacles cropped up, indicating that the Russians ahead knew we were close.

The tribesmen in Afghanistan hated the Russians and British in equal measure, so their loyalty could be easily bought. We passed a goat herd no more than ten years old. He was soon on his heels when we passed no doubt to signal to be aware of being watched.

We turned our horses and started to climb the western hinterlands of the Himalayas, but we'd be prepared this time.

Dawkins carried out his usual regime, scouring the horizon through his telescope for any sign of the enemy. Suddenly he froze and then hushed us with a glance. He descended from his horse, handed the reins to Pia and simply said "Ambush ahead."

Dawkins summoned Mohammed to follow him up to a vantage point. I started to follow but both Mohammed and Dawkins fired warning glances stopping me in my tracks.

The camp was tense until their return, Mango sensed it and had to be soothed by Pia. Mohammed confirmed an ambush. "It is led by a foreigner, moreover their dispositions and behaviour are unfamiliar to me, so I believe this is a Russian coordinated ambush. Alas I cannot help you in unravelling their plan for I know little of Russian tactics," he lamented.

"Unfortunately, I have had the experience before," said Dawkins. And we sat while he outlined the plan. "As soon as I give the signal like this," and he waved his hand as if summoning us to follow him, "Oliver, take your new weapon and peel off. The wagon will be in dead ground; you will be unseen. Make for the higher ground on the right and skirt in as large a circle as possible so, as we approach our assailants, you will be above them and shoot down on them from behind." He continued, "Mohammed ride at the rear and Mango drive the wagon along the track with Pia, I will move between the posts, depending on whichever direction requires reinforcement."

As we approached the dead ground in front Dawkins waved as he had shown us and we carried out his instructions to the letter. I skirted up the slope into a gully which allowed me to remain out of sight. Using bushes, large rocks and all the dead ground possible I found myself six hundred yards above the ambush killing zone.

The altitude and exertion of the climb made me breathless. Adrenaline coursed through my body, making me sweat profusely. My pulse raced.

I reached the top of an arête and crawled onto a ledge. Using a goat track as cover, I moved silently along the ground, just as I had in the highlands of Scotland as a child. The memory of Gilly's voice echoed clearly in my head. "Quietly, laddie," he whispered. "Steady, hold still."

I reached a small bush where I unslung my rifle and pulled back the hammer. I tried to steady my breathing. Sweat rolled, soaking my shirt front and back. In calm silence, I focused down my scope.

A man in Western dress came into view about five hundred yards away. He used a stick in the sand to point out a plan of attack to the five Afghan tribesmen sitting on their haunches alongside him. I watched the gentleman draw the shape of a cross on the ground. I could have easily started picking them off one by one. They would have needed to close in four hundred yards before putting me in any mortal danger, so I knew I'd have a few minutes to escape.

I unslung my rifle and adjusted the sights to 500. I fidgeted for my ammunition and silently broke the weapon, before loading the deadly cartridge into the chamber. I opened the bipod, secured the rifle and lay my body down in the prone position. I wiped the sweat from my brow and slowed my breathing right down before focusing through the scope.

I could hardly believe what I saw. The man in my gunsight was the very same man who had attacked me on the streets of London all those months before! I held my breath and slowly increased the pressure on my finger, adjusting my aim until Pia's crossed strands of hair came to rest in the centre of the back of the man's head. Our wagon would be a mere two hundred yards from the killing zone by now.

I could tell by the way the tribesmen looked at the Western man that he had completed his final instructions, and they were fully prepped for their ambush. This was my moment.

Thanks to the sound delay, they didn't hear my gun's report. Their intensely studious expressions transformed into utter shock as my former assailant's head exploded before them. They were aghast with shock and still trying to take in what had just happened as I reloaded. They had no idea what was coming!

I fired another shot. My next victim spun around, before his entire body was thrown backwards to land, splayed out and arched, over a rock.

102

The smoke from my rifle cleared and I reloaded again, even faster this time. Four of the Afghans had worked out my location and started moving stealthily up the slope towards me. Although I couldn't pinpoint where exactly the attackers were, I placed the crosshairs on a small bush in the centre of two large boulders, and when another tribesman entered my killing area I fired one more time.

A hole the size of a dinner plate carved out his chest, and he tumbled back into the next Afghan's arms, who was also knocked back. His other colleague, however, managed to duck and slip through the gap.

They would have been about two hundred yards away now, but I couldn't see them. All I knew was that on their way around the rocks, they'd have to navigate the largest one straight front of me. I took a fifty-fifty bet on it and rested my aim on a space to the left of the boulder where a small piece of cloth fluttered. I held my nerve and waited. Sure enough, a turban eventually emerged from that very side and within a second, his entire face came into view. He was relatively young and still had most of his teeth. The poor boy was moving cautiously, straight into my aim. Boom! His head was destroyed in a flash—skin, blood and bone splattered everywhere.

There were still two tribesmen unaccounted for. I searched the area to my front, to my left side, to my right. A glint caught my eye. The sun had sprung off a muzzle right in front of me. A chip of stone hit me in the left cheek. I heard a crack and a boom! I turned to see a plume of gun-smoke drift about a hundred yards from me. Blood started dripping down my cheek. I kept my weapon down and peered over my improvised scope. I would have to fire this next shot on instinct. A face appeared near the smoke. I levelled the rifle and fired. This time, the forceful recoil spun the weapon out of my hand, and it cracked against a granite boulder. The man's face was no more. His body, however, stood still before collapsing in one heap.

I knew there was one man left but where was he? I picked up my rifle, ejected the spent case and reloaded it in haste.

My hands were trembling so much that I couldn't marry the chamber with the round and, as I fumbled, I dropped it. I heard a noise behind me and spun around where—to my horror—the last Afghan loomed over me, grinning. He levelled his rifle at my head. He was only yards away. He couldn't possibly miss but, as if revelling in the moment, he took careful aim and clicked back the hammer whilst mumbling something in Pashtu which translated into "God is great".

Chapter 10

I closed my eyes and whispered the first of my prayers to God. A shot rang out. I opened my eyes to witness my assailant flung at least ten yards backwards; his head obscured in a mist of spattered blood, fabric, teeth and brain. Confused, I turned in the direction from where the shot had come. Mohammed was standing a hundred yards away, shrouded in a puff of smoke from his charged weapon.

"You didn't think I would build only one, did you?" he shouted, grinning his toothy grin. "Come on, guttersnipe," he laughed. I creaked to my feet to join him in a stupor.

We searched the bodies for gunpowder and anything else we might find useful. Mohammed found a pendant, it looked familiar. A masonic emblem with a green stone in the centre. By God, it was mine! Stolen from me in the fight outside the Fortune of War tavern months before.

In mid-November we pulled into a village north of Kabul where we bartered our fine, elegant horses for smaller, hardier local equine. We bought thick yak-skin jackets with hoods and gloves to protect us against the tough Himalayan elements. The garments stank of sweat and lord knows whatever else. They were well-worn and, by the smell of them, they'd never been washed. Dawkins looked quite the spectacle seated upon his under-sized mount, dressed as a local, with his feet almost reaching the ground. We were confident now. Provided we carried out detailed reconnoitres, we knew we'd be fine. It was now time to scale the vast canyons, ravines and glaciers of the Himalayas.

The higher we climbed into the Hindu Kush, the stronger my sense that someone or something was stalking us. We had dismounted and were walking the ponies, pulling by their halters. It was my turn to cover the tail end. What started as light snow flurries grew thicker and thicker until, within the hour, we were travelling through a full-blown Himalayan blizzard.

It was during this storm that I first spotted a grotesque, hairy figure out of the corner of my eye. The marauding beast had a hunched back and prowled through the swirling gloom, bent over, growling as it went. The most terrible odour of wet fur and rotten meat lingered in the air. Then it vanished. I squinted, to try to catch another glimpse of it, but the blanketing snow obscured my view.

I had heard stories about the Yeti, who hauled travellers off to its cave where it boiled its victims alive before eating them. I did consider alerting my companions but a part of me wondered whether it was some trick of the moonlight and the howl of the wind. The ghastly vision came and went but I kept my mouth shut, at risk of humiliating myself again, and so my companions remained completely oblivious.

The snowstorm finally abated, and as we set up our camp for the evening this creature appeared again. This time, it stood at full height in front of the wagon. It outstretched its arms and screeched. The beast bounded straight toward Mohammed as I struggled to unsling my gun through my thick garments. My hands were so cold that loading too was awkward. Mohammed looked up, saw the thing coming his way and began mimicking the Yeti, running towards him, arms out and screeching. The two crashed into one another and clinched. Mohammed was knocked backward, and they fell into the snow, rolling, and struggling.

Dawkins and Pia had their rifles unslung and were trying to get a shot, but they hesitated in fear of shooting Mohammed.

Finally, the two bodies lay motionless in a bed of snow. We approached cautiously, unsure whether one or both of them were dead, but before we reached them, they both sprang up, burst into laughter and started brushing the snow from their coats.

"Company," Mohammed announced, "meet our guide!" He embraced the "Yeti". "This is Aafreen."

The "beast" pulled back his yak-skin hood and greeted us with a beaming grin.

Later, by the fireside, I had some questions to pose to our new addition. "Why did you let out that unearthly screeching?" I asked.

Aafreen's strong Kashmiri accent, coupled with this tightly fixed grin which never left his face, made him difficult to understand. "When the wind blows like that, screaming is the only way we could be heard over the wind."

"But how did you create that wretched smell?"

"The yak I was riding died on the way and I skinned it to make a warm coat but there are many—how you say?"

"Sinews?" I suggested.

"Sinews," Aafreen agreed, "that I have missed. They go bad."

"Rancid, yes, I see."

"What about the hunch on your back?" asked Mango.

Aafreen turned his head. "I have to carry everything on my back in a rucksack. It made me hunch over, as you say."

"But you moved like a wild beast," I said.

"The only way to move up here in a blizzard is to bound, or the wind will blow you off the mountain."

We lay around the fire for hours staring into the flames. I must have fallen asleep. I awoke to that terrible smell of rotten sinews. When I opened my eyes, I found a set of pungent, wet socks right next to my nose.

I plucked them from the guy rope where they were drying and flung them at Mango.

"Take your rotten socks!" as they hit him in the face. After a pause and brief inspection, Mango threw them back.

"Not mine; yours." He grunted.

"Where's Aafreen?" I asked.

"Who?" asked Mango.

"Oh, nothing," I replied. I must have been dreaming. "I think the thin air has given me altitude sickness. I feel a tad giddy." Later, I thought that might have been the last of my opium withdrawals.

Our covert journey lasted one hundred and fifteen days in total. We either bribed or captured the occasional tribesmen en route who told us about the progress of our adversaries. Once under our control, they were surprisingly compliant and disclosed a lot of information to Mohammed about their former employers.

Finally, we arrived at the entrance to the secret pass which Pia told us Fagin had travelled along twenty years earlier. We were fortunate enough to happen upon a group of Pundits just as they were surveying the pass on behalf of the East India Company, and after Dawkins had showed them his government credentials they shared their detailed maps with us—quite a stroke of luck, for it really helped us plan the following day's journey. The weather was better now, warmer and less precipitation. The further down the mountain passes we went the more humid it became. Our surroundings went from shrubs to short pines to deciduous trees and then rich jungle.

The ravines were deep, and the waterfalls between the igneous granite cliffs flowed like wedding dresses. Mohammed remained in the lead, constantly checking ahead to make sure the path was safe. Lighting the way with torches and without major incident, we wove in and out of whichever cave system would allow for our large wagon until we arrived on the Indian side of the ravine.

We descended the foothills and entered a village.

The village elder greeted us and insisted we join him for tea and samosas, followed by a delicious goat curry. We warmly accepted his generous invitation for we knew the gesture came at great cost to the village in these lean times of war, famine and drought.

The ponies were considerably shabbier than the ones we had ridden through Turkey. Still, we took immense pleasure in naming them after characters from Homer's Trojan wars: Paris, Hector, Achilles and Agamemnon. Although, Agamemnon was certainly not as regal, nor as proficient as his namesake, poor horse. We scolded him day and night. He was a scraggy looking beast and did not take to me at all.

We soon tired of yelling, "Agamemnon! Move!" and "Agamemnon! Geeup!", so we shortened it to "Agamem". Before too long, he became, "Agam!" and although no amount of shouting would rush this wretched animal, Mango ended up reducing his name to "Aggy".

We arrived in the provincial and predominantly Hindu capital, Jammu, where tall, skinny cows wandered entirely unhindered, wherever they wished. Travelling Buddhist monks also roamed these provinces, they walked in columns through the streets in their bright orange robes, chanting and ringing small brass cymbals to let you they were passing by. They covered their shaven heads with grand, scarlet-coloured caps shaped like cresting waves. Shopkeepers ran out onto the streets offering gifts to the holy men in exchange for blessings.

We passed through the large wooden gates in the inner-city wall. A small contingent of British soldiers in red tunics and white pith-helmets trooped in the opposite direction, swearing at the locals.

It was tense in the city. The monsoon was about to unleash its torrents across this fascinating land. The air was laced thick with spice and the mystical twang of an Indian sitar cut through this world, oblivious to discomfort, fear or misery of any form. Ladies in lavish, coloured saris, their red hair-powder signifying that they were married, demurely lowered their eyes as they glided past. proud warrior Sikhs (with their turbans tied neatly to indicate their grade) smoothed down

109

their splendid beards with one hand, gripping their magnificent sabres which hung centrally from the front of their belts, with the other and talked in booming voices.

Untouchable women, born into the wrong caste, who plied an unchosen trade as whores or lavatory cleaners, whimpered in despair through rotting teeth and blackened gums, pawing the air with their bony hands, begging fruitlessly of the castes who avoided them.

As always upon entering a new village, the local children mobbed our small baggage train, squealing for treats or any morsel of joy we could offer, but we had run out of sweets weeks ago. Once again, I was reminded of the Tyndale slum. How I hated those days and now, instead of shooing away the children, I embraced them and found small morsels to comfort them. Anna would approve.

We halted outside a small, sandal shop. Mohammed dismounted and called out, "Yallah!" The vendor emerged to welcome us with a toothy grin.

"Salam was alyikum," said Mohammed.

"Alyikum is Salam," replied the stranger. The men embraced and Mohammed said, "Allow me to introduce my brother Dipesh." Dipesh took Mohammed's arm before holding his hand over his own heart; he clearly held Mohammed in great regard.

"What is the news?" he asked. "What is new?"

Mohammed met each question with, "Tayib," or "Kull shay Tamam," and a sideways nod, meaning "All is well".

Eventually, Dipesh led us into the back of his house. He invited us to make ourselves at home upon his plump, brightly coloured cushions. His wife passed out a syrupy coffee-like liquid, generously laced with cardamom.

"What is new for you, Dipesh?" Mohammed asked. Dipesh was brimming with all manner of banal news.

"How is it you are called Dipesh, and your brother is Mohammed?" I enquired.

Dipesh said, "Oh, he is not my birth brother, we were together in the army. It is just what we say."

"Dipesh saved me on numerous occasions." said Mohammed.

"And you saved me too, brother," said Dipesh adding "from the Sergeant Major's stick."

And turning to us Mohammed said, "I was really good at cleaning the kit."

"Ask him about the strangers who have passed this way," Dawkins said.

This prompted Dipesh to sit up. "A party of men passed through the town only a few hours earlier. They were heading towards an abandoned temple on the other side of the river. They looked like military officers and one man with them appeared to be bound and blindfolded."

Dawkins rose and signalled for the rest of us to stay put. "Could you lead me to the barracks, Dipesh?" and Dipesh nodded in agreement.

Dawkins returned within the hour with news that he had secured rooms at the officers' mess in the garrison next to the palace. This was indeed a stroke of good fortune.

We unpacked that night after prayers and convened for a meal in private rooms usually assigned to the Colonel and his staff. Our numbers certainly had grown by now. What a motley crew we made around the table! Aware that we were going to have quite a fight on our hands once we eventually faced the Russians.

Dipesh had handpicked several trusted men who had recently served as sepoys in the British Army and seen service on the northwest frontier. Men whom he knew could easily handle themselves under duress.

"We should relocate to the Bahu Fort," Mohammed suggested, "It is used as a religious temple built over one hundred years ago."

"It is situated three miles from Jammu city, on a rock face on the south of the river. It was known as the temple of Mahakali," Dipesh added. "Who is considered second only to Mata Vaishno Devi."

"Should we need to defend ourselves, we will be safest in the area near the cave, where the treasure is buried, as it is solid limestone," Mohammed deduced.

Pia agreed. "Yes, and we could use the river to make our escape."

Mohammed smiled. "Indeed, once we have the treasure, we should obtain a boat."

"There is a small quay used to supply the fort," Dipesh added, "This will make an excellent loading point for the captured booty." One of Dipesh's men entered the room and whispered something in Dipesh's ear. He nodded sagely.

"Lady and Gentlemen," he bowed, "my spies tell me that the Russians are led by a man who calls himself "The Count". He is planning to set off tomorrow to find the cave. He is taking a party of coolies to get through the obstacles. They have bought gunpowder. It looks like they are going to try to blast their way through. We need to get there first, before he ruins everything." Mohammed signalled to our Indian guards who left. Mohammed told us that his brother's friends had left their ponies fully tacked and ready to travel.

"You are all now in great danger," he said. "The Peer Kho Cave is near the fort.

Some believe the bear god, Jamvant, meditated in the cave. Fluorescent algae lives on the stone. They light up when agitated. But many have died in there thinking they can unravel the deadly puzzles that lay within."

Upon hearing this, Pia gasped and sat bolt upright. "Quickly!" she exclaimed, jumping to her feet. "Gather the stores. I know exactly what to do."

We organised our equipment, mounted our ponies and exited the barracks in double file. We trotted down a hill, past the markets and temples. At the bottom of the hill, the path leading to the bridge bisected a road which ran along the riverside. We could see pilgrims leaving the temples on the other side of the river, but there was no sign of the Count or his accomplices.

Dipesh called in at a bungalow on our way to the cave. After vanishing inside the hut for a few minutes, he emerged with four swarthy looking men. At the order the men formed a row and stood perfectly still, as if they had marched onto a parade ground in Delhi, with their rifle butts on the ground and their right hands forming a V around the stock and barrel.

Dipesh raised his chin and puffed out his chest with pride. "These are my friends," he announced. "They fought alongside me in the Sikh wars a decade ago. This is Amar and this, Balbir. Ajeet is here with his brother, Charanpreet. All late of Her Majesty's 31st (Huntingdon) Regiment of Foot." Upon hearing their name, each soldier braced up, ramrod straight, and offered a slight bow of the head. They certainly look the part, I thought.

"These are veterans of two of the bloodiest wars in India. Together we have fought against the Sikhs under General Gough," Dipesh added. He barked orders in Punjabi, and they obeyed without hesitation. It was clear how much they respected Dipesh, and, in turn, he went up in my regard. I had really begun to take to our guide.

"Did you see much action Dipesh?" I asked.

"Oh, yes! We fought many battles." He pulled up his sleeves and lifted his shirt with great enthusiasm to display (to Pia in particular) various bayonet scars and sword cuts around his arms and torso. He hopped along one leg as he drew up his pantaloon to reveal a long scar running diagonally across his taut muscle. "This one on my calf," he said triumphantly. He didn't stop there. Dipesh continued pointing out his various disfigurements as if he were some exhibit at a Brighton fairground showing off his body art or hawking souvenirs.

"I got this at Sobraon. And this one from Mukhi." He paused and pointed to a small nick over his eyebrow. "This one really hurt," he confided in a stage whisper out of the corner of his mouth.

Pia leant in to inspect the wound up close. She appeared as surprised as I upon hearing this for it was small in comparison to the other gashes. That's when Dipesh let out an enormous guffaw and squealed, "I got it from my wife in Jammu. It is always the strike at the heart which hurts the most, is it not so?" We all laughed.

Whilst walking the road, I couldn't help but notice how equally embroidered his friends were with trophies from the past.

Pia turned around and handed me a loaded pistol. "Make sure you keep your carbine close as well." She tapped a large holster on her pony where she kept hers.

Once we had reached the other side of the river, we took the less trodden path off to the left. Our ponies whinged and whinnied all the way up the steep incline.

We came to an enormous rock where Pia (who still led the way) turned towards an even denser part of the forest which stretched up the face of the steepest gradient of the hill. Our ponies grew ever more stubborn, until they refused to climb altogether. We fixed a tethering line between a willow and a limestone boulder and tied them to it.

We prepared ourselves for the rugged climb up a slippery scree slope.

"The cave is behind this waterfall," Pia said.

The cave's opening was just wide enough for a horse and cart to fit through. Our escort of former soldiers stood guard on either side of the cascades in front of the entrance. The walls were cool and damp. Centuries of erosion had smoothed them till they shone. Once our eyes had adjusted to the dim light, we saw how the cave tapered like a long tube into the daunting unknown. "Don't touch a single thing," Pia whispered.

"And watch your step," said Dawkins, "there are human skulls all over the ground." He was right, and they'd been gnawed bare by rats.

Dawkins knelt carefully to pick up a handful of sand. He let it run through his fingers. "Someone has gone to great trouble to cover this floor. The colour of this sand doesn't match the stone on the walls or ceiling. It's been brought in from outside."

A peculiar sound echoed against the walls.

"What was that?" I gasped.

"The floor is moving," Pia said. "It's giving way under our weight."

Mango walked further into the chamber. "It feels bouncy over here," he said, before reeling backwards. "Skeletons!" he cried, pointing to a dozen decomposing soldiers covered in years of dust. Though rotten with decay, we could just make out the red of their uniforms and their Blanco white droopy belts. Their boots had fallen off their fleshless feet and lay strewn at the end of bony legs. Most of the bodies leaning against the walls had spears sticking out of them. Dawkins examined the skull of one of the impaled bodies which hung limply from the limestone wall. He still had his pith helmet on, and an unspeakably large cobweb had covered its jaw.

"He certainly won't be sharing any secrets with us," Dawkins said.

I recoiled in horror as a bird-eating spider crawled out from between the skull's gaping teeth. "Oh, my lord! That creature is bigger than my fist!" I exclaimed. When I stepped back, a crunch and a tinkle sounded out from beneath my boot. It threw me even further off balance. "Broken glass," I said.

"Yes, I know. Look." Pia pointed to the ceiling. A few chemical flasks hung down the entire length of the cave. "I hate to think what was in those when they came down." What's that in front of the far wall?" Mohammed asked. "A statue of Kali," Dipesh replied. "See the ornate stone throne? And her necklace of skulls? That skirt of human arms is holding weapons.

They're swords and tridents." He looked closer. "Two of which appear to be missing." Pia consulted her book. "That's exactly what we have to search for—the missing swords. We have to set them back into her empty hands."

"Who is Kali?" Dawkins asked.

"The mother of destruction," Dipesh replied. "A very important deity in the Hindu religion."

I approached the statue, scanning the area for a sword. I sensed the atmosphere above our heads changing and as I peered up, I noticed that the thick carpet of algae which grew around the flasks had started glowing. It must have been reacting to our body heat.

"Look!" I said. "The deeper we move into the cave, the brighter the moss glows." By the time we reached Kali, the cave was so bright that we had no need for our lamps and blew them out.

The large trunk to Kali's left seemed to be constructed of willow, which was probably why it hadn't rotted in the damp. We opened it with caution and found several rolled-up prayer mats of assorted colours, each one ornately decorated in Sanskrit. We unrolled several of them to examine the patterns of the weave. They all seemed to be identical. Another trunk was about two square foot and carried an Indian emblem, made of brass, of a forward-facing lion's head whose mouth gaped open. His tongue was missing.

"Symbolically, that would be to prevent the lion from sharing its secrets," Pia suggested.

"Like the guy in the pith helmet," Dawkins said, trying to make light, no doubt, in an effort to assuage our evident trepidation (which hadn't worked, I for one was trembling to the core).

A short, hazel stick leant against the trunk with a round piece of metal on one end. Pia consulted her book. "It's a magnet," she said. "We need to use it to attract some kind of key."

She pointed to a golden spot on the far-left back corner. "The maze is in the trunk. It doesn't say exactly where, but it's probably set up on the underside of the lid, I'd imagine. By tracking the path woven into one of those prayer mat carpets, we should be able to retrieve the key through the lion's mouth."

"How do we know which carpet has the right pathway on it?" I asked.

Pia recited from the book. "Find the carpet that is green. Place it down behind the screen. Correctly trace the route and lamp. Place well to truly earn your stamp."

I pulled a few more of the rolled-up mats out of the willow trunk until I found a green one. Like all the others, it had a metal rod at one end. I took the mat and hung it up from two hooks at the back, behind the screen.

"I can't see the details of the path in the weave. Can someone relight a lamp please?"

"I'll light mine," Dawkins said, placing it behind the carpet.

Just like magic, a clear course sparkled. At first, the path looked the same as it had on all the other carpets but after staring at it long enough, one threaded line glowed distinctively brighter than the others. Picking the wrong path would have meant inevitable failure—one wrong move could have triggered whatever was attracted to that magnet to drop into the void of the two-foot box. Lord knew what would have happened had we simply tried to retrieve the key by cutting our way into the box. I called out the path's directions to Pia.

"Go left two inches," I started. She duly followed my instructions. "Now three inches straight ahead. Now right four inches." And so on. There was a faint sliding sound as Pia traced our key toward its open exit point. "Now pull it back two inches towards you." She carried out each step to the letter. She pulled the stick away as it neared the edge, and a small metal disc dropped from the lion's mouth into her hand.

Without moving a muscle, we all watched Pia as she inspected the item in her hand.

"What is it?" I asked.

"Well, it's not a key," she replied, confused. "It's a token made of red wax. An iron, hexagon-shaped coin on the reverse side is what attracted it to the magnet. The design on the front is Ganesh."

"Another important Hindu deity?" I inquired. Dipesh nodded in affirmation.

"Let's try searching the cave for something that matches the design," Pia suggested.

Everyone gathered around Pia to study the emblem, so we knew what we were searching for before scattering to search the cave.

Mango lingered a little longer than the rest of us and then disappeared into another corner of the cave. Within seconds, he called out, "It's here, Miss! It's here. I found it."

Pia hushed him, "Gently, Mango, gently," she whispered sweetly, as she tiptoed toward him. She inspected the hole he had found. "Well done, yes, you found it. It's an exact match."

I held my breath as Pia placed the token, with utmost precision, edge to edge, into the hole until the image of Ganesh married its matching shape, line for line. Click! A magnet on the other side of the lock engaged, and we all sighed in unison. But then the floor creaked. It shuddered and shook. Dust rained down from the ceiling as a two-foot-long door appeared in the wall and two bronze swords fell to the sandy floor with a clang. We all gasped, our hearts pumping. The swords' hilts were wound with copper-wire. Lavish engravings decorated the broadest part of their blades. Dipesh retrieved both swords and walked forward toward the statue, presenting the hilts to Kali, bowing his head in deferential offering, and placed them in the goddess's hands. Nothing happened -at first, but then the statue shuddered, and more dust showered down from the roof.

Chapter 11

With a croaky yawn, the entire statue, base and all, rolled back on unseen bearings and retreated into the recess behind it, revealing a hole in the floor with steps leading into some kind of chamber below. I signalled for Mango to lead, and he reluctantly descended before us.

The air was thick and musty, like an old wardrobe which had not been opened in an age. It reminded me of the first time I stepped through the doorway of our Scottish hunting lodge in autumn, when we visited Mr Brownlow. Our eyes adjusted to the darkness again and Dawkins pointed

"What's that at the far end?" he asked.

We'd barely stepped forward before Pia screamed, "Stop! Look down at your feet." A collection of stone "sticks" approximately one foot long and one inch across were scattered across the floor. At a glance there seemed no more than a few semi-buried on top of the sand, but it soon become apparent that there were many more, so well-coated in dust that they were barely visible. "I think it's a kind of minefield," Pia lowered her voice to a whisper. "Don't disturb a thing, just pick your way through and wait at the far wall until I have worked out this next step in the puzzle." We tip-toed across the chamber with our arms held out for balance. I looked in awe as Pia negotiated it with grace and great balance. Mango on the other hand was a unwieldly fellow and every step he trod was an adventure into the unbalanced.

The monument was seated upon the petals of a giant, pink, lotus flower. He sat no higher than an average-sized man. His oversized Indian elephant head was painted turquoise-green and crowned in a gold and pink headdress. A gold band ringed the middle of his trunk where a small, red stone had been embedded. In the centre of his forehead sat a ruby gem. His four chubby hands were turquoise, like his head. One foot dangled from off the edge of his seat, the other was bent in, as if still unwinding from the lotus position. His ankles were bejewelled in gold bracelets.

He was bare-chested, but an immense, golden necklace, painted with splashes of pinks and purples, hung around his neck. Another statue of similar dimensions sat next to Ganesh.

"Who is that? asked Dawkins.

"Shiva," Pia replied.

"He is much bluer than Ganesh," Mango observed, "and he is angry like you, master,"

"Shiva must have had a servant like you then, Claggage!" I snapped. I was immediately distracted by the wall behind the statue.

"What a backdrop," I said. "Those red flames painted on the wall behind him are rather dramatic."

"Shiva is known as the destroyer," Dipesh explained, "and the mightiest of all gods. He was the one who transformed Ganesh into an elephant after having found him with his wife."

A substantial wooden crate, the size of a tea chest, sat by Shiva's side. It was square and had no lid.

"What are those paintings on the sides of the box?" Dawkins asked.

"Tableaux depicting some of Shiva's many epic battles," Dipesh replied.

A brass Langur monkey's face with a gaping mouth had been inlaid into the mahogany like the lion had been in the last chamber. We peered into the crate and found nine separate, equally sized boxes set out in a grid, each containing one item from a diverse array of seeds, beans, rice, spices and teas. About twenty limestone style "sticks", engraved lengthways with the names of different commodities like haricot, assam and cardamom, lay scattered around the box.

Pia turned the pages of her book and read aloud.

"Our task is to identify the contents of each box and place the appropriate stick in its corresponding hole. Dipesh, since you are blessed with the knowledge of commodity sales, perhaps you'd be best at identifying and calling out the corresponding title. Dawkins, Oliver and I are probably the most agile amongst us, so we'll forage around for the sticks. Mohammed and Mango, you can help us when we need you." Everyone nodded nervously, in agreement.

"The book tells us that some of the sticks are wired-up to booby traps," Pia warned, "so there'll be plenty of red herrings in this cave." She pointed above us to the calligrams where two large, glass flasks hung as perilously as the sword of Damocles. Each contained some unknown, but clearly lethal, liquid.

Bit by bit, as more and more flasks reflected off the dim light, the horror of our predicament dawned on me, for the cork of each flask was held to the roof by nothing more than a single fine, rotten, fraying cord. "One of those things could fall at any time," Pia said, as if we hadn't noticed.

"The slightest jagged movement could shift the draft. Breathe slowly. No sudden movements and no sneezing please."

Dipesh reached into the box and removed a small, green seed.

Like a footman announcing dinner, he declared, "Cardamom!"

"Don't you do a thing!" I hissed at Mango.

We set about searching for a stick labelled cardamom. Hunched over, we scoured every square inch of sandy ground. Methodically, painstakingly.

Dawkins nudged me. "This is like playing a deadlier version of jack straws," he said.

"Found one!" Pia announced. She lay down on the ground to inspect the stick more thoroughly for wires.

"Run your finger in the sand around it," Mohammed said,

122

Pia dragged her finger delicately around the stick through the sand. Within seconds, she froze and stared at us wide-eyed. "Uh oh," she said breathlessly, bringing her finger up to reveal a connecting-wire. Pia looked at Mohammed, "Mohammed, could you tear some fabric off your waistcoat, please, to place on the stick as a warning marker?"

Mohammed tore a strip from his red waistcoat, tied it in a bow, tiptoed over and placed it down upon the stick.

"Another cardamon here," said Dawkins. He too traced around his stick and, once he was certain it wasn't connected, he lifted it above his head, raised himself up from the floor and walked steadily over to the box where Dipesh now stood. A flask tinkled above our heads as it gently clinked against the saligrams.

"Now that you've found the correct stick," Pia said, still prostrate on the ground readying herself to inspect another stick, "take it over to Dipesh and slide it into the cardamom slot until you hear a click."

Dipesh selected one of the pulses from another compartment in the box. Recognising it at once, he called out "Haricot!"

"It's here." Pia had already dug her finger trench. The stick was safe. She held it up in triumph. Mohammed tentatively crossed over to her, stooped and returned to the box to hand it to Dipesh who placed the haricot stick into its appropriate groove.

Pia and Dawkins discovered eight sticks in total over the following hour. I, however, contributed nothing. I did try but was motivated by my survivalist attitude not to risk myself.

Dipesh left the trickiest item till last. When he sniffed it, I thought he was going to sneeze.

He rubbed the textured, black item between his fingers then placed it on the tip of his tongue. His confused expression didn't last long.

"Assam tea," he asserted with pride.

By now the floor was strewn with small, red bows on them but I spotted two untouched sticks in the corner and approached them. There was no inscription on the first stick, so I turned it over. Triumph! I held brandished it above my head. "Assam tea! Assam tea!" I shouted, but in my enthusiasm, I hadn't noticed a wire running through one end of the stick. The wire ran along the floor through the sand to a pulley system.

"Noooo!" everyone shouted. But it was too late. A flask tumbled toward the floor. We all looked on, aghast. The flask fell in slow motion towards its inevitable destination. Mohammed leapt to try and catch it, but his fingers barely skimmed the sides. The flask smashed onto the floor with a sickening crash, releasing a deadly tincture over the sand where it landed.

Chapter 12

We were frozen to the spot. Me, on my knees by the broken flask, Mohammed lying on the sandy floor, the others on their feet staring aghast at the horror of what had just happened. The brown liquid had splattered over the sand. There was nothing to do but await the inevitable. The gas would only take seconds to creep into our lungs.

So, this is it? I pressed my eyes shut, willing a swift and painless death. How futile such hopes were. When I dared open them, it was Pia's cloudy-soft eyes I met first. A pool welled up within her and then a single tear rolled out from the corner of her lash and trailed down her cheek. Dawkins had his eyes darting looking for an antidote. Dipesh cowered in the corner. And Mango was looking at Pia wondering no doubt what she was crying about.

"Allah huwa Akbar," Mohammed whispered, over and over. He was closer to the vial than us.

We watched the small, brown puddle vanish into the sand. But there were no fumes. And I was not choking, not yet dying. I placed the trigger-stick down and reached for a tiny glass shard with one drip of the liquid upon it. I brought it to my nose and sniffed. Dipesh shouted "No don't!" It was a familiar scent. I sniffed again.

"I know that smell, but can't quite place it," I whispered. I dabbed the dot again with the tip of my tongue. "You won't believe this!" I exclaimed. "It's tea."

"Tea?" Pia asked.

"Tea!" I affirmed. "Assam. It must be one of Fagin's jokes. He knew that only an Englishman was likely to think of tea in such a moment."

"We still have one commodity remaining," Mohammed stated. "This cave is much dimmer than the previous one."

"It might be this one," I said, pointing to another stick on the floor.

Mohammed drew his lamp nearer as I drew my finger-trench around the stick labelled assam tea to ascertain that it was not attached to any device. Mohammed took it and handed it to Dipesh who slid it into the last vacant groove.

We could tell from the sound—the way it rolled along inside the box—that the object was circular. When it came to a standstill, a stamp emerged from the monkey's gaping mouth as if the cheeky fellow was blowing raspberries. Pia caught the token in her hand, and we gathered around to inspect it.

Like the first stamp, it was red and had an iron coin within its centre. The image on it was of a leaping tiger with its mouth wide open and one lethal outstretched claw. We began searching the chamber for a similar-sized hole into which it might fit.

The chamber had four sides, so we divided ourselves up; Mango and I looked around the wall on the right; Pia went to the left wall; Mohammed searched the smaller wall by the entrance. Dawkins found the recess on the wall directly behind the statue of Ganesh.

"There is a second opening next to the first. There must be another token we have to find," he said, brushing dust from out of the hole.

"I'd say there's another puzzle in here. Look around for it," said Pia. "Carefully!" she added.

After a few seconds, Pia said, "There is a stone font beside the stairwell here. We must have missed it when we first entered in the half-light."

"Look," I said, "it has a metal lining." I walked over and leant in a little way. "I don't like the look of this at all."

The font was half-filled with some suspicious-looking red liquid. Dawkins pulled the assam stick out of the commodity box and dipped it into the liquid. The limestone stick triggered a reaction which made the liquid bubble, spit and hiss, before giving off an acrid smell.

"This is potent acid," observed Mohammed.

Pia recited from the book. "Within the font your token sits. In the cooling fire. Drain its watchful guardian. If that is your desire?"

"Let's tip it out," I suggested.

"No!" Pia exclaimed, "there are still traps left on the ceiling. The acid could burn through the hidden ropes holding them up."

"Well, we obviously can't put our hands in, if only we had a bucket or any kind of receptacle to empty it into. Any ideas?" I asked.

Mohammed inspected the font up-close, whilst Mango stood leaning against the wall near the entrance. He was scratching his chin, as if considering options to our conundrum. I hadn't noticed it until now that, despite the heat outside and his profuse sweating, Mango was still wearing his enormous, leather storm-coat with its massive pelmet attached at the shoulder. His corduroy breeches were held up by a belt and, to my amazement, peeping out from his left pocket was the end of the stick which we had used to solve the first puzzle with the carpets and the magnetic stamp.

Dawkins was distracted by my expression and noticed it as well. "Mango, is that what I think it is in your pocket?" Mango looked down with an innocent expression raised one eyebrow, as if he had forgotten that he'd pilfered the stick in the first place. "May I please use it?" Mango handed over the implement with the eagerness of a border collie.

Stroke of genius! Dawkins submerged the magnetic end into centre of the font and as he drew the stick out of the liquid, a token emerged on the end of it and the font began to drain.

The token must have been acting as a plug.

The next token we plucked from its corrosive captor was a gold coin. Mohammed dowsed it in water from his canteen to remove any acid and pulled it away from the magnet on the stick.

"What is it? Pia asked.

"It's a python," I said.

"Wrapped around the limb of a tree," Mohammed added. I carried it to the hole and tried work out where it might belong. I was just about to place it in a vacant slot when Pia grabbed my arm.

"Hold on!" she said. "Look. The impression in the hole is not a python, it's a bear. We need to find a hole in the shape of a python."

"And a coin like a bear." Added Dawkins

We had learnt from the last trial that the statues were the key to unlocking the chamber. "There must be another trial somewhere else in the chamber," I concluded.

Mohammed. "Yes, something's not quite right," he said. "Here." He held up his lamp and illuminated the necklace. "You see these two objects? They're strangely out of place, don't you think? Could they be mirrors perhaps?" He slid his hands between the mirrors and Ganesh's chest and held them away from Ganesh's chest to show the rest of us what he meant. "Yes, they are mirrors!" One was shaped like a teardrop, the other, an equilateral triangle, both the size of a child's hand. And look here," he said, indicating the side of the base of the statue, "it's a handle."

Pia turned to face Mango, who was standing next to the handle. "Mango, can you rotate it, please?" Mango leaned forward and did as she had asked. He began turning, as if operating a giant musical box and it creaked into action.

Mango turned faster, until pearls of sweat dripped from his brow. The statue's eyes began to glow, brighter, then brighter still. Faster and faster, he turned, until the statue's eyes emitted two blinding streaks of light onto Ganesh's vacant hands.

Pia stared wide-eyed at the deity's empty hands and said, "I think I know what to do!

Everyone, look around for something—anything—which would fit those mirrors inside it."

Enshrouded in dust, at the foot of the wall alongside me, lay two sticks. Whilst the commodity limestone sticks would have dissolved in the acid, these sticks were different. One was about a foot long and made of wood, with a two-inch slot carved, at an odd angle, into one end. The other had a similar slot cut into it, but it was about two feet long and twice as thick. At the bottom of each stick, another notch indicated that they might lock the rods into their respective receptacles at precisely the correct angles.

Pia took the sticks and fitted each one of them perfectly into Ganesh's vacant hands, where they locked into position.

Mohammed attempted to remove Ganesh's necklace, but the fragile string disintegrated in his hands and various trinkets tumbled in between the deity's crossed legs, along with one of the mirrors, which shattered into a hundred glittering shards—along with our hope, it seemed. Our fate was now, literally, in the lap of a god. After an awkward juggle, however, Mohammed just managed to catch the other mirror before it too was destroyed. And then our hopes were dashed, yet again. "I'm sorry to say that the silver is peeling so badly that the mirror is entirely unreflective," he announced, peering into the small looking glass. We stood inert, defeated, and silent

"Dawkins," Pia whispered, "do you have your signalling mirror from Mehmet's box of tricks?"

"Brilliant! Yes, I do!" he exclaimed, reaching into his jacket pocket. Anticipating that she might ask me too, (it was the only item I had bothered to bring along from that box) I produced mine with a flourish (though she seemed none too impressed by my theatrics at such a moment).

Pia ripped some fabric from the hem of her skirt, pressed a ball of wax from Mohammed's lamp and jammed the mirrors into their slots.

"Mango, start turning!" Pia ordered, and Mango did as he was told.

Once again, the whirring sounded through the cave, and Ganesh's eyes began to glow. After a few rapid turns, a beam of yellow light led a trail from one mirror and to the other, illuminated a bead on the wall opposite, where it fixed upon a hole which had formerly been shrouded in darkness and impossible for us to have seen. Even if Mohammed had shone his lamp over that wall we would never have noticed the hole as there were dozens of them, and they were all identical in size and shape.

I held up the python stamp, checked it matched the hole exactly and inserted it. Sure enough, the magnet's familiar click sounded on the other side of the lock, triggering another stamp to vomit from one of the holes and fall at my feet. This one had the cypher of the bear engraved upon it. I returned to the second hole behind Ganesh, inserted it in its correct receptacle and turned, triumphantly, to Pia, but her nose was buried deep in another passage of the book.

She shut the book and headed back to Shiva, where she gently levered the arm which brandished the mighty scimitar and twisted it ninety degrees, until the scimitar was horizontal. Nothing happened. We looked around at one to the other, but then a low rumble kicked in and a spattering of dust showered down from the ceiling. The statue pulled away from the wall with a creak, revealing an archway behind it.

Mohammed held his lamp up and led us through the chamber through the other side of this portal was rectangular and smaller than the others. "Brahma," Dipesh said, lighting up a statue in the far-left corner. Dipesh nodded.

Pia was already on her way, walking towards it with her eyes closed. "Pull down the stone god's jewel," she recited the earlier lines from her book. "Sinister is blessed, dexter is damned."

He pulled on one of the rods on Brahma's necklace, taking particular care to bias towards the left side. That familiar moment of suspended silence ensued before the rumbling and creaking sounded. The statue slid across the floor, revealing a small opening, just wide enough for one crouching body to squeeze through.

Once again, Mohammed lit the way and, one by one, we passed through.

The glistening opulence which regaled us on the far side was almost beyond description. It is unlikely that a more magnificent sight had ever been seen before. Fagin must have been in a hurry as were scattered across the floor curtain after luminescent curtain of strung pearls, not yet donned by bride or mourner, draped over piles of wooden chests. We feasted our eyes over golden spools of thread, balks of priceless silks and jewellery boxes of all shapes and sizes. Tea chests were crammed with cups and cutlery. Chinese boxes with intricate ivory-inlaid veneer—this belonged on some lady's dressing table, not strewn across dusty floor. Our stunned faces reflected back at us from the surfaces of the porcelain cups and polished jugs. Glorious, gold-framed mirrors hung from the walls.

Golden statues with watchful eyes followed us about Fagin's cave as we marvelled at the golden chains and silver medals encrusted with large semi-precious stones, endless trunks filled with gold and silver coins, the plates, jugs, the tea sets. We were wealthy beyond our wildest dreams.

My eyes settled on a large wooden trunk with barrel top and rusted iron-bands which held the trunk's spars together. An old padlock, the kind which had been used by the East India Company some twenty years before, dangled from the lock at the front. The initials I. F. were carved onto a brass plate on the lid.

"Fagin?" Dawkins whispered, as if saying the name aloud might raise him from the dead.

"Isaac," Pia nodded. "My father. His name was Isaac."

131

Mohammed waved his hand around the priceless booty which surrounded us. "What on earth could be so priceless," he asked, "that amongst all this glory, he would lock one single box?"

"Let's find out," said Pia. She took a strong blow to the padlock with the stock of her rifle, leaving the lock dangling redundantly on the hasp. Dust sprang from the lid at the shock of the blow, and a rusty squeak rasped through the still air as we slid the bolt and lifted the lid back to reveal a collection of diamonds. Some were no bigger than apple seeds, but they were as clear as pure spring water. Others were as large as a cobbler's thumb. There were rubies from the deepest blood-red to subtlest rose-petal tint, deep azure sapphires, turquoise and pea-green emeralds and Imperial indigo amethysts as big as quail eggs. This dazzling trove of gems danced before our eyes.

Unaware that I was watching him, Mango scrabbled around on the floor, picking out yellow, lozenge-shaped stones. He popped them into his mouth and sucked them a little before removing them to hold them up and inspect as they twinkled in the lamplight.

"Mango, take off your coat, you're sweating all over the treasure."

He shot me a glance before dropping the garment in the corner behind a trunk. He turned back to face me and froze. The unmistakable click of a shotgun's hammer sounded behind my head. The clinking sound of diamonds camouflaged the sound of the gun hammer, so our colleagues were oblivious to the threat at first, but soon enough, Mohammed, Dawkins, Dipesh and, finally, Pia noticed how stock-still Mango and I were standing, and they gasped in unison.

I lifted my arms cautiously as I turned to find one man armed with a pistol and another, with a shotgun. More men crept in behind them.

The eldest of these unwelcome guests spoke first. "Lay down your weapons and stand over there," he ordered, pointing to the wall furthest from the chamber's entrance.

"He told you to drop your weapons," another man with an eastern European accent, asserted. "That means now!" Two of his henchmen sprang forward and kicked the weapons, as we lay them down upon the floor, into the far corner where we couldn't reach them.

"Where are my men?" asked Dipesh.

"Oh, they're dead," said one of the henchmen. And he fondly tapped a modern looking crossbow which he then levelled at us.

Mohammed took his chance. He reached out and grabbed one of the men as they moved in but was blasted straight through the heart, with a single pistol shot. His body slumped to the floor, dead.

I was slacked jawed, "What have you done?" I yelled. "You bastard! A shot like that—Christ! Are you stupid or just bloody mad? You could have brought these walls down on all of us." But the walls and ceilings had remained intact, thank heavens.

The assassin, whom I assumed was the leader, ignored us, and turned toward a gaping-mouthed Pia. "Thank you for getting us through the obstacles so quickly, my dear," he snarled.

Another man appeared in the chamber's opening. He was dressed like a local townsman but blindfolded. The leader turned to his accomplices and ordered something in Russian, which I translated as, "Throw the wretch to his friends." One of the thugs shouted to the blindfolded man, "You! Get over there." He shoved the man towards us.

"Merrick-Jones?" I exclaimed. "Is that you?" It was that same poor lieutenant whom I thought had been vaporized in Crimea! So, the prisoner all the villagers along our route to Jammu had told us about was Merrick-Jones, not Vladimir. But his face wasn't blindfolded at all—it was a bandage which was wrapped around his head to protect his flash-burned eyes. "We couldn't find you after the explosion on the redoubt," I whispered, dumbfounded. "We thought you were dead."

I took a closer look at our assailants and realised that one was yet another of the men who'd accosted me in the alley outside the Fortune of War tavern all those months ago. Another man entered the chamber, and I recognised him at once.

"Vladimir!" I cried out, "Thank the Lord you are here."

Merrick-Jones was standing bedraggled and whimpering by my side. "Hey, old boy," I whispered, "how are you holding up?" Merrick-Jones merely grunted something inaudible and tumbled onto the ground at my feet. I looked to Vladimir, but he was pointing a pistol directly at me. "Pick your friend up," he commanded, nodding to Pia and me.

I stared back at him, bewildered. "What on earth are you doing, Vlad?" I rasped.

"Oliver, what in heaven's name is going on?" Pia asked, bewildered. "You know this man? He has a gun aimed at your head."

"I can bloody well see that, Pia!" I replied, "Thank you." It was the first time I had ever been discourteous to her, and I felt instantly ashamed of myself.

Dawkins stepped forward. "Look here," he reasoned, "whoever you are, there is enough treasure in this cave for everyone. Why don't we simply pack it up together and get away before the locals realise what we're up to? They're sure to kill the lot of us if they catch on."

Vladimir laughed. "You're not going to leave here alive, my friend."

Pia must have been sizing our opponents up, and I suspect she felt that if she had been armed she could have defended herself. The fear in her eyes transformed into frustration and then rage.

"You lot, fill these up," the older Russian ordered, tossing a pile of hessian sacks before us.

We spent the next two hours filling the sacks with treasure while the Russians trained their guns upon us. Another two henchmen took turns pulling the laden sacks from the chamber, struggling with the weight as they dragged them across the sand.

At one stage, our team of four just happened to be stooped over a box containing a collection of ornate, tribal daggers. We were facing the same direction with our backs to our assailants.

I looked at Dawkins as he assessed one of the daggers for weight and quality, but even he, with all his secret service training, was clearly reluctant to attempt a counterattack. After calculating the distance between us and our enemy, he sighed in resignation and tossed the dagger he'd been musing over into my sack. We all, reluctantly, followed suit. I tried to reason with my old friend, but he was cold to me, I wondered if he knew his sister had passed away. I thought about breaking the news but no good could come of it. Once the cave was stripped of its most valuable assets, Vladimir commanded us to sit on Fagin's empty chest. "There's no escape for you now," he said, smiling. He scoffed at the look of dread on our faces, and we watched as the Russians reversed out of the chamber, then the last of the henchmen reached in and snatched our only remaining lamp.

The light dimmed as it exited, leaving us in darkness. The sound of the statue as it returned to its original position. The lock engaged. We were locked in doomed!

Chapter 13

I sat in the dark blinking, trying to digest what was happening. Our trusted friend, Mohammed was dead, and I felt the same pang of desperation as when dear Anna had passed. And now of all the ways a man could die, slow asphyxiation was perhaps the better option in the face of the other wretched, poison-soaked traps Fagin had set. I felt strangely numb as I mused over my squandered education, Fagin and the accident which had maimed Mango. Anna also appeared in my thoughts, along with the rookeries of St Giles and the Jago.

Dipesh began whispering to himself, and I could hear the click-clack of Mango's fingers fidgeting as he picked on a hangnail.

I have no idea how much time had passed before I heard Pia frantically brushing her hands against her body and erupting into a screaming fit. "Something just crawled across my face," she cried. "Are there spiders in here I hate spiders. There it is again! Ahhh... No, hold on. Sorry. It's... it's a strand of hair blowing. Wait! There's a draft coming from somewhere."

Mango scuffled in the direction of his dumped coat. He struck a match and lit one of our special candles that Mehmet had issued to us in Istanbul.

"Where did you get that, Mango?"

"From your box, Master Oliver."

"You are an utter buffoon! How dare you steal from my box." Mango hung his head. "What else did you take?"

He didn't dare look me in the eye. He was shamefaced. "I took something from all the boxes, Master," he said, with a peevish squint, "not just yours."

Mango poured hot wax onto the closed lid of a trunk and stuck it in. He had put his coat back on and began emptying his pockets.

Candles, pens, survival knives, compasses, lock picks, a collection of diamonds, a golden snuffbox, a dagger. The lid of the trunk was soon festooned with articles purloined (however innocently) by my kleptomaniacal servant. We gathered around and helped ourselves to our implement of choice, leaving useful trinkets for Mango as a reward for his accidental ingenuity.

"Look at how that candle is flickering," Dawkins said. "Air is getting in somehow. There must be a cracked seam. Let's each light our own and follow them to the spot where the flicker intensifies the most." We proceeded to explore every corner of the chamber.

"It's here somewhere," Pia said. "See? My candle's flickering the most here." We lifted all the candles up into the corner of the chamber to find a draft teasing a tangle of shimmering cobwebs and a crack in the wall. A clay patch in the shape of a door had been clumsily camouflaged behind a cloak of dusty cobwebs.

It was barely visible, but its texture was decidedly different from the rest of the wall. Dawkins dug around the crack with his knife. The clay crumbled. He jabbed a little more until more and more clay fell away. He sheathed his knife and pushed his fingers into the small hole he had made. Eventually, he attacked it with such gusto that the hole was soon big enough to fit one's head through. Mango and I joined him and, soon enough, a large portion of the wall lay in pieces on the floor.

A beam of dazzling moonlight flooded the cavern making Dawkins' eyes sparkle with satisfaction. Everyone's excitement was quelled soon enough, however, as the light revealed our friend's dead cadaver.

"May I have your water canteens, please?" Dipesh asked, his face grave and forlorn as he stood over his brother-in-law's body.

We handed over all that we had. Dipesh undressed Mohammed and washed the body three times. Among the less expensive and bulky items the Russians had left behind was a bolt of gold silk.

We cut a piece from it and Dipesh wrapped Mohammed with loving care. He then laid him on one side and, with the use of a compass, made sure that his head was pointing towards Mecca. Once he had completed his barely audible Salat al-Janazeh, he covered Mohammed's body with a light layer of sand and walked with great dignity to the place where we all stood. Pia was the first to embrace him. We each offered our own compassionate gesture of care.

We stood there together, poised at the opening to the cave on the edge of a sheer rock face, staring out into a moonlit night beneath a starry sky as it shone over a forest canopy one hundred feet below.

Dawkins was the first to break the silence. "That bolt of cloth," he said, pointing back to what remained of the roll of golden silk. "Let's cut strips and make a rope." We all agreed.

First, we unrolled the cloth before cutting it into long, two-inch strips. Dipesh spliced two together, using wire from my Tomahawk handle. It wasn't long before we had created a sturdy rope, at least two hundred feet long.

Abseiling down such rope was sure to shred our hands, however, so we searched the cave for some solution. One of the trunks had a collection of cushions in it and with those we were able to construct padded gloves.

We gathered our discarded weapons and loaded up as much ammunition as we could. Dawkins removed his watch and put our new rope through the loop in what Dawkins described as an alpine hitch.

We looped the rope through the brass handle of the largest chest in the chamber, one which had (fortunately for us) been fixed to the floor with bolts, before doubling it back down the cliff face.

I had never abseiled in my life, and I must admit, I didn't have much confidence in the system.

"Mango is the heaviest, he should go first" I said."

"That way, we will be sure that the rope can carry a hefty weight and the rest of us will be safe." Mango retreated unsteadily back into the cave. Fortunately, Pia volunteered to be the first to descend. She manoeuvred herself and the ropes into position and with no trepidation, backed towards the opening, whilst we took her weight.

"Lean back, Pia," Dawkins instructed, "or it won't work." Well aware that she was placing her very life in our hands, she leaned back until the rope held all her weight. "Now walk down the rock wall."

At first, Pia stepped back slowly, but as her confidence grew she sped up. Dawkins had tied a piece of red silk five feet from the end of the wire to warn the abseiler that she was reaching the bottom and, as the red flag flashed passed the karabiner, Pia applied her brake and swung back and forth a few times before dropping herself safely into the branches of a tall pine tree.

Mango was next, followed by Dipesh and the injured Merrick-Jones, who required much gentle guidance for he was clearly the most frightened of all of us. He seemed to have no comprehension of where he was or what he was doing. Despite this, he managed to swing out on the red flag's cue and throw himself courageously into the void where he landed in Dipesh and Mango's strong hands.

I was next. I have no fear of heights (thanks to my holidays in the Scottish Highlands) and if I do say so myself, I glided down the rope with a certain finesse and elegance. Finally, Dawkins who, at the end of his descent and once the flag had passed his karabiner, braked, took one end of the rope, swung himself into the canopy whilst gripping the rope tight and leapt like a monkey into the treetops. The other end of the rope flew off and back up the rock face with a whirr and flick then tumbled back down about him. He coolly retrieved the rope, coiled it up and tossed it over one shoulder.

One by one, we climbed down the tree until we were all safe, our hearts still thumping, on the forest floor.

We were now on the far side of the hill opposite the cave's entrance. We traversed steadily across the escarpment, losing altitude with each step until we reached the raging river below. We walked upstream with caution for we knew the Russians could still be nearby, and we soon heard their boisterous bellowing from behind an ancient wall.

Dawkins held his mirror on the end of his stick and raised it over the wall. The Russians were loading the sacks of our treasure into a large jolly boat. A few hundred feet further upstream on the quayside was the place Dipesh's family had safely moored a boat for us.

"It's best we don't confront the Russians here. Tensions are too high," Dawkins said. "Let's ambush them down the river, away from the town. We don't want to spark a gun fight. That would alert the villagers to the desecration of their deities and have them after us too." We all agreed.

As luck would have it, whilst searching for a better lookout over the river, Dipesh found a boat with several running boards missing upturned by the shore. A barricade to hide inside.

After about an hour of peering through the boat's hull four Russians aboard a large rowing boat passed the wall and sped downstream. The instant they were out of sight, we raced up to untie and hop aboard our boat and drifted out with the current. Mango and I took the oars and rowed, with Dipesh at the helm. Pia and Dawkins kept armed vigil at the prow whilst Merrick-Jones sat in the bilge.

Once we entered River Tawi's main eddy, the boat picked up speed and soon enough we were headed towards the Indus.

There is no doubt about it, traversing Kashmir and the Himalayas' hinterland by boat has advantages which cannot be matched. It is by far the fastest and most exhilarating means of travelling across India.

My morale increased with every mile and soon I felt like a veritable Jack-in-the-box. Our boat was spacious and comfortable.

The family had provided us with enough victuals to sustain us for a week, had we required them. We got a lot of distance between ourselves and the caves of Jammu in that first hour.

In the early evening, we were coming around a bend when we spotted the Russians' boat pulling up to a bank in the distance. We ducked into a small inlet on the opposite side and remained hidden until just after daybreak when they set off again. We headed west for the next day, surveying the splendid landscape and local wildlife along the riverbanks.

After several hours, the tempo of the river picked up considerably. As it narrowed, the banks on either side grew steeper. The jaws of a giant chasm penetrated the midday sky up ahead. A thick plume of water vapour rose like smoke from a dragon's mouth. The forest grew denser, and the Himalayan blue pines were replaced by a thick jungle canopy of Chinua trees. Ariel-root banyan trees propagated the area, and epiphytic figs strangled their hosts. They clung onto the mature trunks, sucking all life from the phloem which ran like arteries through the trees.

Rival troops of macaque monkeys cackled and cawed with chatter, announcing our arrival to all who would listen. Their mocking calls reminded me of bickering rival gangs in the slums of London. The deafening caterwaul was punctuated here and there by the trumpeting of wild bull elephants seeking out their mates or the roar of a panther, or tiger patrolling and marking its domain.

"Did you hear that sound? That is most certainly a panther," Merrick-Jones said. He knew the call from his childhood.

As the chasm loomed closer, the jungle sounds were soon drowned out by the rumble of a different kind—crashing, violent and constant. The humidity grew almost unbearable. Armies of bullet ants, laden with cargo, raged in single file through the rotten flora on the jungle floor, like a convoy on their way back to barracks.

Huge, venomous millipedes perambulated along, and beetles hopped from orchid to orchid.

Oversized bees buzzed, seeking nectar, whilst a small jungle bear looked on longingly, wondering where their nest of honey might be.

"The river splits in two at the hill and rejoins itself on the other side," Merrick-Jones told us. "The left side is slower, safer. Whereas the right fork will lead us into steep and deadly rapids."

Dipesh made a swift decision. Guided by an urge to avenge his friend no doubt, come what may, he swerved the boat, in one violent turn, to the right.

"Well, that's that decision made, I guess," said Dawkins. "Now there's a fifty-fifty chance the Russians did the same."

"They didn't. I am certain of it," Dipesh replied. "Why would they take such a risk? In any case, we have the advantage. Don't forget, they don't even know we've managed to escape the cave. Mango and Merrick-Jones, you lie down there in the hull. It will stabilise us."

We were soon at the mercy of the tumultuous rapids. Granite boulders rose like hunched titans bathing waist-deep in the foamy waters. Their smooth, shiny surfaces were uncannily flesh-like. They stood in waiting, to the left and right, ready and willing to smash our small lives to pieces. Dipesh deftly negotiated through each treacherous eddy, water chute, back tide and wash-through. We almost capsized several times.

"Quick! All this side!" Dipesh screamed, and we all leant to the left. The next moment he was ordering us to, "Grab my legs!" At which we leapt aft and held on for dear life. At one precarious turn, the boat began rotating around the edges of a steep, gigantic whirlpool which threatened to drag us down into its vortex, to sure death. "Tuck your feet in under the running board and grab that branch," he yelled.

"Let go now!" We were catapulted out of the whirlpool's pull and, were saved from capsizing on exit.

Pia and Dawkins remained port and starboard amid-ships respectively, pushing us away from the rocks on either side. Dipesh stood at the stern, steering us with the rudder whilst I stood at the prow, searching for menacing rocks below the water's surface.

Adrenalin pierced my veins the instant I saw the danger. "There!" I pointed. "And there!" Dipesh reacted on each warning, pulling the rudder in the direction to which I pointed so the boat swung violently away from the hazard.

We plunged down several feet on several occasions as the boat tipped on its fulcrum point, showering us with water and almost catapulting Dipesh himself overboard. Every second filled us with dread. The crashing of the water combined with the uncalled-for heckling from the laughing audience of macaque monkeys. Felled logs swept passed us from time to time. They were un-steered of course and smashed to smithereens against the bathing titans, like some portent of our own fate.

The river calmed as it broadened on the other side of the island mound, and we emerged from the watery terror, bruised but relatively unscathed.

When the two rivers merged, a family of wild pigs on the left-hand bank scampered off into the jungle. Dipesh guided the boat further downstream towards the left shore and landed in a small inlet where we jumped out. Feet on land! Such a relief. We tied the boat to a nearby mango tree.

"We need to get in there a few hundred yards," Dawkins said, pointing to the pitch black of the jungle. Dawkins and Dipesh departed to reconnoitre a route, while the rest of us unloaded our provisions. I indicated a spot to Mango where I thought we might hide. As Dawkins and Dipesh disappeared, the rest of us trudged into the unknown. I ran the silk rope from where Mango hid so he could signal us if he saw the Russians. We reached a clearing and set up camp.

Merrick-Jones set to preparing a pot of curry and I produced a makeshift table by lashing the oars between two trees and placing a footboard across them.

Dipesh and Dawkins soon returned with news. "The Russians are between us and the rapids," Dawkins said. "They're about a mile upstream. We need to ambush them. There are five of us and five of them."

"Six," Merrick-Jones added, grumpily.

"Hold still, Merrick-Jones. I'm going to remove these bandages."

The scabs around his eyes had fallen off, revealing bright pink, healthy flesh.

"Open your eyes," I told him. Merrick-Jones stood there, blinking in the half-light of the jungle. "How many fingers am I holding up?"

"Three," Mango replied.

"Not you, Mango, I meant Merrick-Jones."

Mango held up his own hand and asked Merrick-Jones, "How many fingers am I holding up?"

"Shut up Mango!" I growled and returned my attention to my patient.

"I can see," Merrick-Jones muttered. "It's blurry but give me a few minutes."

"Do you really think you can manage?" Pia asked.

"Oh yes, just give me a few minutes."

I sat in front of Merrick-Jones and inspected his scars. Dipesh had put a pot of yoghurt in our victual pack, and I gently applied it to Merrick-Jones's pink flesh.

144

"What about fighting? Do you have any fight in you?" Dawkins asked. "I wouldn't go that far," Merrick-Jones replied.

"But don't forget, we have that element of surprise over them," Dawkins said. "They think we are dead, and the locals don't know the treasure is missing from the cave."

"Except us, here in this jungle," Dipesh added.

"What do you suggest?" Pia asked.

Dawkins looked down, rubbed his chin, as if churning something over. After a moment, he smiled and said, "I have a plan."

Chapter 14

Merrick-Jones was not ready to fight so he agreed to stay in the camp where he could make himself more useful organising firewood and such. We set off to follow the river upstream, keeping close to the banks and out of sight.

After we'd journeyed an hour or two, Dawkins said, "We'll need to keep vigilant and quiet from here on." It seemed we were approaching the Russian encampment.

After sundown, we stopped to hide amidst the foliage and wait in the dark whilst Dawkins went on ahead to observe their camp. He returned a few minutes later and briefed us. "It looks like there are only four Russians sleeping at cardinal points around a central fire. Oliver, you are to shoot the third sleeping body, at the position pointing westerly. Pia, you shoot the southern body, and Mango, you the northern one." North was the only point of the compass Mango had bothered to learn, so it made sense to allocate him that one. "Dipesh, you have the most easterly position, on the far side of their fire." We nodded in agreement. "I will stand ready," Dawkins added. "If any one of them manages to run off, I'll be bringing them straight back down."

The night chorus of shrills and clacks was just starting up. We cocked our weapons and headed forth, without cracking even the tiniest twig. The Russians felt so safe, so confident, that there was no one trailing them that they hadn't even posted a guard, and the dying embers of the enormous fire they'd lit illuminated the four sleeping shapes where they lay as if it were bright as day.

We huddled down on the edge of the clearing. Dawkins used hand signals to silently signal the tactics of our plan of attack. I had no issue shooting such cowards whilst they slept, for these same men had set upon me in London, stranded me, and left me to die in the cave.

I looked over to my other team members who seemed focused about what we were doing. As Dawkins whistled, we raised our arms and fired.

I smiled. My shot had hit its target in the back. Pia seemed equally happy with her shot. However, there appeared to be something not quite right about the way the bodies of Dipesh and Mango's victims were lying on the ground. I had seen a lot of dead bodies, and their death pose was all wrong.

We began to close in on the encampment to inspect our quarry when gunfire rang out from the other side of the clearing and a bullet whipped by the exact spot where I had been standing seconds before. Pia ducked. Something had barely missed hitting her too! The various pistol flashes gave away not only our positions but also theirs. Both parties ran forward, hunting their respective foe, ready for the full-scale attack which was to follow. I tossed my empty pistol to one side and drew my tomahawk and as I had already prepared my pen in the other. I charged into the battle, which was met in the middle of the clearing around the fire, only to discover that the Russians were armed with the same pens as we were!

We sprayed with our pens and lashed out with our tomahawks.

Chaos ensued as combatants left, right and centre sprayed chilli and pepper at each other. We could barely make out who was who. So much spray flew through the air that it seemed both sides inadvertently incapacitated their own members, showering their opponents' faces with the blinding concoction till every man and woman on the field was left desperate and half-blind, straggling and crashing about amidst a cacophony of wails and screams. I did manage to get close enough to one assailant, slashing him in the arm, but his injury wasn't fatal.

I tripped over one of the "bodies" we had shot earlier. They were not bodies at all!, strategically placed logs covered with blankets.

Dawkins seemed to be the only one who hadn't been affected by the spray. I saw him taking aim at Vladimir, but he couldn't get an accurate shot as the battlefield was too muddled, what with enemies and colleagues alike wheeling left and right.

After a few moments, he blew the preordained whistle, signalling an end to the attack. We disengaged and retreated to the spot from which the whistle had called, leaving the Russians rubbing their eyes in the centre of the clearing. As soon as they realised how isolated and exposed they were, they turned and ran off into the forest.

"Water! Water!" I screamed. We were all eager to return to camp where we could calm our burning eyes in the river.

The Russian boat sat abandoned in the inlet and the Russians had obligingly failed to unload the boat of their booty. There was nothing for it! We simply untied the laden vessel, climbed aboard and pushed away from shore.

By the time we returned to camp morning was already creeping over the horizon. Merrick-Jones had collected enough wood to fuel a fire. He further surprised us by producing a large piece of sausage which we divided amongst ourselves and chewed. The savoury morsel cheered us no end. After our well-earnt breakfast, we packed up quick smart and boarded our boats. Dipesh, Merrick-Jones, Pia and me and the Russian boat while Dawkins and Mango launched us into the river and then climbed aboard their own.

The river was calm; it flowed only little faster than a brisk walk. There was no way the Russians would manage to keep up with our pace through such thick jungle. The boats were drifting too close to one another, however. Something had to be done.

"A lot of what we are carrying is worthless," Dawkins said. "We can't carry the weight of it all. We're going to have to pull the gems out from various statues and plates."

"We should moor up ahead, in that inlet," Pia shouted, pointing over to a space near the northern riverbank.

We pulled in and transferred half of the treasure sacks to Pia's boat before setting out once again.

Dawkins and Dipesh steered whilst the rest us set about extracting the stones from the various deity's statues and plates encrusted with the jewels.

We placed the most valuable gear in a sack and ditched the de-jewelled statues and plates into the river. I'm not a superstitious man but peering into the clear river and spying Ganesh as he stared back up at me was somewhat unnerving to say the least.

After travelling for most of the day, our stomach rumblings began to drown out the clink-clank of the jewels.

"How about I try to catch a spot of dinner whilst you keep beavering away at getting the boat's weight down," I suggested. "I think I saw a passel of wild pigs further back." Everyone nodded enthusiastically. Mango moved to join me, but I dismissed him with a wave.

Confident that the Russians would be miles away, we pulled up and moored. I left the others to set up camp and walked upstream a few hundred yards. One can become quickly disorientated in the jungle, so I was careful to keep the river to my right at all times. I soon arrived at the small gully where I had seen tell-tale trotter prints in the mud near the water edge and made a mental note to return at sundown, the most likely time for a family of pigs to congregate at a river for a drink, when I would seize one of the piglets. I smeared mud and wild pig-muck all over my clothes to disguise my scent—a trick I had learned from a Scottish ghillie while shooting with my great benefactor, Mr Brownlow, in the glens— then covered myself with rotting foliage from the jungle floor and waited for the sun to set.

The sun fell, and the first little pink snout emerged, twitching, from the dark undergrowth right on cue. There were four. They moved cautiously, snorting and sniffing the thick jungle air. Their mother followed close on their heels. I drew my legs up underneath my body and, slowly but surely, eased more pressure on my feet which I had levered against an old log, until I felt myself sliding silently closer and closer to my prey.

The piglets lapped the water at the bank with their mother snuffling around at the rear, completely oblivious to the danger I posed. The largest, male piglet was my intended target, and I was only about a foot from him. I taughtened my sinews and prepared to pounce. I counted down, silently. Three, two, one.

Squeal! The sow let out a massive scream and all the piglets scattered, leaving me flat in the mud. A small boat had triggered the sow's alarm. The boat had slewed into the inlet, and I was laid out in its path. The prow slid up to the bank, stopping right by my prostrate midriff. I curled around the bow and as the occupants dropped off the boat, their muddy splashes covered me. One of the men stood on my ankle but I managed to hold back a yell.

I was sure they were Indian natives, searching for the culprits who had looted their temple. I could not understand what they were saying but by the tone of their chatter they were excited.

They loosely tied the boat up, removed a load from it and headed into the jungle.

They were back soon enough to fetch another load. I didn't move a muscle. Every time one of them came near, I held my breath. I lay in that mud whilst they unloaded and prepared to set up camp. They to-and-froed into the jungle for what felt like forever.

When they finally lit their campfire, the light it emitted spread all the way to the bank where I lay. I was paralysed by fear and watched from the shadows for an hour as their fire grew larger and larger. All the while smelling the fumes of succulent pork.

My friends would be growing anxious about my absence soon. They would be ambushed if they came searching and started calling out my name. I mustered as much courage as I could to manoeuvre my knife through the rope which secured the boat to shore. Then I slid down the side of the boat and dragged it out into the flow of the river, holding tight to the fraying rope.

Much to my relief, the primary current eventually picked the boat and forced it downstream, toward my party and safety.

I grabbed hand over hand on the rope, until I was able to pull myself up onto the boat and steer with a paddle to our own little mooring point. I heard the unmistakable chattering of angry Indians in the jungle upriver, behind me.

Mango and Dipesh were on guard near my pack, but the rest of my party were fast asleep.

"Quick! Grab everything!" I said. "The Indians are coming!" Dipesh and I returned to the Indian boat to snaffle all we could—food, clothing and weapons.

My startled friends, grabbing all they could, ran toward our boats. Dipesh stood by the stolen Indian boat, holding the golden Shiva the Destroyer statue over his head. He threw the war god forcefully into its hull, holing it in one go. The irony of this gesture and the choice of statue was lost on none of us. The boat soon filled with water and sank, until nothing but running boards were visible in the river.

We all travelled in our stolen Russian boat and towed own boat containing our rations and store behind. Once safely aboard, we sat in a circle, ate a plate of cold meats and drank water purified by Dipesh whilst I told them my story.

"It was a shame you didn't catch the piglet," Mango said.

I clenched my jaw and side-glanced him.

Dawkins managed to divert the conversation. "Let's put some of the smaller gold aside, to pay for provisions, guides and transport. We may as well leave the rest."

Pia glared at him. "After all I've been through, what my clothes went through," she said, holding out her long, shredded skirt.

His suggestion came as quite a shock, to everyone but especially to me. Dawkins placed his hand on my shoulder and reassured us.

"There will be enough for everyone. The heavy statues were almost worthless but trust me, the gems they were encrusted with, are not."

"Let's use this small water butt as a safe," Dipesh suggested. After a flurry of activity all the diamonds and gemstones pearls and coins were safely in the water butt.

"Well done, Oliver," Dipesh said, "you have served us well."

"Well done, Oliver," Mango echoed, "you have served us well." What was extraordinary about Mango's impression of Dipesh was he had sounds exactly like Dipesh had—the same tone, accent and timbre. He was full of surprises that man—some good, some plain old annoying.

We tied the boats together and, even though I was shattered, I steered while the others slumbered. I smiled to myself, satisfied to my core at how we had pulled off this great adventure. Perhaps that's why I could carry on. Behind the calm, a low, distant rumble crescendoed steadily. Water vapour was rising on the river's horizon, and I realised that we were approaching it alarmingly fast. I woke the others, and we steered onto the nearest bank. Dawkins went for a reconnoitre, taking Mango with him for company. When they returned, Dawkins called us all together.

"There is a large waterfall ahead," he said. "It's too rapid for us to traverse. We walked down a well-worn path and found a village at the base.

"The villagers were pleased to see us, and they gave us these."

Mango pulled something out from behind his back. It was a garland of orange orchids, which he placed upon his head, proudly, as if it were a crown and did a twirl, to show it off. After breakfast, the next morning, we packed our hiking equipment and loosened the moorings, until the boats drifted out, one by one, into the river.

We stayed in the hamlet for several hours, soaking up the hospitality and mirth. Curious children plucked at our clothes and giggled. Even though the villagers were as poor as church mice, they offered what they had. Young ladies brought us tea and regaled us with plates piled with fresh nuts, berries, scented oils and herbs. Mango made himself popular by throwing a gaggle of boys into a pool, after which they'd splash their way back to the edge and gleefully prepare to be flung into the water again and again.

When we bade our farewells, Dipesh paid the village elder with a bag of gold, which he dropped into a large skiff. He then gestured for us to the same with our bags and we obediently (though slightly bewildered) put our own bags in the skiff.

We remained silent and befuddled whilst he approached each of the fishermen standing on the shore and handed them a large amount of gold.

We watched in amazement as the fishermen took their axes to each of their boats. Genius idea! But I wondered if our pursuers would not take great umbrage to this if they thought we had done it out of malice.

We were able to relax slightly for the rest of the journey, knowing that the Russians and the Thuggee Indians were stuck in central India waiting for the local population to repair their own boats, which would take at least three days.

Every day that passed carried us further away from Jammu and our pursuers, further from the lies, deceit, betrayal and closer to the Indus, Karachi and London. We made our way through rapids, whirlpools and around waterfalls until, finally, we entered the tranquil Indus which led to the Bay of Bengal and the Arabian Sea.

We succeeded in reaching the Port of Karachi. And made our way to the Consulate where Dawkins explained who we were and what we were about. It was at Karachi that our noble friend, Dipesh, announced he was leaving to return to Jammu to sort out the mess the Russians had made.

"You know, if Dipesh takes most of the treasure back to Jammu, he may save the city from mutiny or rioting," Dawkins declared, "which, in the long run, means we will end up saving the Empire twice."

"My good god man, we've been through so much! And what do you mean, twice? What on earth are you talking about, man? You have to be joking!" I protested.

"All in good time, Oliver, all in good time," he replied. "We only needed a small box of the diamonds, rubies, emeralds, pearls, topaz, jade and a mere portion of the gold for our actual purpose," Dawkins said.

I sat up bolt upright.

What was he suggesting? For our actual purpose? What was going on here? Were we giving much of the treasure back to city's elders?

"Even just a few of the diamonds would set us all up for life, after all," he added.

I begrudged parting with some of our treasure, but something was seriously amiss.

Still, I had no alternative but to swallow my tongue and trust that Dawkins knew what he was doing. Our brave friend was reluctant, but he agreed to take a large part of the loot back to Jumma. Even Pia handed over a gold bracelet (with a fair degree of truculence) as a gesture of trust and sincere friendship.

Merrick-Jones seemed relieved, in fact. "Is it good karma?" he asked.

"Yes," Dipesh replied. "Excellent karma."

Mango examined the contents of his pocket and handed over a broken compass.

"Thank you, brother," Dipesh said.

"Thank you, brother," Mango mimicked. Dipesh laughed .

We said our farewells to Dipesh. He blessed us and set off up the mountain pass, towards Jammu on a mule we had purchased as a surprise gift, laden with sacks of gold and silver for him and the people of Jammu disguised as baskets of sugar loaves.

I found a compass in the market which I paid far too much for, but, given the many challenges to which Mango had risen, it was the perfect gift to thank him for his unquestioning loyalty and courage. He seemed genuinely touched when it was presented to him. We made our way down into the town centre where we found a small restaurant.

"You're the only one who speaks the local dialect, Merrick-Jones," Dawkins said. "Perhaps you could find us some lodgings nearby?"

"Yes, of course," Merrick-Jones replied.

Dawkins handed Merrick-Jones a bag of coins and led the rest of us inside, to a back corner so we could keep an eye on the door. We ordered coffee.

Dawkins checked and double-checked that no one was in earshot before leaning in as if he had an announcement to make. It seemed an explanation was finally on its way. "I have a confession to share," he whispered. "Something I've known all along." What he went on to tell us took me entirely by surprise.

Dawkins paused to clear his throat. "There is a good reason we are not keeping all the jewels for ourselves."

"Why the hell not, Dawkins? This had better be good." I exclaimed.

"Calm down and let me explain. You see, two years ago," he continued, "the government almost went bankrupt. Lord Aberdeen ordered the Crown Jewels be broken up."

"Why?" I asked.

"In order to pay for the Crimean excursion," Pia answered.

"You are in on this as well?"

"Of course. We are a team," she replied.

I was incredulous. "They were all sold off?"

"Every bit of them. Yes," Dawkins replied, "but the government underestimated the loyalty of the British public."

I exclaimed, "I bet they did! I am furious, especially as Prince Albert is gaining in popularity," I said.

"It's probably because of the new ideas from the Great Exhibition," Dawkins added. Pia stared at Dawkins and said "Correct. The government fear that if the British public find out what they've done, they would revolt. The Russians have done the same."

"So, that is why the Russians wanted the jewels so badly," I uttered.

Dawkins continued. "Our mission is to return to London and, with the help of the Crown Jeweller, to replace the stones back into the regalia."

"You mean, we have to give up all our loot?" I asked.

"Not all of it. I have a plan," Dawkins replied.

Chapter 15

Dawkins's declaration not only astounded me, but it also made me rather proud of my old friend. Once upon a time, this boy was no more than a thieving ne'er-do-well; the fact that he was willing to give up even a morsel of our loot in order to remain loyal to his mission on behalf of the Crown was astonishing. He had come so far. I was witnessing an unexpected maturation into sage manhood.

"I hope you understand now why we gave so much to Dipesh. Can you now understand how he is saving his city."

I was speechless. I understood entirely but was still stunned by the turn of events.

"We'll pay a dhow captain for passage from here to the Red Sea, then catch a ship from Alexandria to Marseille, from where we'll catch a train to Antwerp and, finally, hand these stones to a cutter, who can replicate the stones we require. Once those are cut, we can return to London and restore the regalia to its former glory. No one need ever know they aren't the original jewels."

It wasn't long before Merrick-Jones strode into the room, excited. "I found a place to stay. It is just around the corner," he said.

The apartment was not far from the café. We spent a lovely evening around the table reminiscing and marvelling at our adventures.

Merrick-Jones had recovered very quickly, his dressings no longer needed daily attention, which meant that he was ready for us to hand him over to army doctors in the barracks in Karachi so he could be treated appropriately, at long last, before being repatriated. He was not only visibly surprised, when we presented him with his own small bag of jewels, but filled to the brim with gratitude, which manifested itself in a constant round of handshaking and grinning, accompanied by yet more handshaking.

"And what will you do with your newfound wealth?" I asked him.

"I'm leaving the army to return to university," he replied. "I have always dreamt of being an architect. I much prefer building things to destroying them."

We headed back to our apartment where we gathered around the table to spill out the contents of our various bags, boxes and pouches of remaining treasure.

Painstakingly, gem by gem, Dawkins sifted through the complete collection, matching each one with diagrams from the illustrated book entitled *The Crown Jewels*, which had been written by the Beefeaters at the Tower of London. The redundant jewels and coins we had decided to discard were heaped into a pile on the far side of the table. Once Dawkins was satisfied, he had the correct type of stone and a (roughly) correct carat-weight and clarity, we divided what remained of the discarded booty between the five of us

Amongst the discarded booty were a good deal of lozenge-shaped diamonds, which I suspected Mango had swallowed in the cave with the intention of retrieving them later. I was keen for him to be reissued those exact same stones and gingerly slid them toward him with the edge of a pencil.

My give-back gesture was a small box containing the most beautiful diamonds and rubies of the entire bevy. They were certain to fetch me hundreds of thousands of pounds. Pia had an extensive collection of fabulous pearls.

That night, I sewed my diamonds into the sleeves of my thick surgeon's dress-coat. Pia sewed her pearls into her petticoat hem. I never asked Dawkins what he did with his,

Mango had brought a sumptuous meal of goat curry up from the café, which we devoured before Dawkins outlined our strategy for the return to London.

"We'll go as far as we can by sea, before taking the short camel-train to Alexandria. Many a frigate sails from there, and what is useful for us is that we will fall under Her Majesty's Royal Navy's safety.

Dawkins left for the port before dawn, to negotiate our passage to Egypt. He returned at sunrise with the news: we were to depart at the turn of the tide. This was only two hours away, so we packed swiftly and made our way down to the quayside to meet our captain and his crew.

Luxurious dhows lined the quays, their sails furled so that only small darts remained. They flapped in the breeze like a flock of courting birds ruffling their feathers. They were so newly built that the smell of their fresh varnish still permeated the air. Our merry band perambulated along without a care in the world and my spirits soared when I spied the extravagantly decorated vessels, I assumed were the very ones we would be voyaging upon.

We marched straight past those vessels, however, and, as we rounded the last of the beautiful boats, I realised that we were headed for the most ramshackle vessel on the wharf. The only boat with torn sails and sprung planks above her devil board. Upon seeing us, her snaggle-toothed captain grinned like an idiot. He shook our hands vigorously, with palms as rough as pumice from years before the mast. His skin was tanned and wrinkled, as weather-beaten as his ancient ship. We walked gingerly up the gangplank and climbed down onto the dhow. Here we were, entrusting our fate once again, to the devil of destiny.

The captain stoked the twelve sailors into action by yelling an unintelligible tirade in what seemed to me was gibberish, but to his crew were clear precise orders.

Several of them leapt up and pulled on the ropes at once to raise the settee-sail, whilst others cleared away the scraps of food, cups and plates on the deck to prepare to embark.

A small Arab boy (he couldn't have been much more than nine years old) scurried enthusiastically amongst this motley crew.

He wore a tiny brimless cap upon his head, and a winning smile embellished his face. The boy's dish-dash was soiled with the putrid stains of fish guts.

He tugged at my sleeve and beckoned us all to follow him below-deck, where he showed us to our cabin. Everything stank of rotten fish down in the hull.

The cries of dockside hawkers selling their wares sounded through the portholes. I stowed my possessions with unusual care, into a corner of my allocated space and rolled my thick, black coat into one end of my hammock to serve as a pillow.

It wasn't until I felt a change in way the dhow rocked, and the hawkers' shouts had faded into the distance, that I realised we had pulled away from the dock. I went up on deck to find Dawkins and Pia at the prow watching a pod of dolphins soar before the bow, darting through the wake as we pushed through the warm Arabian Sea. The entire sea was soon alive as the two-metre-long dolphins were joined by their friends. Together they spun and leapt like some aquarium's dolphin show as they chased a shoal of yellow-finned tuna.

I turned back around to find every crew member facing west by northwest, kneeling in prayer on the deck upon their multi-coloured mats. Judging by the array of bowls and puddles of spilt water, they had already washed their hands, feet and faces. The crew bowed, dutifully, murmuring and muttering in unison, following their Iman who led the prayers from the front.

"I thought they were supposed to face east?" I whispered from the corner of my mouth.

"The Iman has a compass," Pia explained. "They are facing Mecca."

"Oh."

The dhow continued chasing the setting sun. By six o'clock, the orange sky had evolved into a deep velvet blackness.

I sauntered to the stern to view the vanishing Indian subcontinent one final time. A small jolly boat was being towed behind the dhow. It bobbed back and forth at the end of a few yards of rope.

The sky turned soon enough, spattering starry dots across the horizon in every direction. I'd never seen such an array of bright colour in a night sky. You've not witnessed the truly multi-dimensional depth of our galaxy until you have seen stars shoot through one of those Arabian nights. It's a scintillating panorama. I felt as if I could almost reach up and grab one and, as we rocked gracefully beneath the swirl and spangle, the subtle scent of something resembling sweet curry, though not quite as strong, floated up from the dhow's galley.

A guest upon any luxury dhow moored off the slave-traders' berths is rarely better fed, and I was famished so I headed for the tiny galley where two crew members were mincing dates and crushing down on them with their bare hands, into a soft sticky toffee which I knew to be called aloo. They blended in some orange blossom honey from a clay pot and offered us a plate of the tangy stew. It was served with chapatti bread.

A magnificent feast. I devoured my entire bowl and, without a moment's hesitation, approached the chef, bowl in hand. After dinner, the same crew member who had led the prayers and whom I assumed was the elected religious leader, began singing a series of Omani poems. They had the same metre as a limerick, and the final line of every poem was repeated by one and all.

Dawkins' attempt had us laughing uproariously, but soon enough it was me who was trying to crack one and I became the butt of the joke. A word to the wise: never compare an Arab to a cat, unless it's a lion. The Arabs went strangely quiet. They simply stared at me, not a single smile amongst them and no one addressed me or even acknowledged me after that.

As the night drew on, the swell began to heave and, by the time we retired, menacing white horses were riding the peaks of the waves.

I dozed intermittently in my hammock, and at one stage I realised I could no longer hear the stream of Arab commentary, laughter and squabbles which had been so prevalent before. There was a flash and, seconds later, the crack and rumble of thunder. That cloudless, starry sky at six bore a fully-fledged monsoon by midnight. I climbed back up on deck and discovered, to my horror, that the crew and the jolly boat we had been towing, had vanished. I urgently called to the others.

"It would seem the crew had more faith in rowing a boat they weren't familiar with, than a ship they knew as well as a sister," I observed, as they joined me on deck.

"Get the sails down!" Dawkins ordered.

We floundered along through enormous seas for some time, until we spotted land, a mile off our starboard side.

We got the main sail down first then went to the mall-triangular-jib, secured at the bow. We were flicked about like a bagatelle ball. The challenge was not so much staying upright but staying on deck at all!

Suddenly, the billowing jib sail was ripped, something cracked just above my head and the spar hurtled to the deck, stopping only inches from my face. To make matters worse, the halliard rope holding up the jib caught the strain and detoured the swinging horizontal spar away. The tension pulled a marlinspike from its hole, hurling it lethally across deck. Dawkins had grabbed the ship's tiller, and he was struggling.

Pia, Mango and I tried hauling in the remaining sail. Boards sprang up all around us as we struggled to keep the fast-disintegrating dhow afloat.

Dawkins shouted through the pounding rain. "Get your gear together. Find something that floats. Anything! We're going to be sunk in minutes."

I couldn't make out what he'd said, but Mango had heard him clearly enough.

I usually found Mango's mimicry of Dawkins' voice amusing but this time, I found it utterly disconcerting. I passed the order onto Pia, and we ran below to collect all our valuables. I also grabbed a machete I'd seen in the galley. I ran to my hammock to retrieve my coat and, as I lifted it, its contents squealed. Good gracious me! The sailors had left the wee cabin boy behind.

"Ayesh ismak," I managed, a smattering of Arabic I had picked up from the evening's entertainment.

"Isme Ali," the boy replied slowly, as if addressing an idiot.

Together, the boy and I returned to the deck. Dawkins pointed to a square wooden frame with small square holes and shouted, "Get the cargo grate and tie yourself to it".

A lightning bolt struck the mainmast with a powerful clap-thwack, and the mast disintegrated at once, bringing shards of smouldering wood crashing down around me, several of which fell through the grate, and began igniting the cloth in the hold below. Waves crashed over the bow and before we knew it, the dhow was sinking.

Pia and the boy held tight to each end of the grate they were tied to. I grabbed for the mast but missed. My heart felt like it had shot to the moon as, in that instant, Mango grasped my wrist and drew me in toward him. The boat sank beneath us as we floated off and away into a blinding onslaught of salty sea-spray. The waves' power was too much; everyone was coughing and spluttering. We were in a truly desperate situation.

Mango helped tie my wrist to the grate with a length of cord whilst I tried to wipe the torrents of rain from my face and squinted off toward the dark hollow where the dhow had sunk, taking my friend, Dawkins, with it.

Boxes and bails bobbed in the waves but no Dawkins. I scanned the waters frantically, and listened out, amidst the wail of wind and boom of breakers, for his voice.

"Jack!" Pia shouted, pointing to an area twenty feet from us.

Miracle of miracles. There he was! Splashing about as he struggled to free himself from a knot of ropes connected to the dhow.

But we couldn't get to him, we were helpless in the face of this cacophonous storm. He couldn't hear us calling to him, he never once looked our way. Despite my stinging eyes, I was desperate to keep him in my sights, but the swell swamped us time after time until, one blink, and he was gone, obscured amidst the boxes and pieces of ship.

I wept, moaned and howled like a child, but my tears bled into the green sea. Gone.

Pia screamed over and over, "Jack! Jack! Jack!" until there was nothing left but one final forlorn, "Jack".

My thick, sodden coat was dragging me down beneath the waves. I thought I would take it off and lay it across the grate and just as I had managed to spread the coat a wave flipped us all over and I managed to catch a last piece of cloth. But it was dragging me down. Reluctantly, I let go of the cord.

I could feel the coat clawing at my legs before drifting away from my body, as if it didn't want to leave me. I could not bear to watch my treasure sink, but I held onto the hope that it might wash ashore and find a new friend strolling on some desolate shore or be caught in some fortunate fisherman's net.

We pushed Ali onto the centre of the grate where he clambered up and sat crossed-legged, his eyes wide and petrified. The rest of us clung to one another other with one arm and gripped the ropes with our other. Our hearts and bodies were utterly broken. We bobbed there, sobbing in the night, mourning the loss of both my best friend and our fortunes.

At first, the rope merely chaffed my skin, but it didn't take long before it had dug a path into my wrist and of course, the constant wash of saltwater only added to the agony.

It wasn't until after the next wave washed over us that my eyelids and lips began to tingle.

I'd been stung by something. A flash of lightning illuminated hundreds of floating bubbles—baby jellyfish! Deadly? Perhaps. Perhaps not. The unknowing only added to my distress.

A phosphorescent glow ahead signalled the crashing of waves upon a shore, and we kicked our way towards it. With the wind behind us and the swell moving in on the tide, we headed easily into the beach.

A single lightning strike flared up, and Ali pointed to a colossal silhouette. What was it?

Another strike but longer this time, and as the monsoon shifted off and away, Ali pointed in the direction of the shadow once again.

"Jebel Akhdar!" he cried, as a shimmering emerald mountain rose before us from the sand dunes in the distance.

A burst of orange brought on the day. Flotsam from the dhow stretched out along the shoreline and we were washed up with it. Bedraggled and bereft, though the rivulets which ran down Pia's light chocolate skin managed to make her glimmer. We collapsed above the seaweed line and slept for what must have been hours, for by the time we awoke, scorching late-morning rays pelted into us.

I stared down the beach and noticed the grate washed up on the edge of the surf.

I could not believe our luck! Both Pia's brown leather pouch bag and the sleeve of my coat had managed to get tangled in the grate and travel ashore with us.

Ali was beside himself with excitement. We had no idea why. He wanted us all to see something. He took Mango and Pia by the hand, pulling their arms practically out of their sockets, forcing us all to follow him down the beach.

We walked for about a mile, scanning the landscape as we went for any sign of Dawkins, whether dead or alive. But nothing.

After two hours or so, fishing nets appeared, strung out in the distance, and we soon we came upon a village.

"Seeb! Seeb!" the boy cried out, dropping Pia and Mango's hands, at long last, and running towards the nets.

At the first house, the boy turned around and gestured for us to follow him.

"Yallah," he shouted, "Kaleena neroh!"

"Come on, let's go!"

Chapter 16

The first few houses we trudged past were each enclosed by a smoothly rendered, brown mud wall. Each front door was built from ornately decorated palm wood, the only wood available in this part of the world. Their intricately carved frames were painted in varying green and brown tones with square-topped, thumb-thick nails lined up in neat rows, one foot apart.

Groups of young children gathered around us, excited to see strangers in town. They laughed and shouted, holding out their tiny empty hands for us to fill but we had nothing left to offer them. Still, they were enthralled by our smiles and handshakes which we had in abundance of course.

A small boy recognised Ali and ran off shouting. Within a minute, a deep voice boomed through the village, scattering the children left, right and centre. At first, I assumed the children were being told off, but it turned out to be a game the children were familiar with, for when the man belonging to the voice arrived, he swiped his camel-cane in jest, within a whisker of their toes and the kids giggled deliriously. Ali gushed with joy before leaping into the man's arms, embraced him with all his might, and the children emerged again from their hidden holes to encircle the pair in celebration.

"Salam wa alaykum, Abu," said Ali, looking into the man's face with a grin the width of a yawning hippopotamus.

"Wa Alyikum is salam, awalad!" the man replied, squatting down on his haunches to hold Ali out before him with both arms extended, to stare, disbelieving, into the child's lively eyes, which mirrored his own exactly, and glistened as he crouched deeper to embrace Ali once again. The boy shook his head in disbelief. The man too. Tears flowed and grins grew even wider, spreading across the faces of these two reunited souls.

The man kissed the child on his forehead and nose before drawing him back in for yet another hug, looking to the skies and cheering,

It wasn't until he stood up again that I realised how tall he was and how muscular his frame. His features were chiselled, his skin a dark tan and his hair was hidden by a smartly tied turban. A noble nose, not too big nor hooked, but very thin, like an arête in the Cairngorms. His long beard was tweezed and trained, not a hair out of place. It underlined a strong jaw. His dish-dash was brilliant white, and his brown leather sandals exposed a set of perfectly manicured, polished toenails.

Until now, he only had eyes for Ali but the instant he realised he had company, he bowed and said, "Welcome to my village".

"Come; come and sit in my majlis. We must celebrate the homecoming of our son. I am Ali's father, Yoseph."

"Oliver," I bowed.

"Pia," she said still dabbing her eyes (both in grief for Dawkins and joy upon watching this pair reunited, I imagined).

"Pia," repeated Mango sagely.

We entered Yoseph's bayt and shuffled around his brass-topped coffee table, before sitting down, cross-legged on the floor, upon his array of grand, decorated cushions.

A baby started crying in the other room, and a woman entered. It was her exquisite dignity and poise, as much as her stature, which suggested she might be the matriarch of the family. She dropped her stoic guard the instant she spotted Ali, confirming to me that she was indeed Ali's mother, and there was a great deal of commotion amongst the three other younger women who followed her in—Ali's older sisters perhaps—who fussed, hither and thither, over the boy, incredulous that he stood before them. Then they were scolding Ali harshly, pointing accusatory fingers this way and that. Next, they began caressing him, swamping him in doting affection, pulling the child into their chests and chattering in incomprehensible Arabic whilst thrumming their tongues against their top lips, as tears of joy streamed down their faces.

The high-pitched cries they emitted reminded me of the whooping sound those notorious Cherokee Braves who went to New York after white man "befriended" them. I'd seen them myself when I visited America in my school holidays.

Eventually, they turned to face us and bowed their heads to the floor.

"These are Ali's sisters," Yoseph said, "Mariam, Ruth and Saleema."

"Shukran, Shukran," they repeated in unison. The matriarch barked orders at the others, and they scattered like startled deer into the adjoining room. When they re-emerged, the tallest of them was carrying a water jug and bowl. The smaller woman had fetched an old Arabian-style coffee pot with a long S-shaped spout which emerged from the pot's base. Tube-shaped cups made of glass, with a gold-gilt lip and handles too small to fit my fingers through, were brought to the table neatly displayed upon a round silver tray, along with a plate of dates and pomegranate. Saleema poured a viscous, black coffee into our cups. The cardamom aftertaste was so strong that hours later, even the slightest belch brought the flavour back up.

After coffee, Mariam and Ruth washed our hands and feet with rose water before dowsing them in fragrant oil. I could hear still the baby whimpering from behind the curtain, and the low murmuring of an Arabic lullaby. The matriarch flicked the middle daughter out of the room. When the young woman re-emerged through the beaded curtain, she was carrying the source of all the crying. She took the young babe over to the fire in the centre of the room.

From behind the same curtain emerged a much older, wizened woman (presumably the mother-in-law). She started bellowing orders and gesticulating with great animation. I couldn't hold back a small smirk on seeing Yoseph so awkward and somewhat impotent in the presence of these Amazons. The baby was crying rather unnaturally, I thought, not like a baby crying because it is uncomfortable or merely hungry.

169

This was far more anguished, and no matter how hard Mariam tried, she could not comfort the child. The elderly lady instructed the girl on how to unwrap the child from its swaddling and hold its little, naked body along one forearm. She plucked a glowing stick out of the embers of the fire, and, to my horror, I spotted the ring of spot-burn scars around the navel of the poor child. Pia stiffened and nudged me hard in the ribs. I stood up and walked over to the girl.

The hag kept up her commentary at the top of her voice. I could see the sorrow in the younger girl's eyes and stood up to walk over to her. Everyone, bar the hag, seemed tense and upset, which only egged me on. I held my hands out toward the babe and the girl turned away from the impending torture and handed the infant over to me, intuitively trusting me. I laid it gently on the brass table-top and pressed down on its abdomen with my index and middle finger. The infant pulled his feet up and clenched his fists, before letting out a pathetic squeal. The poor little lamb had colic.

I took the smoking stick from the woman's grasp, and she looked on, babbling her incomprehensible commentary, nodding approvingly but to her dismay, I tossed the stick back toward the fire, where Mango kicked it the last few inches and into the hearth.

"Would you bring me the oil bottle from the side table?" I asked Pia, "The one the girls used to wash our feet please."

I rested the child on my arm while Pia poured oil onto my free hand, and I gently massaged the boy's abdomen. The baby calmed down, eventually, and I handed him back to the girl whilst offering the hag the most withering look I could muster. She scuttled away, muttering.

We all feasted whilst recounting the extent of our adventures as best we could via a mixture of Yoseph's translations and our dramatic re-enactments in mime. Ali shared his stories to the family too, and we discovered how he had been stolen by Zanzibarian pirates before being sold on to the dhow captain a year ago.

As the village elder, Yoseph kept abreast of the comings and goings of harbours further down the coast. He was from an extremely high-caste family and was highly educated. He knew that Portuguese tea clippers often moored in Muscat harbour to replenish their water supply and other stores.

"I can take you to Muscat in the morning," Yoseph told us. "We have a date harvest and a herd of goats to sell at market."

Fuelled by Ali's stinking clothes, an open bonfire blazed away outside. I sat myself down across from Pia and Mango and we all contemplated the silence, mesmerized by the amber, scarlet smoke flames and smoke. On cue, the goats started to nibble at the dates tied to the donkeys but were soon shooed away by an angry goat herd. Pia wept and though Mango did his best to comfort her by placing a blanket about her shoulders, she shrugged it off. At this, he too began crying.

Knowing I could offer little comfort myself; I returned to the house and my bed. On one hand I had lost my childhood friend, and we had bonded somewhat over an adventure, On the other Jack had lured me into deadly danger. There again it was Jack who had forced me to give up my vices and lastly our mission had died with him.

On the subject of jewels, Dawkins had kept the extra but as far as I could tell he was also the treasurer of the adventure, so it looked like we would have to forfeit some substantial treasure to even get back to England, even if we had some.

The Iman's call to prayer rang out from the mosque's minaret across the village at daybreak. None of our party took part in the prayers; we left our bayt and headed to the stone sump to bathe in the well-water which ran along a twenty-foot aqueduct before overflowing, after which it served as the entire village's water source.

All the villagers washed in the sump. There was nothing resembling soap, only hundreds of fish to feast on our dead skin.

Our ordeal at sea had chapped everyone's hands and lips, and what with the stream of potent coffee we had imbibed, the culmination of our adventures and a mild case of heatstroke, I know I was not alone in feeling exhausted after a fitful sleep. My blistered sunburn had died down, somewhat, but I still ached all over.

After we had bathed and returned to Yoseph's house, the mother beckoned us to follow her into the room next door. A pile of local clothes had been laid out. Mango and I had a square brown coloured cloth about a yard in length, to cover our heads and a white dish-dash and brown leather sandals. She gestured for us to put them on. Where were our clothes? Pia was visibly anxious, and I too started panicking at once.

I uttered "The last of our bloody loot was sewn into the lining." As if she had read our minds, the mother looked over to the corner of the room where our clothes had been carefully tied up into bundles. I recognised Mango's enormous jacket had served as wrapping for his pile of freshly laundered clothes. Pia's was wrapped in her own skirt. They were each tied up with rough twine.

We dressed, and Ali showed me how to tie the turban in the local fashion. The two elder daughters tended to Pia. Once we were all dressed, we went out into the courtyard, where Yoseph, the mother and grandmother finished loading bundles of dates onto three donkeys. The beasts looked completely dwarfed under their enormous cargoes, it was quite comical. Yoseph called us over to him.

"Ya!" he shouted, with a toss of his head. Donkey after donkey emerged from alleyways on either side, led by their masters and laden with all manner of package—dried tuna fillets, sheaves of wheat, more sacks of dates, driftwood from the sea and date palm leaves. A bleating herd of floppy-eared goats were rounded up in the rear by young boys flicking wispy canes. Five camels lumbered along in the rear of the caravan.

Their long lashes blinked the flies off their faces; their tails wafted at random over their haunches.

The voyage was noisy and filled with laughter and jokes, all in Arabic of course.

"Ya Mohammed!" an owner called out.

To which another owner replied at the top of his voice, "Ya Abdul!"

Their chorus of voices never ceased. They yelled obscenities at one another, and personal quips whose context I often missed.

"Abu Moosa," someone might cry out, casting doubt upon the parenthood of someone or other.

"Ya Ali!" Moosa replied, before making some joke about the boys having fornicated with goats to beget his fellow merchant.

The journey from Seeb to Muscat is a day's walk at donkey-plodding pace. Our path followed a featureless shoreline, which was essentially just an extension of flat land running from the mountains to our north to the sea. The route was lined with coarse-grained sand and small acacia bushes. We occasionally passed other caravans returning to their villages from Muscat, which lay beyond the mountain passes.

Mango was in splendid spirits and, much to the amusement of one and all, skipped along impersonating every voice in the convoy.

It was a pleasant journey, given the travails we had endured up to this point. We camped outside the gates of Muscat's fortress wall. The boys tended their goats, the camels knelt, chewing their cud. The six of us sat on a carpet before a tuna fillet. Five trails of salad divided the bulky cone of rice, which was piled on top of the fish, evenly into six portions. Much to her annoyance, Pia had been seated with Mango and the goatherd boys.

"After all I've done," she muttered, "I get seated here, alongside the goat boys, for goodness sake!"

"It's how it's done here, Pia" I said. "We have to fit in as best we can to avoid standing out. Judging by the grim-looking faces of those gate guards, the worst thing we could do is to draw attention to ourselves by behaving differently from the norm." I felt for her, of course, but what else could I do? She shrugged and folded her arms.

It was a strange mood that had descended upon us although we were safe at last, our mission was dead in the water just like our friend Dawkins and Mango would not accept that Dawkins was gone. "He'll turn up he's a dodger he'll come soon with the treasure too." he insisted

Yoseph gestured for us all to start eating. I held back a moment, keen to adhere to local customs and make sure that I followed our host's etiquette.

He grabbed a fistful of rice, squeezed it into a tight ball between his fingers and palm, topped it with a lettuce leaf and some porridge, and proceeded to thumb-flick it into his mouth. He chewed away with an extremely satisfied smile.

I reached forward confidently, ready to follow Yoseph's lead. I thought I was mirroring Yoseph's exact moves, but it seemed not. Before I knew it, my neighbour to my left had grabbed my arm and forced my hand back into my lap. The Arabs began laughing, mocking me. What had I done wrong?

Only then did it occur to me. I had used my left hand, and Arabs wipe their bottoms with their left hand. I should not have tried eating with mine!

I acknowledged my shame and, much to my neighbour's amusement, sat on my left hand for the rest of the meal whilst concentrating on my thumb-flick technique with my right.

After the meal, we sat around the fire listening to recitations of poetry from the herdsmen, stories about genies from the womenfolk, and tales of Ali Baba from Ali, whose translations were very entertaining.

As the night's entertainment wound down, I felt impelled to walk down to the shore. I spotted Pia's silhouette standing on the shoreline staring out to sea.

All along the shore were various other fires, each fuelled with driftwood, or palmwood from the interior beyond the mountains.

Each fire had its own compliment of traders enjoying the night sky with their families. They chatted and sang or merely stared up at the vast and complex mystery of the Lord's good works.

It was hard to believe this was the same sea—now so innocent, so sleepy—that had taken our friend, only a day before. Its ripples stroked the sand along the shoreline. A goat bleated from time to time. A shooting star flashed across the horizon. As I walked further from the campfire's yellow hue, I too looked up. God's colours grew more and more intense, more glorious and awe-inspiring.

This would be the first time I'd had a chance to talk with Pia since we entered Seeb, some thirty hours earlier. The prospect had me feeling elated.

As I approached, I realised her shoulders were shuddering. She was clearly weeping. I didn't want to startle her, so I cleared my throat. She turned slightly, and her tear-smeared cheeks shone in the moonlight. Dawkins and Pia had grown so close and none of us had yet had time to reflect on the reality of our loss. Now, here we were. Safe enough to finally sink into the reality of our feelings. At risk of either one of us being overcome, I moved with steady care and place my arm about her, then pulled her tenderly into me with a squeeze.

She turned her face into the crest of my arm and sobbed into my dish-dash. "I loved him."

"We don't know for certain that he is dead," I said. "We didn't actually see him go down," I added, in the hope that it would help. But she only cried louder.

My head was in a whirl. I loved my friend, and was certain he was dead, but I loved Pia in a unique way. With Dawkins gone, I guessed I had a chance to fill the aching chasm left by my own dear wife's absence. I wanted Pia's pain to abate, but I was grieving too for he was also my friend.

We stared at the gently lapping sea. It was so still that the stars refracted on its surface. They had same depth they had held the night before the storm.

Pia composed herself and with no further words we retired to our separate tents. I slept sounder that night than ever.

The sun had barely risen but the herdsmen and traders were already beginning to stir. Off in the distance, to the southwest, the imam called for prayer. Then the trumpets ordered the guards to change over and take post. We fed the animals and prepared them for the final leg of our journey before doing the same for ourselves. Prayers hummed on in the background, whilst we filled our goat-skin bottles from a nearby well.

The caravan trundled the few hundred yards towards Muscat's still-locked gates. The trumpeters sounded another tune and the mood within our caravan grew strangely morose. The mighty gates to Muscat's outer wall opened and twenty or so Omani palace guards marched out and took post along the outside of Muscat wall. Various caravans who had been camped outside overnight began moving toward the gates. Traders with heavy sacks across their backs, shuffled through with their frankincense, gold, silver and leatherwork.

Everyone was headed towards the central marketplace.

Our party remained uncharacteristically quiet. I sensed that everybody in our caravan knew something we didn't, and their subdued manner made me extremely nervous. An imposing-looking guard halted us as we approached the gates, and two soldiers marched forward from the wall to remove half goods from the donkeys' backs and place them on an ever-increasing pile next to the wall.

The herdsmen didn't say a word; they merely smiled with resignation and walked through the gates without so much as a backward glance. I was appalled to see the same "taxation" happening when other traders, departing with goods they had bought in the market, were stopped, only to have their goods halved by the pilfering soldiers!

Those guards were supposed to be protecting the gates on behalf of the traders but were stealing from them instead. The so-called tax was effectively seventy five percent by my calculation.

It was our turn. As we were walking, the bulkiest of the guards grabbed at our branches of dates. Yoseph bristled as he glared at the guard who was untying half the harvest.

Another guard then turned his attention to Pia. She had respectfully dressed in the style of all the other Arab women entering the city, with full black purdah but, as I was to discover soon enough, guards seemed to treat all the women in the same way, with impunity.

The Muscat guards knew they held all the cards and could take whatever they wanted. First, the guard placed himself between Pia and me, then he grabbed at her waist with both hands, leering and grinning with his coffee-stained teeth. Sweat trickled down his temples to land and wallow in the mangrove roots of his stubble.

Naturally, I pushed forward to offer her my assistance, but Pia escaped his clutches as nimbly as a monkey, ducking beneath the belly of a camel. The guard managed to grab the trail of her long, black robe but I pulled him around and struck him in the gut.

He was wearing body armour, so nothing I did affected him. I stood trembling, holding up my fast-swelling hand and sweating profusely. Someone clawed at my collar from behind and a blunt object hit the side of my head. My last conscious memory as I slumped to the sandy floor, was of Yoseph shaking his head disapprovingly, and hauling his donkey train past the guards into the city, with Pia, her dignity still intact, and the other women by his side.

I came around to find myself locked in a dungeon. Through the grated slit above me I could see the main gates rising to the sky and deduced that I must have been near the entrance to the fortress. I was fixed to the wall by a heavy iron chain about my waist, and the back of my head throbbed.

A bump as big as a plum, soaked my finger in sticky blood when I rubbed it. I'd been stripped to the waist, and my body was smattered with bruises—black, blue and yellow. As I tilted to one side, I ran one hand down my torso. I breathed in and out. Several ribs were bruised, perhaps broken. I could tell I had been beaten even after I had lost consciousness. The saliva I hawked when I coughed carried the metallic flavour of blood and I must have been in shock because I was cold, very cold.

The sun streamed in through the bars in the wall. A plate of stale flatbread lay on the floor across from me. A large brown rat stalked around the wall's edge; he was headed towards the plate. Horrified, I turned away only to find another black rat headed across the floor in the same direction. The floor was partially covered in straw saturated in vomit, putrid faeces and urine which had spattered into my cell from an open sewage gutter which ran along the middle.

An iron lattice door stood on the other side of the gutter wall. It was built of flat bars of thick, interwoven iron and had fat rounded rivets mounted at the joints. Red rust ran down the bars from the rivets and, next to the door, I suddenly spied the hairy, naked legs of a person hanging from solid iron manacles chained to the wall.

The sunlight streaming through the bars was bright. What I could make out, however, was that the man was as beaten and bruised as I was. A small circle of blood had pooled below his filthy feet. By my estimation, the poor man had lost a pint or so.

The heavy stomp of footsteps echoed down the corridor and there was the clinking of keys at the lattice door. The unwilling iron gate opened with a high-pitched creak. The guard marched into our cell, keys in his right hand, a flaming torch in his left.

178

The torch illuminated the room, and, to my bewilderment, I saw that it was an unconscious Dawkins who was hanging from the wall. The guard prodded him before turning his attention to me. He planted the torch into a bracket on the wall and then lifted me up by the hair.

"You come with," he grunted, through ochre-coloured teeth.

Another guard entered and unlocked the padlock at my waist and tossed the clanking chain into the corner. His breath reeked of the by now familiar odour of coffee and cardamom.

Dawkins hung limply but his swollen left-eye opened a tad before closing again so I knew he was alive. If the guards had noticed I am certain they would have assigned him yet another vicious blow.

One of the guards pushed me across the room towards the iron-gated entrance. I paused near my friend for just a moment before the guard forced me from the cell and launched a gelatinous hoik at Dawkins.

My escort propelled me out of the gatehouse, and I stumbled up a short street lined with houses and shops. Salesmen bellowed out of doorways in some animated tongue I did not recognize, out-pricing one another's wares and no doubt bragging about how his very own grandmother had lost her sight trying to stitch the ornate work, a common selling trick in all Arab souks. The shops were crammed with silver khanjar daggers, with their beautifully carved ivory hilts resting at-ease in their sheaths.

Old men sucked on hookah pipes in the date-laden cafés, reciting poetry. The sweet smell of frankincense perfume permeated the air.

I estimated the hour to be around five o'clock. The sun was low in the west, and an imam had begun calling his followers to dusk's prayers. Soon, other imams started up, calling the faithful to prayers from the dozens of minarets scattered throughout the city.

A bonfire was being built with date palm trunks in the marketplace square. A grand, iron throne stood by the pile of twigs.

I threw the soldier escorting me a quizzical look.

"There. Rebellion. Sud," he said, pointing south. "We break it. Leader want throne. We give him throne. On fire. Ha, ha, ha, ha," he laughed.

They were going to fry the poor chap alive.

"We give crown too." He pointed to a small cauldron on a nearby fire into which men were dropping rusting swords. Another laugh from my escort and I shuddered to the core of me.

Chapter 17

I couldn't be sure how long I had been locked up, but it felt like I had not eaten for days. Simply imagining a drooping date palm and its branches laden with bunches of the yellow beads of yet to ripen dates was all it took to get my mouth watering. My culinary reverie was interrupted by several military horses as they galloped in through the city gates behind us, cutting a gap through the crowded street.

"Yallah, make way for the prince's hunting party!" the riders shouted in Arabic as they whipped any guards standing idle for their slovenly ways. Random passers-by also suffered the brunt of the horsemen's ire. The rhythmic whooshing sound of their canes never let up. I could smell the linseed oil on the polished leatherwork, and its silver lorinery sparkled in the morning light. Each horse was crowned with a braided mane. An erect peacock feather waved prominently above their brows.

One rider, on an unremarkable horse came into view. He led a mule with three dead jackals, blood dripping from their snouts, tied over its back. A pair of finer, black Arab horses trotted side by side behind them. Each rider reined their horse with a right hand and held a large, hooded hawk with the left. In my youth, I had spent a week in Twist flying kestrels with Mr Brownlow and had learned that falconers' gloves are always left-handed.

A moment later, a lame, white stallion clip-clopped by. The horse's bit, bridle and other lorinery was brightly polished gold (it was certainly not brass). His saddle was topped with a plush, silk cushion and ornate Arabic script was carved on the ivory stays. The pommel, too, was ivory, and it had an extra seat at the rear with a back-support made of black veneered wood, decorated in gold-leaf writing. The poor beast was bleeding from its withers and fore legs. Lacerations spanned, like sunbeams, from its chest. The rider's apparel, which would once have been of first-rate quality, were now torn and scuffed.

A larger black steed loped alongside the stallion ridden by an impressive specimen—a Nubian, high-ranking officer.

He was wearing a charcoal painted breastplate shaped like the chest of a roman god. His centurion-style, raven-coloured helmet was embossed with gold and a long white ponytail streamed down from its crown. A short, pleated skirt (roman style) made of leather hung from his waist, ending halfway down his sturdy thighs. His chocolate-coloured legs shimmered with sweat. His shins were also armoured with black and gold legging-plates and his reins, which were unusually thick, were of twirled silver tile with gold thread. The Nubian's muscular arms were statuesque, in almost a godlike way. The whites of his eyes shone bright against his chocolate skin as he stared around wildly, seeking any small transgression on which to land his wrath.

From the rope-burn scars around his neck he had most likely once been a slave. I also spotted the raised welts on our dark lord and surmised that the kiss of some cruel trader's whip had left them there. The markings were criss-crossed on the underside of his ulna indicating that he had adopted the classic pugilist stance to protect his head. A sheath, housing a classic scimitar sword—no doubt razor-sharp—protruded from his back-plate. Every inch of this man was threatening. Even his horse let out a contemptuous fart and shat at our feet as it strode by.

The dishevelled Arab adolescent riding the white steed held a blood-splattered rag over his eye. Every man fell to his knees upon seeing him, their hands laid flat out on the ground, their faces in the dirt. No one dared look the rider in the eye. With the flick of a wrist my guard ordered me to join them. I did so, at once, only to find myself inhaling one glorious glob of steaming, hay-laden horse turd. It was in this undignified position that we waited until finally, the Sultan's son had passed us, and we were able to dust ourselves off as they vanished around the bend.

We came upon a twenty-foot sandstone wall with ornate, wrought-iron gates straddled by a pair of parapets. Beneath the white canvas which billowed in the gentle desert breeze above the sentry posts two sentries, dressed in white linen, stood motionless.

Their eyes were steel as they scanned their area of duty. Their polished silver breastplates and helmets glinted in the sunshine.

My escort hollered over to the left guard who turned around to shout down to an invisible doorkeeper. After a jingling of keys and the clunk of a lock, the left gate opened. It was only a small picket-gate, but large enough to allow one person at a time to pass. I am of average height, but even I had to duck my head to get through the entrance. I shuddered as I tilted my bare neck forward. Any defender could have sliced through it in a trice with utter impunity. A thick wooden board lay across the base of the door to trip the unwary, a design feature which ensured that any would-be assailant would be at a disadvantage from the outset of his attack.

Once I'd straightened up, I found myself looking at one of the most beautiful gardens I had ever seen. It led up to the palace's awe-inspiring marble facade. My guard took me to the palace baths, where a couple of adolescent boys stripped me and sponged me down. After an hour soaking and sponging, I was so relaxed that I drifted off to sleep, I don't know how long I was gone but when I awoke, two beautiful, caramel-coloured women were luring me out of the bath to wrap me in a large cotton sheet, before leading me by the hand down a corridor to a separate room where, to my delight, I found Mango waiting.

I ran straight to him. "Oh, my good fellow," I gabbled, "you are here, but how? Why? Hmmn?"

Mango put his finger to my lips, and, with a glance, he glanced over to a man seated at the back of the room. The man was unlike our burly guards. Aside from his white dish-dash, he wore a white, brimless cap like an upturned cup with a flat bottom, intricately embroidered in pastel blue around the edges. His turnout was flawless, his beard immaculately trimmed and his skin a tone lighter than I would have expected. The room was square. A large opening led to a balcony overlooking the inlet which led to the Sultan's personal harbour. The walls were of shiny, white marble with veins of brown and gold meandering ets through the slabs.

Inlaid pillars of chestnut-brown wood and gilt-gold held up an opulent marble ceiling. Resplendent, slit-woven kilims were scattered over the tiled floor. They were exquisite and caressed my soles so gently that I involuntarily slid my feet sideways along the nap to the edge of each rug. Despite the searing heat outside the room was cool. A continuous bench of mahogany covered in silken cushions lined the walls.

An ornate, pewter water jug surrounded by four matching cups and fruit bowl stood on a large, copper roundtable in the room's centre. I could not keep my eyes off the sumptuous collection of dates, pomegranates, oranges and grapes and eagerly sat down to consume the exotic fruit.

No sooner had we sat down than an enormous door, ornately decorated and built from Burmese mahogany, opened before us. Two men strode purposefully towards me. I recognised Yoseph at once. The other man gestured for me to stay seated. He must have been the guard captain. He was tall and elegant.

"Captain Ahmed, Captain of the Palace Guard," he said, by way of introduction, in a decidedly British accent.

"Your English is impeccable," I replied. "Where did you study?"

"I worked in the consulate in Calcutta before coming here, to this palace. I will be translating for you. By the way, your friend Yoseph has been extremely helpful."

"How so?" I enquired.

"Whilst in the market, a herald was sent back from the Sultan's son's hunting tent with a message that the prince had ridden through an acacia bush whilst chasing a jackal in the desert.

A thorn had embedded itself in his eye and the Royal Physician, here in the Palace, announced that he would treat it by pouring salt into the eye, allowing his tears to wash the thorn out."

184

"That is ridiculous!" I proclaimed. "Salt would merely dissolve and cloud the eye; he'll be blinded for life."

"Quite. Having seen you using modern medical practices and knowing of the Royal Physician's habit of employing ancient therapies, Yoseph made his way to the palace, at significant personal risk to himself, I might add, to insist on an audience with the Sultan. He described how you had previously put a stop to a barbaric cure which was about to be undertaken in his own house. The Sultan then ordered you to be brought here.

"Yoseph explained to the Sultan, the circumstances behind your unfortunately arrest and His Majesty agreed to your release on the condition that his son's sight be saved.

"A failed attempt is not an option. Do you agree to cure the boy?"

I really had no choice, of course. "I will require various medical instruments; an ophthalmoscope for a start."

This was an instrument I had heard rumour of having been invented in Germany. I had no idea, however, how the implement worked but, in any case, mentioning such a device sounded impressive. "Along with some tweezers, small clamps," and just for good measure I added, "and my two assistants Pia and Dawkins."

Ahmed noted everything down as I dictated.

"Yoseph told me about Pia but who is this 'Dawkins' you speak of?"

"He is hanging in the cell where I myself was held."

Ahmed bowed slightly and left the room.

Servants came and went, busying themselves lighting oil lamps on the walls as darkness fell, refreshing the fruit bowl and refilling the water jugs. Mango occupied himself by sewing the rips in his shirt.

185

I dropped off to sleep several times, then woke myself with a jolt and looked around the room, embarrassed, only to drift off and jolt myself awake again. Eventually, the door opened and Ahmed strode in, followed to my absolute joy by none other than Dawkins and Pia.

Mango leapt to his feet to throw his arms around the two. I too went to hug Dawkins but as I approached him, he slumped down upon a silk chaise longue.

I sat down gently, beside him, as if mirroring his unsteadiness would help ease the pain of his bruises and raw wrists from the manacles. A semi-healed slash hung low along his left brow, his bottom lip was thick and split. If he ever wished to breathe properly though his broken nose, it would require setting straight.

The man in white whom I had first noticed sitting in the corner of the room, had still not uttered a single word. It was obvious to me by now, that he had been tasked with eavesdropping. For this reason, I was careful to speak only in veiled speech when briefing Dawkins and Pia. They seemed to catch on pretty quickly, and our silent attendant leant forward intently every time the three of us conversed. Furthermore, he picked his moment to serve us with fruit or lemonade every time we started whispering. We grabbed the chance, however, when he was called away, to catch up properly and it was during one of those opportunities when he recounted his story about how he had fought the storm.

"How on earth did you manage to survive?" I asked.

"I untangled myself from the rope and swam to the surface," he explained. "I clung to whatever flotsam I could and once I was washed ashore.

I wandered into a nearby fishing village.

The villagers were suspicious of foreigners and called the local militia. A cavalry detachment was dispatched to pick me up and I put up quite a fight but soon found myself hanging in the guardhouse."

Later that evening, Dawkins, Mango and Pia washed before we made our way through to the white marbled dispensary. Pia had tied her hair into a bun and tucked it beneath a white bonnet from one of the Sultan's wives.

The oil lamps flickered incessantly but it was amply lit for the purpose and though, of course, there was no ophthalmoscope, there were other appropriate tools as I had ordered the Omani medics to prepare, and so the operation went ahead.

Our teenage patient was led in wearing fine clothes and a large, woollen patch over his left eye.

The Court Physician strutted into the room. "The prince has had a light dose of lithium," he announced. "Now, follow me to the treatment room." He shot me a scornful glance and departed in a pompous huff, mumbling in Arabic as he went.

The boy stumbled slightly as he walked, so he was certainly already woozy. As we lay him down, Dawkins handed me some contraption he had fashioned out of metal with which to support the large telescopic lens that the medics had borrowed from the Sultan's impressive telescope collection.

I peered down the lens into the boy's eye. My instrument was about six inches wide; the thorn looked like a little finger embedded in the lower part of the eye. Fortunately, the needle-like object had missed the iris, lens and suspensory ligaments. It really was quite a miracle that it had only punctured the eye's sclera. The onlookers did not know it, of course, but this was to be the simplest operation I had been involved in. However, as this was, in a manner of speaking, a sort of theatre, I would also ensure that it was the most theatrical operation I had ever carried out.

The appearance of the lad's eye was indeed dramatic—very red and no doubt painful for the patient. I had already briefed Pia and Dawkins about making the operation seem impressive, and they did me proud.

Despite the occasional wince from Dawkins who was still a little tender from the shipwreck and subsequent beatings, both were making an enormous fuss of passing me the largest instruments with expansive gestures worthy of any operating theatre back in Bermondsey. We carried on our charade as I extracted the thorn, making every detail seem more complicated a procedure than it was.

Finally, I stuck a small swatch of fine linen, fashioned by Pia, down over the eye and covered it with a fawn leather patch.

"The sclerotic and choroid ciliary body had been lacerated," I explained to the palace physician. "It will remain sore for some time and should stay covered for at least two weeks. Clean the dressing daily and only lubricate with the purest of water. No salt. If you follow these instructions to the letter," I paused for dramatic effect, "then the eye is surely saved." I stood tall and lifted my chin slightly.

Dawkins and Pia, knowing the stakes here, donned their sternest of expressions and patted their hands together as if clapping whilst they whispered with feigned sincerity, "Well done. Well done, Doctor Twist."

Sultan Thuwaini bin Said al-Said thanked us for saving his son's eyesight by inviting Dawkins and myself to a feast. I was to be guest of honour. We were offered smart white dish-dashes, elegantly trimmed with gold braid. Their collarless necks were round with string tassels tied at the throat. We were also handed a black cotton shawl, also trimmed with gold, and smart brown leather, thong-styled sandals.

Meanwhile, Pia was sent to the royal dressmaker where she too was to be fitted with more appropriate evening wear.

We were led into a larger room. The first room I had seen in this palace had been lavish, but this room was decorated to another level.

The colourful silk carpets on the immaculate marble floor had been hand-stitched in Tehran and were breathtakingly beautiful. The patterns in the maze of carpets which covered the room were mesmerising.

Vast dark wooden beams built from imported Burmese rosewood, carved with wriggly gold-leaf designs and Arabic quotes from the Quran hung overhead. Their silver inlays were polished to a glimmer. In this rectangular majlis, a single marble bench, scattered with large blue plump cushions with delicately platted tassels, lined three of the white walls.

There was no bench on the wall through which we entered, however, simply a long row of servants standing with their backs to the wall, carrying trays of pomegranates, oranges and lime juice with mint leaves.

The room was uncluttered, and the oil-burning lamps poised atop scores of columns, were each made of solid gold. Frankincense from Sur smouldered in orbs, which were also made of gold. The aroma was fantastic; unlike any scent I had ever inhaled.

A trio of Omani performers knelt near a pillar in the centre of the room. They sang of the Sultan's magnificence. One musician thrummed a drum on its side with a drumstick bent at one end at a right angle. Another played an oud lute, and a third clapped vigorously.

As each verse ended, everyone in the room ceased whatever they were doing or saying and shouted, "Sahir!" I later discovered this translated as "True!"

Portraits of the Sultan in various periods of his life hung on the walls, without a single reference being made to the previous Sultan, who had died under suspicious circumstances earlier in the year. Every portrait bore some comment referring to the Sultan's majesty, mercy, benevolence, courage or some such virtue.

The Sultan himself stood at the door by my side. He was in his forties, about five foot seven and was morbidly obese.

His podgy skin was not much darker than mine and, though it was a cool evening, he was sweating profusely.

His moustache was full and bushy, and he had grown a tiny goatee beneath his lip.

As each court member filed in, the Sultan greeted them with a sentence in Arabic. I assumed mine translated into, "This is Doctor Oliver, the one who saved my son's eyesight."

Every man who entered had already removed his sandals. Every man wore a turban, denoting his place of origin and thus his status. Some were neat and tidily tied up, showing they were from Muscat or Ibra or Sohar.

Those whose turbans were more loosely bound, were likely from Nizwa Fort. The several colourfully dressed gentlemen who arrived donning turbans which fell loosely around their shoulders, were most certainly members of fierce Bedouin tribes from the interior. Every man carried his bonduke with a matchlock firing mechanism, their thin wooden butts were fragile by Western standards, although decidedly more ornate. Their barrels were exceptionally long, and their bore smaller than the standard British infantryman's rifle.

Each man shook my hand and said, "Salam wa alyukum." Although I knew only too well that their greeting was insincere for both Dawkins and I were little more than Abyad adoo, Arabic for "white-eyed enemy".

The Sultan nodded to a man whom I assumed was the head servant who shouted, "Yallah". At this, the Sultan led Dawkins and me to a raised table surrounded by prepared cushions, in the centre of the room. Much to her indignation, however, Pia was led to an anteroom to eat with the wives and daughters.

The Sultan sat before anyone else, of course. Enormous dishes of rice were carried in. The head servant clapped, and the band started up once again. Then came the meats—chicken, goat, tuna and even camel.

190

Assuming the empty cushion by the Sultan was designated for me, I too went to sit down, for it seemed the only space left to fill. The Sultan lifted his hand, stopping me in my tracks, and said, "La, la, Awlad".

He gestured to the servant, who scurried off. The Sultan's son arrived.

"Salim bin Thuwaini!" the herald at the door announced. At which, the musicians stopped playing, and four men placed a plate, almost as wide as the table itself, down, piled high with stacks of food. Still more followed.

A bowl was carried to Dawkins, and he lifted it to his lips at once, ready to drink the contents but the head servant removed the bowl, then sprinkled Dawkins' hands with rosewater and gestured for him to wash them. When he was done, another servant dried them. I followed suit. The atmosphere in the room changed; voices faded until we all sat in absolute silence whilst the son walked around the table. The guests stared at the bandages around his head, and some whispered covertly amongst themselves.

He took his place and nodded, begrudgingly, in recognition to me. A hardened blend of bitterness, hatred and resentment oozed through this fifteen-year old's every laboured gesture.

As many adolescents, he shrugged off his father's loving pats and gestures, but in such a way that seemed beyond the usual teenage tantrum.

The discomfort in the room was palpable throughout the rest of the meal. The Sultan, however, chatted away with joviality, oblivious to his son's surly demeanour. Or perhaps he was pretending not to notice. or he had grown immune. All the same, I found it disconcerting. No one dared touch the food, though the aromas at that table had us giddy with anticipation. Everyone waited. And waited.

Finally, the Sultan stretched his arms out before him, like some

191

athlete warming up, and reached across the plate to rip a rasher out of the cheek of a camel's head, which had been carefully balanced upon a jebel of rice.

Talking and eating, the Sultan gleefully gobbled up the various treats reaching hither and thither with his sleeve accidentally collecting rice and scattering the food that did not entirely pass his rigorous assessment.

Suddenly, the murmur of voices fell silent. No one moved. The Sultan was pointing. To his throat. His face had turned crimson. His eyes began to bulge. It was alarming, to say the least. He clutched at his throat.

He pointed to his face now. Next, he was convulsing. Choking. His ministers watched on. Motionless. I was the only one who stood. I crossed over to him, swiftly.

Two bodyguards moved in to stop me, but Ahmed ordered, "Kif!" They relaxed and let me pass.

I swooped around the Sultan and picked him up by the armpits. I leaned him over and gave him a heavy smack with the palm of my fist, right between his shoulder blades. A semi-chewed date flew out of the Sultan's blue face, and he let out an enormous gasp.

The guests all stood and applauded, whilst the son gave me the most disparaging look I have ever seen before returning to his feast.

The Sultan was bursting with gratitude. He summoned Ahmed over and thus ensued a brief exchange between them before Ahmed turned to us to say, "After the feast, the Sultan wishes to show you his treasury."

Once the Sultan had had his fill, he flicked his hand, and a swarm of servants descended on the feast. The plates were removed, in silence, even as I gnawed on, and the table was cleared mid-pineapple.

The servants left, the Sultan clapped his hands, and a new set of servants emerged carrying small bowls of rose-scented water.

They proceeded to wash and dry each of our hands. Bowls and servants vanished and the majlis was returned to its original state of quiet repose. When the Sultan rose, the guards by the giant mahogany door stiffened.

The Sultan pointed toward Dawkins and me. "Yallah, Kalina Narooh," he said, waddling away.

The Sultan led us through his colourful, exotic gardens. Small water bowls sat along the edges of the path; other bowls brimmed with small seeds.

When the Sultan stopped at a corner, he tapped the path with his spindly cane, and a short man, wearing a white dish-dash and brown Omani turban, emerged from the shadows. He held a pewter water jug with which he refilled one the empty bowls with water.

"The Sultan is fonder of his birds than his people," Ahmed whispered.

The Sultan shouted at the water-carrying man, and two guards ran forward to drag the poor soul off to God knows where—a fate I find difficult (even to this day) to contemplate. We passed an ostentation of peacocks which let out the ghastliest scream whenever we were near.

We approached an iron door, and the Sultan pulled a large key from his belt, with which he unlocked the massive padlock on the gate. This was the entrance to the treasury. The architect had evidently designed this building very specifically knowing it would serve as the treasury. For a start, the door was only able to be opened wide enough to fit one man though. A stone had been laid, just inside the mighty door. Another security feature which had been very well thought out indeed were the three large trunks which were placed in the room. They were certainly too big to have fitted through the doorway, so the walls must have been built around them, thus ensuring that if the treasury were ever robbed, the thieves would only manage to take a small proportion out at one time.

After wrestling for some time, with a smaller key on his belt, the Sultan finally managed to open a smaller, yet denser door. The eyeful of gems and diamonds behind that door utterly disarmed us, for they were beyond even Fagin's treasure in India.

Dawkins stared, intently as if counting the inventory. And as we looked around the treasury I looked back at him. He was murmuring something to himself. Dawkins looked like he was checking off a list inside his head.

But I was very excited as I was sure the Sultan would treat my quick thinking with a jewel or too. I was wrong, just viewing the treasures was to be our reward.

We surveyed that room in wonder but after a moment, I felt something in Dawkins' manner change. I glanced at him, then followed his gaze. He was staring at a very large emerald which was precariously perched upon a bed of gold coins and his expression changed from intent concentration to quiet contentment.

Chapter 18

The Sultan smiled. "I see you are admiring my latest acquisition,"

"Breath-taking," Dawkins replied. "Where did you buy it?"

"I am not at liberty to say but I can tell you that it cost me more roubles than I care to admit."

After our short viewing of the treasury, we left to return to our bedroom. It was the first chance I had to ask Dawkins why his entire demeanour had changed when were in there.

"What happened?" I asked him. "What was it you were so intensely mulling over?"

"Oliver, I have great news," he replied. "I have solved the conundrum and now understand why the Russians were so desperate we be left for dead in the cave at Jammu, and why they wanted to prevent us from reaching the embassy."

"Tell me," I said.

"There was a sizeable green emerald in the treasury. You may have noticed it."

I shook my head.

"I had been briefed on the story behind such an emerald," he continued, "and I am sure it is the same one. The emerald is part of a set. Informants amongst British collectors leaked rumours which led to the Secret Service unearthing the news about the melting-down and sale.

"We consulted with experts to attain dossiers on the size, shape, carat, colouring, style of cut and imperfections of every jewel known to be in the collection, including the centrepiece. We have been trying to identify stones from collections across all the countries around Europe and tracked down some of the smaller ones over the years, but nothing substantial enough to confirm that the rumours were true—until now!

I believe that stone I saw in there is the centrepiece they described and, therefore, conclusive proof that the whole collection has indeed been sold."

Dawkins had been specifically instructed to look out for the centrepiece as part of the confirmation effort, so he knew everything about it.

"Dawkins, you have such an eye for detail, such a brilliant memory," I said.

"Those jewels are from the Russian Crown Jewels," he said, ignoring my compliment entirely. "I am sure of it. They have been melted down to pay for their involvement in the Crimea. The Russians didn't want this information getting out. And no wonder! The tsar's excessive extravagance in times of war has already pushed the Russian people to the brink of revolution. This would topple him. They're even closer to revolution than the British are."

Determined to prove what the Russians had done, Dawkins called us together that night to discuss a plan on how to steal back the jewels.

We also needed an escape plan, of course. He assigned Pia, Mango and me with tasks regarding the burglary. Whilst he was to arrange and manage the actual escape.

I was to manufacture the skeleton keys but first I had to steal them from the Sultan. To this end, I set about following the Sultan around the palace. The Sultan often walked around the court with his camel stick, silver belt and khanjar. Upon spying a crack or scratch on the floor, he would stand and tap the floor until a flunky appeared, to whom he would report the damage.

"If it is not fixed by sundown tomorrow then—Chop!"

I required more tools than the surgical instruments I had been provided with, the kinds of implements that marble stonemasons use:

A file, loadstone and some form of thin metal which is possible to cut and smooth down; something like a mason's trowel.

Dawkins and Pia later appeared in my room and the three of us slipped out onto the balcony, out of earshot of our eavesdropping servant.

Just before dawn, I made my way through the palace to scratch an unmissable gouge into the marble floor right next to the Sultan's bedroom doorway. I hid and waited for the distinct clink of his silver-toed cane pointing out my handy work. Within minutes, a stonemason arrived. As soon as he started work, Pia came and distracted the hot-blooded fool whilst Mango swiped first his trowel, then his saw.

Another scratch appeared the following day, and one more mason lost his loadstone. It didn't occur to us until Pia told us what was likely to become of these poor fellows (the harem was the source of all manner of rumour), that our actions had effectively sentenced these poor masons to the chop! But it was all in the name of the Empire, of course. Like in any war, or similar conflict, there was no space for commiseration or regret on behalf of the enemy, no matter how innocent their fate found them.

Next step was to attain a pattern for the key. I had noticed red marks on the Sultan's white dish-dash where his keys hung around his waist indicating that the keys were a tad rusty. This would serve us well. The challenge was, however, thinking up a way to separate him from his keys. I formulated the perfect plan to be executed at yet another of the Sultan's banquets.

After we'd completed our feast of goat, cooked deep in the ground with herbs and spices, Dawkins and I started a food-throwing game with the Sultan. We aimed all manner of morsel into his mouth. Naturally, the Sultan liked to win, so he caught every morsel we shot at him, without missing a single grape, corn kernel, walnut, chicken piece or sultana.

We laughed uproariously, jollying on until the inevitable moment arrived, when the Sultan started feeling stuffed. So stuffed, in fact, that he was forced to loosen his belt. I was rather proud of this plan, I must say, for it went exactly as it should have. We played on until the Sultan removed his belt entirely, placing it on the tablecloth in front before him.

We continued to distract the Sultan. Over the following hour or so, I deliberately knocked over a candle, so its wax would flow straight onto the keys. Not only did the rust from the keys leave clear, traceable outlines on the cloth beneath them, but as they lay there in the heat (and with a little help from a weighty pitcher which I "clumsily" placed down over them), they sank millimetres by millimetre, into the cushion of the tablecloth, leaving an impression as defined as if we had pressed the form into wax ourselves. The royal locksmith himself could not have cast a better mould. Ingenious, no?

I watched the servants sweep the tablecloths away, careful to remember which linen basket our potential templates were dropped into. The instant that basket was left unattended, I signalled with the flick of a hand for Mango to pluck the cloth from the basket and hide it beneath his dish-dash.

Meanwhile, Pia had been plotting possible ways to distract the peacocks surrounding the treasury. She later told me that during dinner, she had secreted a handful of sweetcorn from her plate and tucked it into a pocket beneath her burka. She then soaked the kernels in marsala wine overnight. A brilliant ruse.

One would imagine that escaping such a walled-off city would be the greatest challenge of them all. Ironically, however, this ended up being the most straightforward part of the entire scheme. The city had been designed to prevent people from getting in, not out, which meant all their defences were geared for that objective.

The Sultan's reign had always been a precarious one. Given its instability, it was hardly surprising to discover that there was a system of secret exits.

This collection of gates was known to very few people, but Pia had overheard the women gossiping about the location of a network of escape routes somewhere at the rear of the city when she spent time in the harem. Dawkins sought them out on one of his many forays into the garden and reported back to us that, although they were locked from the outside, they were easily opened from the inside via a quick-release bar.

"What will be your task?" I asked Dawkins.

"I will befriend the Sultan's horses."

"How so?"

"I'll gain access to the stables by feigning an obsession with all things equine," he replied. "By all accounts, the Sultan keeps a remarkable collection. I'm going to wander down there on a daily basis."

"But how are you going to befriend them?"

"By taking apples from our bowl," my devious friend replied, nonchalantly pointing to the fruit bowl on the table in front of us. "Each horse will get an apple every time I visit.

They'll stop shying away from me eventually. In fact, I anticipate that they will be eager to approach me and gobble up my sweet offerings within a few days."

There was a crunch from behind me. I jumped.

Mango, of course. He stood there munching away at a crisp red apple. He'd got me! And I almost smiled at his little ambush. Sometimes, I wondered if he knew exactly what he was doing—perhaps not as clueless as he seemed.

"That should be enough to get to Sur," Dawkins observed. "Sur is a fishing port about two days' ride south of Muscat.

Once at Sur, we will need to find a most excellent dhow to spirit us away to Port Said."

This would require bribes and travel expenses beyond what we had in our possession. We somehow needed to acquire more gold coins. Our separate plans began to coalesce one by one. I set about fashioning the relevant keys with my template and tools. Pia did her part and Dawkins his.

We feasted well on our final night, and then the four of us snuck down into the garden. Stars glistened in a tranquil night sky, the giant moon sat poised and so close that every crater seemed as clear as the blue veins and arteries on Pia's majestic neck. It was almost as if we could pluck it from the sky and take a bite from it. (Not the neck, you understand.)

Getting past the first gates to the treasury was simple. After feasting on the Sultan's leftovers the guards had slackened off, falling fast asleep.

The largest peacock in the muster loomed large at the door to the treasury. He opened his beak, ready to squawk his first defensive squeal but Pia, just in the nick of time, tossed a scattering of her laced kernels his path and he retreated, satiated, into the shadows. Another greedy peacock appeared and then another, but within half an hour the birds were settled in a deep, drunken doze.

With our bird-brained alarms disarmed, we stole across the garden towards the mahogany door where it shone, pitch black, with its giant bolts protruding through the boards. The spikes on each bolt were ornately carved and superbly finished with gold leaf. I inserted the largest of the home-made keys into the first gold-coloured padlock. It opened quickly with a click and a slight squeak. I raised the latch. Such was the workmanship on the hinge, that it opened without so much as a squeak.

It was not until the second lock that we encountered a problem. Its key was too wide. But I had come prepared. I drew a file from my pocket and began filing away at the key. After a few unsuccessful efforts, the lock finally gave up its security and opened. We were now in the inner sanctum where we went to work in earnest.

Moonlight streamed through the iron bars, glinting off the spread of jewels in a dazzling display of opulence. Dawkins roamed around that room like some shopper browsing a haberdashery shop. He scrutinized every emerald, ruby and amethyst he plucked out of the piles, holding them up against templates he had drawn on a flap of silk, ripped from Pia's bloomers. He gently placed both the Russian emeralds into his small bag. Meanwhile, fool that I am, I loaded my pockets with gold coins.

Pia picked her way through the diamonds before loading an enormous sack with pearls, rubies and other fine gemstones. Dawkins gave a low whistle, indicating that we should wrap up. The weight of the gold in my coat pulled down hard on my shoulders and the bulging pockets clanked against my legs, making it awkward to walk. Pia did her best to put some of my gold into her sack. She even slipped some of it down the top of her lace blouse and into her girdle.

We exited the treasury, picking our way through the maze of collapsed peacocks, we walked calmly down the garden steps towards the stables. Dawkins popped into a bush on the way. He had stowed a haversack there earlier and filled it with wine-laced apples.

All was serene in the stables, where those elegant white horses sighed through their nostrils, scuffing their hay and toeing the ground impatiently. They ate our apples with gusto and, after about twenty minutes, their demeanour changed. Pia approached the Sultan's horse. She blew gently into his nostrils, making him putty in her hands, then saddled the four Arab stallions which Dawkins had identified as being the best amongst them. We mounted the steeds and trotted out of the stables.

Not a guard was to be seen. We rode on toward the bush where Mango lay in waiting. He pulled a bough aside revealing a tunnel which we rode through until we emerged by an unmanned gate.

Dawkins dismounted and handed me his mount's reigns. He walked stealthily towards the camouflaged gate and pushed the bar.

It grumbled and creaked open. The horses complied silently as we walked them through. Dawkins shut the gate behind us before scouring the ground for a boulder large enough to wedge the door shut.

"Psst," he whispered.

I dismounted, handed my reigns to Pia and helped Dawkins roll the stone into place, just as the first call for morning prayers rang out across the city.

"Allaaaaaaaaaaaaah Huw, Akba, Allaaaaaaaaaaaaah Huw Akbar, Allaaaaaaaaaaaaah Huw Akbar."

The sound started me and as I stumbled, coins from my pockets clinking deafeningly onto the marble.

A commotion bubbled up from the other side of the gate. Our flight had been uncovered. The blood-chilling yell of the Chief Executioner, Erasmus, howled across the gardens. I envisaged that monster of a man I had seen escorting the Sultan's son from his ill-fated hunting trip.

Our fate, should we fail to escape, would be in that sadistic lunatic's hands.

Terrified, we galloped off into the desert, with voices behind us shouting.

"Yallah. Yallah."

Alarm horns were going off. We could only imagine the chaos as the cavalry soldiers, half asleep and in a state of undress, tried to follow us on their inebriated horses. Laughing now, we sped into the southern desert mountains, making sure to keep to the coastal path en route to Sur. Mango led, riding like a lunatic, his reins were flailing all over the place.

Chapter 19

We rode hard those first three hours. Our horses began to flag and froth a little, so Dawkins decided it was time to rest. We watered them in a wadi near a village. The mountains around us were largely barren, but there were enough green shoots around the small pools left by recent rains for our animals to graze on. Looming boulders were scattered across the landscape. They must have been shifted by the lethal force of those rare and unheralded torrents which occurred in those parts. Some surfaces had eroded enough after hundreds of those events, that they were shiny smooth; others were still covered in sharp protrusions, suggesting that they had only recently been deposited. The wadi would have remained dry riverbed for the most part, but flash floods had left pools of stagnant water; good enough for horses though not for us.

Nosey locals recoiled on seeing us. Out of fear it seemed. With our scuffed dish-dashes and worn sandals, we looked like Arabs especially after having spent months under the scorching Afghan sun. After India, the shipwreck and our time at the palace, we carried an air of "local" about us, I guess. Coupled with our fine saddlery, ornate, embellished bridles and distinguished horses we may have passed as tax collectors or civil officers, never a good thing in the eyes of a poverty-stricken villager.

I kept to the back with my Keffiyah wrapped close around my face, as was traditional with the Arab headgear in dusty conditions. Had anyone looked up closely, my blue eyes would have been a sure giveaway, but Dawkins, Mango and Pia, what with their dark eyes and hair, were just the part.

Resting for too long was certain death so once our horses' thirst was sated, we set out once again, though at a slower pace this time, since we figured enough distance had been made between us and our pursuers. Dawkins, Pia and I took turns looking back, keeping a lookout for anyone on our trail.

We caught sight of the harbour of Sur at midday on our second day.

On our descent, we looked over our shoulders and spotted a plume of dust rising from behind the jebel we had just ridden down. The mounted cavalry was close on our heels.

Dawkins had a knack for knowing the ergonomics of a place and quickly established where the best dhow was moored. He approached a fine-looking vessel. Its small crew were lazing around on the dockside. Dawkins waved to the captain.

Despite his broken Arabic he managed to negotiate not only our passage to Suez but that of the horses as well. It was fortunate for us that the captain was already about to set sail for Zanzibar. He happily agreed to the extra money we offered. He was the type who regarded the last man who had remunerated him as his best friend (until the debt owed was paid, that is).

Pia and I nervously searched for signs of the cavalry entering the village. A hullabaloo was sure to herald their arrival.

The call to midday prayers started "Allaaaaaaaaaaaah Huw Akbar."

"Allaaaaaaaaaaaah Huw Akbar."

"Allaaaaaaaaaaaah Huw Akbar."

We jumped. Even after all this time, the cacophony still caught us off-guard, as it always arrived without preamble. The crew stopped what they were doing and prepared for prayer. They washed and dried their hands. An elected imam knelt, and the other crew members followed suit.

"Allah hu Akbar," the imam chanted.

The captain didn't seem to worry about the prayers. He simply kept going about his business, so we loaded the horses while the devout crew prayed on.

"Bis mu Allah…"

They prayed on the quayside for what seemed an eternity.

204

There was a noise further up the other end of the quay and a kerfuffle by the souk. A tall official pushed his way through a throng of market goers. A black horsetail streamed from his helmet like a long plume. My heart sank. It was none other than our nemesis, Erasmus, followed by thirty cavalrymen donning their white horsetails. They pushed and shoved their way through the crowded market.

"Allah hu Akbar."

A chicken cage was hurled into the air before crashing to the ground, releasing its captive hens who clucked into the chaos and ran erratic circles around the legs of passers-by. A vase of oil was flung across a table, ceramic pots and pottery vases smashed and tinkled down the marble, which was now covered in oil, adding havoc to an already unfolding disaster waiting to happen. Raging soldiers slipped over one another, abusing the nearest merchant as they fell.

"Bis mu Allah."

Furious gesticulation, crates flying, wilder beasts than mere chickens were now let loose from their pens. A bolt of cloth was flung to the right, another to the left and a third over his shoulder, as Erasmus swung wildly through the vortex of this catastrophe.

Our crew prayed on. "Allah hu Akbar."

Erasmus eventually made his way through to the other side of the protesting crowd. His golden armour glinted in the sunlight.

The ebony skin on his Nubian arms was glistening with sweat after the long hard ride, and his muscular chest bulged rippled. He must have been at least six foot seven—a formidable sight to behold.

The crew ceased their prayers, straightened up and started muttering amongst themselves.

Alas! The instant Erasmus spotted us, his teeth bared, and he picked up his pace, racing down the quay towards us.

He pressed one hand against his thigh to still the sword in his hilt and thus avoid tripping himself up. And still, the crew gabbled on, unperturbed by the impending danger, oblivious to our panic.

Erasmus was now running full pelt down the quayside with a clatter of soldiers on his heels, pointing and shouting. I glanced across to Dawkins as he loaded the last horse onto the dhow's deck. Rivulets of sweat were trickling down his face. It was all I could do not to push the crew aside and carry out their duties for them. Mango gibbered incoherently as he tugged on a rope. The executioner hurled to one side anyone standing in his way. Several of them landed in the harbour, others were thrown against the sandstone wall. Fresh pomegranates flew, crates of oranges tumbled, and bolts of silk unravelled at the hands of his wrath. Until Erasmus himself was flung against a neatly stacked pile of crates, which toppled left, right and centre, tumbling like die or toy blocks. This was no kids' game, however. I was so stricken with fear that I swear I was close to soiling myself.

To our enormous relief, the crew stopped their worshipping and stood. We were surely about to be saved. Not so.

Much to our despair they began shaking hands, congratulating one another on how well their prayers had sounded today and how strong their resolute faith. Meanwhile, Erasmus pelted down the pier, screaming in anguish.

The crew boarded just in the nick of time and managed to cast off the very moment Erasmus reached the edge of the quay.

They released the last line, and the dhow creaked away from the wharf as painstakingly slow as an old man's knees.

Erasmus sprinted towards the boat, letting out a mighty roar as he leapt into the air. Only a few feet more and we would have been free to sail away, but the dhow jolted to a halt, and everyone aboard lurched forward.

The useless crew had failed to cast off the final line correctly. I looked around in panic to see the Nubian mid-air, his scimitar gleaming in the sunlight. In a flash, Mango drew his sword and cut the rope in one slashing stroke just as Erasmus soared behind us, legs cycling in the air and, much to our relief, plummeted ignominiously into the harbour water behind with a splash.

His black mane flicked this way and that as he fought to stay afloat, but he was soon dragged beneath the surface in a gurgle of bubbles. The rest of the soldiers skidded behind him, using their outstretched arms to try and brake. Several of the luckier ones managed to teeter to a halt on the wharf's edge, whilst others failed to stop in time, launching those up front into the salty depths and almost certain death under the weight of their resplendent armour.

The dozy captain remained oblivious to all that had taken place behind him. He carried on as if an entirely commonplace departure had taken place and even took the soldiers' waving fists as a friendly farewell, waving back at them with a merry smile as the dhow slipped away and glided out across the harbour.

We stationed ourselves behind the crew who had conveniently spaced themselves out along the gunnels and, on Dawkins' signal, we heaved the unfortunate crew into the water. The Arab sailors hurled a barrage of abuse across the harbour at us as we left.

Now for the captain, who stood at the helm stunned and confused as we drew our daggers and headed his way. He twitched at his belt, only to discover that his scabbard was empty and the Kanjar he was groping for was now being brandished by Mango.

He took his chances and ran to the deck's edge before leaping overboard to join his crew who were treading water twenty yards back.

Dawkins took the tiller while Pia and I handled the jib at the bow.

We took turns manning the mainsail once it was set and reached down the coast of Oman at an incredible pace, confident that we'd call into the village of Salalah by the next evening, without risk of capture, since our stolen boat was faster by far than any messenger on horseback.

The majestic dhow sailed on through a tranquil Arabian sea. Dawkins steered and Pia remained on deck, tending to the horses with buckets of cooling water, whilst I went below deck to take stock. Much to my delight, the hold was overflowing with dates and pomegranates intended for the markets of Zanzibar. A slaughtered goat lay ready for cooking, and a crate of plump chickens started my belly rumbling.

We ate heartily that night. And afterwards, Dawkins took time to explain our position.

"First," he said, "during my time in the special division of Scotland Yard, aside from the Crown Jewels of Britain, I was also briefed on the Crown Jewels of other monarchies. But my mission was to find gemstones which can replace those sold, take them to our Antwerp experts for replication so the Crown Jewels can be replaced. I identified which stones from the Sultan's treasury could replicate the iconic stones that are missing, and I confirm that we most certainly have replacements for The Black Prince Ruby and Stuart Crystal, as well as Edward the Confessor Sapphire."

Dawkins pulled a handkerchief from his coat and unwrapped it, revealing two large sapphires and two red stones, one smaller than the other. "Now, bring out whatever you have left," he instructed.

We emptied our own pockets, blouses and sack onto the table to form a pile of diamonds, sapphires, rubies, emeralds and gold coins.

"I also noticed two emeralds in the Sultan's Treasury," Dawkins continued, "which I have seen before. They were from the Russian Crown Jewels, which means the Russians have melted their Crown Jewels down as well.

Russia is far more politically unstable than Britain so, if we have ample proof that they have done such a thing to the national treasure, then we can hold them to ransom. Their population will surely revolt if such news gets out."

He then revealed the very same emeralds of which he spoke.

"There is, however, a third emerald," he said, "hidden on an amulet. That amulet was a gift from Emperor Yunghan of China in 1810 and the third emerald, of which I speak, replaced a pearl in the original. A British spy smuggled it from Russia as a message to tell us the Crown Jewels had been broken up. Fortunately for us, Oliver, you are in possession of that."

"Me?" I asked, utterly bewildered.

"It is the masonic pendant."

Dawkins ignored my dumbfounded gape and continued, "Our problem is that we cannot trust either the governments or the monarchs; they change too frequently for relations to hold."

The midday sun bore down with unprecedented strength. Pia and Mango lay bolts of cool, water-soaked cloth over the horses' backs. We rounded the Cape of Aden by early afternoon, to head north into the Red Sea. Sunset sank over the horizon as we glissaded atop a sea of glass. Flying fish flew across the bow, and a pod of dolphins surfed behind them in the boat's wash. We made out several schools of tuna but no fishing for us. A green turtle bid us luck with the triple bob of his head—a good omen indeed.

We gathered speed as soon as the wind, which came in from the port and stern, billowed our sails.

I had never sailed so swiftly and, if the grins etched on their faces were anything to go by, nor had my colleagues.

The cerulean sky was clear, and the salt spray brought much relief after the stultifying heat.

The horses too seemed to appreciate the impromptu shower. They swished their groomed trails, shook their manes, whinnied and issued approving snorts.

We passed hundreds of dhows bearing north, south, east and west upon the Red Sea over the next couple of days but finally, we approached the village of Suez. We prepared the horses with meticulous care knowing they had a hot journey ahead. I focused on ration supplies whilst Pia and Mango loaded our belongings and the few weapons we had—machetes—upon the horses. Once we arrived at Suez, we tied up, unloaded the horses and abandoned the ship to set off up the rugged trail to Port Said in the north.

We travelled north with no incident, though we did pass several French surveyors seeking some way to connect the Mediterranean with the Indian Ocean. The concept, of course, was ludicrous and ambitious to the extreme. It also seemed to my mind, just one more reason for tribes on the left bank to war with those on the right, until the inevitable invasion by foreigners took place, an entirely new enemy was created, and the cycle started again.

As soon as we arrived in the bustling city of Port Said, Pia and Dawkins split up to find the best options in the port for a passage back to Europe. Mango and I tended the horses and Pia returned within one hour, with news about a former French battleship which had been converted into a steamship. It had the potential be a one-hundred-and-twenty-gun ship, but its current voyage was merely a trial, which meant that it had nothing more than a skeleton crew.

The magnificent ship was called the *Ville de Paris*. It was the ship which saved us by destroying the patrol boat before we entered Sebastopol's battle.

They had finished a refit in Marseille and were on a short test voyage before returning. The captain, Rennie Le Breton, was thrilled to offer us berths as they had so many vacant, and he yearned the company of gentlefolk.

We eagerly accepted his kind invitation and, in exchange for his generosity, we gifted him our magnificent horses. He showed his delight by extending every possible luxury to us, inviting us to dine with him and the officers, regaling us with the tales from the Crimea, updating us on the progress of the war. We in turn shared our own stories, although of course, we held back on the more murderous, mutinous details of our piracy, jewel theft and deceit. Consequently, there were holes in our accounts, but such factual paucity was made irrelevant for our trip was only short. What's more, the captain drank such copious amounts that much was lost in translation in any case.

We arrived in Marseille two days later. We thanked the captain profusely and promised a letter from her Majesty's government, which pleased him enormously. In return, he proceeded to open a magazine and present us with six pistols, designed by no other than Samuel Colt himself. He parted with the baby Dragoon Five shooters willingly (one could almost say joyously), plus several pistols and ammunition.

Chapter 20

Marseille is a rough port even by British standards. Walking those rickety, rain-swept streets in the company of a single woman and loaded up with so much treasure had us all feeling rather ill at ease. Pia, however, proved herself, yet again, as a competent fighter, fending off an uninvited embrace from some over-amorous drunk. The sailor was left with a bruised and battered undercarriage, an unsightly swollen lip and a bloodied split above his blackened eye. Soldier, sailor and docker alike stayed well clear of Pia from that point onwards, as if they sensed the inherent mettle behind her pluck.

We arrived at the newly built Gare de Marseille and bought three first class tickets to Paris. The train was to leave at nine a.m. Dawkins sent me to the port's main square with detailed instructions.

"Oliver," he said, "I need you to buy three identical carpet bags. This long," he demonstrated with his hands, "this wide and this deep."

Mango and I headed off towards the largest of the market squares. Dawkins and Pia went to buy wine and fresh eggs. I watched as they crossed the road, walked up an alley and came back, fifteen minutes later, with a bundle wrapped in paper and tied with string. They strolled past several shops before popping into the Bureau de Post and remerged a few minutes later. During this time, Mango had supplemented the food box with the supplies Captain Le-Breton had ordered for the ship's galley. A little later, we rendezvoused at the station café where we drank thick coffee until our train was due to depart.

Light rain had started, Dawkins, Pia, Mango and I walked down the wet platform, found our carriage and boarded the train at precisely five to nine. Rain splattered against the glass of the carriage windows which were smeared with filthy, smoky soot. We settled into our seats just as the station master blew his whistle, to which the train driver replied by pulling a rope leading to a valve and emitting a high-pitched "Poop! Poop!"

The train controller, an officious, pompous looking man, signalled the driver with his green flag and we rolled away. Staring past him to the top of the platform, I noticed a group of people arguing with the station staff.

Dawkins sat opposite me by the window. "Did you notice those three men by the pillar?" he asked.

"No," Pia and I replied in unison.

"I think I recognised one of them from the cave in Jammu," Dawkins added.

Pia stared out through the train window whilst Mango munched and crunched through the contents of his voluminous haversack. I stared back at Dawkins, hoping to elicit more information, but Dawkins nonchalantly carried on sorting through his kit pack until he found the peeled boiled egg he sought and gleefully popping the entire thing in his mouth.

At that, the train pulled out through a swirl of steam and smoke, and we were on our way.

The beautiful French countryside rushed by, and Pia busied herself with her carpet bag.

The three identical bags, lying side by side, looked peculiar and just a tad too conspicuous, in my opinion, so I pulled one out and shoved it beneath my seat. Dawkins did the same. I must confess that, after all the to-ing and fro-ing, I had no idea which of the three was mine.

We slowed as we entered the town of Avignon, where the train was filled up with water from the bowser and imported a load of coal. Passengers disembarked; passengers alighted. Our carriage door opened to the enormous silhouette of a bald man in his fifties. He must have weighed eighteen stone and was a rather peculiar sight in his black cardinal's three square-ridged biretta and a fluffy tuft on top.

213

The hat only added to his towering six-foot five height. His hood gathered around the back of his neck and a white cord was slung around his broad waist.

As he stepped forward into our carriage, his toeless sandals peeked out from under the hem of his full-length monk habit. The light shone on a cheerful, round face. A pair of circular spectacles rested forward on his corpulent red nose, the bifocal lenses of which made his already frog-like eyes bulge even larger beneath his magnificent pair of ginger brow-bushes.

His carpet bag was intricately woven with the Passion of Christ on one side, and the Nativity on the other. A wooden rosary with a four-inch wooden cross rested on his ample chest.

"Bonjour," he said, in flawless French as he raised his hat "Est-ce que cette place est occupée?" pointing to the vacant seat.

"Non, elle est disponible, monsieur," Pia replied.

"Thank you," he replied, in equally perfect English.

"How could you tell I was English?" Pia asked.

"Your accent, my dear. Enchanted to meet you. May I introduce myself. I am Father Vincenzo," he paused. "Vincenzo Spano," he added and reached one of his finely manicured hands out, then bowed before reaching across with his other, to take both Pia's hands in a firm, cup-like grasp, all the while, looking down over his rims, deep into her eyes, as if inspecting her very soul. "God's blessings on this journey," he grinned. His accent was a mixture of Flanders and Scottish.

His gaze was concentrated and intense as he took each one of our hands; first Dawkins, then me and finally Mango.

"I am what is commonly known as the Pope's Enforcer. The reason for my visit to Avignon today was to sack the bishop," he merrily informed us.

214

"Why so?" asked Pia.

"Let's just say he had some unusual methods when accounting"

Father Vincenzo Spano felt deeply blessed by his religious calling. Despite his parents having started out as humble folk, by a stroke of good fortune, his father became a Flanders mill owner. Although he sought little more than to live the simple life of a monk, he rose through the clerical hierarchy to become Abbott of the monastery in Bruges on Donkey Lane.

"Where Charles II hid in exile, before the Restoration," he added.

Dawkins' interest was visibly piqued upon hearing the Restoration mentioned. It was, after all, the Restoration which had led to the creation of the Crown Jewels and the pursuit of those jewels which had catapulted us into these adventures in the first place.

Our train struggled on its way up the escarpment of the Massif Central region. We had decelerated to walking pace and may have stopped altogether if it hadn't been for the mistral tailwind. Father Vincenzo's monologue eventually trailed off and after a short silence he reached into his bag, drew out a large, tattered Bible and opened it carefully to a place reserved by a red leather bookmark.

I looked back into the carriage, and my heart practically sank through the floor. Pia was nestled into the arms of Dawkins. They were both entirely oblivious to all. He stroked her black hair as he stared nonchalantly out the window and she lay against his chest, her eyes closed and her gentle smile wide.

Soon enough, the train slowed, and Father Vincenzo Spano closed the hefty Bible he had been reading, placing it in his lap just as the Lyon sign appeared. We ground to a squeaking creaking halt.

We were all of us, entirely off our guard when the carriage door was flung ajar and three men rushed in.

The man at the head of the trio levelled a pistol at Dawkins' head and gently squeezed the trigger.

The gunman's lock came down and there was a flash of gunpowder—but no retort.

The shooter looked visibly shaken that his pistol had failed with a fizzle. I was frozen to the spot. Pia and Dawkins recovered much quicker than I, however. They leapt to their feet as Father Vincent lifted the Bible from his lap and belted the pistol from the assailant's hand with it. The second man pushed past, only to be met by a punch to the right ear from Mango. The man turned and having finally come to my senses; I inserted two fingers up his nostrils from behind and jerked him backwards. Spotting the target of an open throat, Pia backhanded his Adam's apple with her closed fist, incapacitating the man at once, lurching him forward so he collapsed in a heap. Pia's expert punch had clearly collapsed the man's windpipe, he clutched at his throat and was left on the ground, gasping for air.

Pia and I turned to help Dawkins, still grappling with the shooter, whilst the third man took this opportunity to seize one of our carpet bags. Father Vincenzo tripped the man over.

Subsequently, the thief's planned graceful descent through the train door was transformed into an undignified plummet from the carriage onto the platform, where he lay sprawled out, bag and all, facedown at the feet of the station master.

He stood, raised his hat to the station master and proceeded to run towards the exit. I wish I could portrait that station master's expression when, yet another man—this one, blue in the face— flew past him in the air, clutching at his throat, after having been skilfully propelled by a sandaled kick au derrière from Father Vincenzo.

I can only imagine the already bemused station master's shock as the original shooter was ejected by yet another of Father Vincenzo's dexterous manoeuvres.

He grabbed the assailant's buttocks and propelling the fool, face-first and with a sickening thud, into a water-tower, where he slid into an unconscious bundle on the sooty ground.

"Tout le monde à bord pour Paris," the station master cried.

The whistle blew and the train started to slowly set off for Paris.

We stared at the space which had previously been occupied by the now missing carpet bag. I knew what everyone was thinking. Who's was the bag that was stolen?

After a rather uncomfortable silence, Father Vincent leaned in and whispered, "Well, they were clearly no ordinary thieves. I believe you were being targeted." To my surprise, he added, "They were Russians."

"How do you know that?" I asked.

"During the struggle, dear man, they were cursing in Russian. If you are headed for Paris then I suspect you are in for more trouble. The city is filled with Russians at the moment, as they are preparing to sign the treaty which will end the Crimean war. You should avoid Paris at all costs, would be my advice." He thumped his Bible for emphasis before completely changing his tone. "What is your ultimate destination?" he asked.

The blood must have still been racing through my body—before I could stop myself, I blurted out, "Antwerp".

Pia and Dawkins shot me a pair of piercing glances, and I shrugged.

"Antwerp," Father Vincenzo repeated, nodding slowly, as he pieced together our undercover plan.

Despite the four of us being alone in our compartment, Father Vincenzo looked over his shoulder to check no one was listening before leaning in to whisper, "It's none of my business but as you are heading for Antwerp, it can only mean one thing: diamonds."

"If I'm right then don't go on a Friday expecting to get work done on the Saturday. That's the Jewish Sabbath. Every dealer, cutter and assayer will be forbidden to help you in any way until Sunday."

"Of course!" I said. Why hadn't we thought of this?

"So, what do you suggest?" Dawkins asked, tapping his chin and tilting his head with an almost panicked desperation. The misfired weapon had clearly rattled him to the core.

"Come back to the monastery with me. Not only do we have warm beds, but we have our very own brewery. Furthermore, whatever it is you might be carrying will be safe behind our walls. You will be safe in my Carmelite utopia." He grinned that cheeky grin of his and nodded as if the decision had been unanimously agreed upon.

"If you don't mind," Dawkins said, "may we have a moment to discuss your offer in private, please?" He pointed to the small space to Father Vincenzo's right, and Father Vincenzo shuffled six inches sideways to occupy it.

Once settled, he began chanting. "Risi Dominus Frustra," he sang, before removing his rosary from his robe pocket, running five large beads through his fingers and reciting a prayer. "Our Father…Hail Mary…I believe in God. Eternal Father, I offer You the Body and the Blood, Soul, and Divinity of Your dearly beloved Son, Our Lord Jesus Christ, in atonement for our sins and those of the entire world…"

"Risi Dominus Frustra," Mango echoed. "Our Father…Hail Mary…I believe in God…" The longer Mango mimicked; the redder Father Vincenzo turned with rage. He looked across at Mango, inspecting him for a moment. I was terribly embarrassed, but relieved when I realised that he seemed to reach the conclusion that Mango was simply not all there. Father Vincenzo took hold of the ten smaller beads and continued reciting.

"For the sake of His Sorrowful Passion…" As he continued praying.

We discussed the pros and cons of visiting the monastery. It took no time. We were all of one accord, there was no better alternative than to accept his offer.

None of us knew which bag was missing, of course. Although we each of us had something to lose, in my heart of hearts I hoped that Dawkins' bag was there. He had the most crucial jewels to cut.

There was nothing we could do; we would not have the chance to check the bags until Father Vincenzo was out of the way, and we were alone.

I asked Dawkins to send London word by telegram, requesting a meeting with Antwerp's contact (the Crown Jeweller).

"I'll do it tomorrow," he replied.

Father Vincenzo sat bolt upright. "While our Lord Jesus was on the cross," he declared, as if addressing a congregation.

"Two robbers were being crucified at the same time. As all three poor men's heads drooped and life ebbed from their bodies, two ravens flew down and perched upon the robbers' heads.

"One of the ravens lifted the first robber's head and cawed, 'Repent!' The robber confessed and asked for God's forgiveness. Once the first robber confessed, he passed away, and his soul left his body.

"His soul travelled up to heaven and the gates flew open to angels singing and archangels playing trumpets. There, at the entrance, our Lord Jesus Christ welcomed him.

"The other raven lifted the second robber's head and said, 'Repent!'

"But the second robber said, 'I'll do it tomorrow.'

"The raven cawed, 'Christ!' and flew off. Of course, the second robber was not allowed to enter heaven.

"That is where the expression 'to procrastinate' comes from."

"What happened to the other robber?" Mango asked, much to my annoyance.

"He was sent to hell, a fiery lake of burning sulphur where demons tormented him day and night and his worst fears were realised long into eternity."

Father Vincenzo's tone was flat and plain-spoken, as if he'd been asked for a recipe for a cake.

Dawkins agreed to send the telegram from the city walls of Paris. On approach to the city, the train slowed considerably, and we dropped ourselves from the carriage, one after the other, until we each sat in an extensive line, dishevelled and dusty, on the levee bank of the track.

We made our way to the main square of Bercy. It wasn't long before Dawkins pointed out an inn with one of those unmistakable archways indicating the presence of stables, horses and carriages. We entered the courtyard, where a set of six bays stood ready to be harnessed to the next incoming carriage. Father Vincenzo entered the inn to organise a carriage to Bruges.

The inn booth was small, but we managed to tuck ourselves away in a corner. The garçon came over and greeted Father Vincenzo like an old friend. Thanks to Father Vincenzo's discrete company, no more questions were asked. He seemed particularly proud to show off his extraordinary linguistic gift and ordered us each a hearty serving of pot-au-feu in perfect French dialect. Once the meal arrived, Father Vincenzo passed blessing over the food, and we followed with Grace. Much to our surprise, a still-steaming loaf magically appeared in Father Vincenzo's hand and as he held it up above the table, I found its aroma so fresh and comforting that it made my mouth water. Mango looked wide-eyed at the loaf and reached out with his licentious paws. He was just about to rip a chunk from it when Father Vincenzo began chanting yet another (but shorter, thank heavens) melodic prayer in Latin.

Pot-eu-fer was delicious—oxtail, leek, carrot and potato, in an aromatic broth which had no doubt been slow-cooked over several days.

"You won't find a jug of blonde in any other part of the world. It was brewed in this very region." Said the tipsy cleric

The beer was so strong that you could almost taste the earth in the hops. So too, the Camembert and Brie which was served after the meal on our naval biscuits. To clear our palettes, we finished with forest apples and freshly picked berries.

The innkeeper was a jolly chap and seemed well acquainted with Father Vincenzo; perhaps he'd sacked many bishops in the area. The innkeeper clearly enjoyed our more sophisticated company after the navvies who frequented the province since the new railway was built.

It was on our second pitcher of beer that the innkeeper announced, "Votre voiture est prête, messieurs et mademoiselle, et quelques couvertures à ma charge."

"Bon, d'accord. Je vous remercie, monsieur," the cleric said.

"What did he say?" I asked.

"He told us our carriage is ready and that he has added blankets free of charge."

"Please, thank him on our behalf," said Pia.

"I just did. Come on, let's gather our things." It was then that I remembered, we still didn't know which bag was missing.

We climbed into the covered landau, and the footman closed the door after us. I sat beside Father Vincenzo with Pia opposite me. Dawkins seated himself last. He was the only one without a bag.

I was alarmed when I noticed that the footman was armed, but as Father Vincenzo didn't seem perturbed by it, and had travelled this way many times, I did my best to put it out of my mind.

A whip cracked and the carriage lurched forward. We left the inn, and Paris behind us. The coach was warm and had been stocked up with tasty food and ale. We rocked metronomically through the countryside and soon fell asleep, only to be woken a few hours later, as we entered the grounds of Cathedral Saint-Gervais-et-Saint-Protais de Soissons.

The Dean emerged to greet our carriage. He seemed visibly shaken when he saw such a high-ranking cleric at his parish so late at night.

He kissed Father Vincenzo's ring and after a brief conversation, the two hugged. The Dean then called out to two lesser clerics who shuffled from the cloisters to greet us before showing us to our comfortable but humble quarters.

As soon as I was alone in my room, I looked in my bag where, much to my relief, I found my coat, sleeve and diamonds intact.

At four a.m. I was awoken by the ringing of bells and a harmonic choir singing psalms. The scent of incense wafted through the windows and under the doors. A jug of icy water stood in the centre of a pottery bowl in the corner of my room.

Once refreshed, I entered the corridor and knocked on Pia's door. Much to my dismay, Dawkins was the one to open it. Pia was sitting on the edge of the bed and looking very glum indeed.

After a moment, she broke the silence with dismal news. "Dawkins' bag is the one that was stolen."

I must have turned pale as Dawkins passed me a mug of water at once. Fortunately, there was a chair at hand, and I promptly sat down, my body almost numb with shock. "What are we going to do now?" I asked.

"Carry on to Bruges and then Antwerp," Dawkins replied.

"Why would we do that? What point is there?"

"Because that missing bag contained nothing more than my dirty washing." He beamed, a cheeky glint in his eye. "The gems were packed off in the egg crates and sent by post to Antwerp in Marseille. They will be waiting in Antwerp for us when we arrive. Besides, Father Vincenzo is starting to intrigue me. Come on, let's get some breakfast."

"You devil you!" Pia laughed. "You could have told us earlier, Jack," she added, walking to the dining room with a renewed spring in her step.

Now that the Crimean war was nearly over, the mood in Britain was considerably lighter which meant that we were able to take our time travelling to Antwerp. Over the following days, we made approximately thirty miles a day, resting at night in the various monasteries, convents and cathedrals en route. The seventh century architecture of Saint Vaast Abbey in Arras was fascinating, as was the Basilique-Cathédrale Notre-Dame-de-la-Treille in Lille with its stained-glass windows which, when the sun shone through, flooded the nave with subtle hues. It was so much more elaborate than any cathedral I'd ever seen in England.

Father Vincenzo proved to be not simply an inspiring travelling companion but the most informative and entertaining host. He showed us many extraordinary things along the way, and being a very educated and connected man, he spoke French, Flemish, Latin and English fluently. I imagine that Dutch, German and Greek were his forte too. As his guests, we were greeted in every religious establishment with the same graceful and courteous welcome.

Chapter 21

It was Monday, March 3rd, 1856. After scoffing a hearty porridge, we bid adieu to our generous guest and boarded the train to Antwerp. We placed our two valet bags in the luggage rack above our heads and settled into our three-hour journey. We travelled first class and, thankfully, this short trip was uneventful, with no excitement and no danger.

It was a warm spring day in Bruges. Apple and cherry blossoms lined the route out of the city. Monks would eventually ferment the fruit from those trees to brew their world-renowned liqueur, which they used as currency to pay for the generous hospitality offered so widely to the amiable Father Vincenzo Spano.

We arrived at Antwerp Central Station at around lunchtime, to be met on the platform by Mr Royston Strickland. Mr Strickland was the eminent British Crown Jeweller, whose task it had been to break up and sell the Crown Jewels in the first place. He expressed his relief at having received Dawkins' telegram and told us he would, with immense pleasure, reconstitute the Crown Jewels with gems supplied by some of the best gem cutters in the world.

"Good afternoon, gentlemen hand lady," he said, doffing his top hat ever so slightly. He appeared uncomfortable in the presence of our lady for some reason, he seemed to avoid eye-contact with her, which made his manner come across as haughty. "This way hif you please." He scurried down the platform in an effort to keep apace of Dawkins' enormous strides. "I trust, sir, that your mission was been a complete success. Absolute discretion is the watchword," he warned us.

Mr Strickland was a thin, nervous, little man. His fingers were unusually bony, and he had an almost weasel-like demeanour. He talked through his nose and had the peculiar and unfortunate habit of adding an "h" to words where no "h" should have been.

Dawkins nodded. "Is it far?" he asked, in a hushed tone.

Strickland pointed with his cane, "Noh, noh, just h'across the road."

I followed behind the two men, and realised for the first time, how tall Dawkins really was—at least six foot two inches in his stockinged feet, by my estimation. He had grown a fine pair of mutton-chop sideburns since our escape from Oman. Prince Albert himself would have been proud of such a set.

Whilst in Bruges, we had shopped for attire more suited to the circles of refined European society. I wore a long, white carriage coat, a crisp white shirt, black waistcoat, a brown Derby, felt bowler hat and had tied a blue, paisley kerchief about my neck. Dawkins wore a morning suit, including a tall stovepipe top hat. His wingtip collars kept his flamboyant, red bowtie from drooping like a sad clown's mouth.

He and Mr Strickland, were dressed almost identically which would have, undoubtedly, upset Dawkins to the extreme.

Pia evidently got quite a kick out of dressing up in fussy flounces, playing the role of the fine young lady. She was a vision to behold, in her mauve high-collared tea dress, dramatically pulled in at the waist. Her extravagant bustle swung like a pendulum as she walked. It was only when she had to rearrange herself, from time to time, beneath the whalebone corset (which must have strangled and pinched most dreadfully) that her mask dropped. That gleaming pitch-black hair which I so loved was hidden away under her neat bonnet, but I was no less hypnotised than usual. Her buckled shoes popped out from beneath at least eight petticoats. I am certain she knew the impact she had made as she smiled coyly, those scintillating eyes accentuated by a modest application of makeup.

The station was crowded, but we kept our wits about us as we negotiated our way through the throng. Beneath our calm exterior, we were all anxious. This was possibly the most vulnerable part of our mission. Our pistols were primed and the bags we carried were strategically positioned well enough to deter any would-be assailant.

We crossed the busy road and followed Strickland into a small shop, lined with trays of exquisite rings and bracelets. He led us to a formidable-looking wooden door with steel bands crisscrossing like some fortress gate. He hit the cast iron knocker three times, the clank of which echoed around the room. Within seconds, a viewing panel slid open and a pair of chestnut brown eyes, illuminated by a single tallow flame, stared out through the slit to scan our ensemble. Several bolts were slid across, grinding in their sockets, and the shop owner behind us rushed to his front door to lock it. He turned to face us, with one motionless hand poised in his breast pocket. He was clearly armed.

The keeper behind the door looked us up and down as if ticking us off some imagined checklist. Once satisfied, he beckoned us to follow him through and up some narrow stairs. At the top of the stairs, an older man introduced himself as Isaac Horowitz. He was reputed to be the foremost diamantaire of his day, the Michelangelo of diamond and gem cutting. Behind him, a brightly lit studio was filled with eleven apprentices all of whom, we would come to learn, were related to him.

"Welcome, welcome, come into my office, lady and gentlemen." He greeted us warmly before addressing Pia directly. "Me Lady, some wine?"

Pia demurred and he raised his brow as if in hope, before shouting something in Yiddish to one of his apprentices.

Isaac wore a long overcoat and had a straggly beard. His thick-rimmed spectacles were perched, triumphantly, upon his strong, aquiline nose. He was typically dressed for an Orthodox Jewish gentleman.

We were directed to hang our coats in the corner of the room, where a tall black hat had already been slung.

"I have been fully briefed on the job at hand," Isaac said. "Please, this way." He gestured towards a custom-made, teak table. A narrow wooden ledge, standing an inch high, ran around the perimeter to prevent gems from dropping off the sides.

An internal gutter led to a hole in one corner through which stones could be funnelled into the cloth pocket which dangled underneath. A badger hairbrush (usually used for shaving) was attached to a fob chain and used to sweep the gutters. Even the brush had its own cup to rest in, ensuring not even the smallest stone would be lost. "Show me what you have," he said, laying a large velvet cloth down.

Dawkins walked to the table and reached into his bag. He produced one brown, paper envelope sealed with gum Arabic, then another and then another. Isaac opened each package eagerly but with great care and poured the contents onto an ever-increasing pile. The mound of carmine, iridescent, violet and azure gems piled high on royal blue velvet was stupefying. It was the first time we had seen all the treasure in one place.

Mr Strickland unveiled a piece of vellum and began reading from the list. "Now," he said, as if announcing members in a royal cortège, "we require two thousand 'Eight hundred and sixty- 'eight diamonds, two hundred and seventy-three pearls, seventeen sapphires, eleven emeralds and five rubies."

The diamantaire began counting out the various gems and distributing them onto their respective piles. He was calm and measured. We turned our attention to the most important stones.

"The first 'is the Stuart Crystal," Strickland announced imperiously (his haughtiness had started to get on my nerves). "This gemstone is one hundred and four carats, oval-shaped, one and a half inches long and one inch wide. It carries one or two blemishes. It is a sapphire of cobalt blue with a hole drilled through one end so it can be worn as a pendant."

Isaac searched through the pile and plucked out a blue stone about the size of a man's thumb knuckle. He wrote what I assumed read Stuart Crystal in Yiddish upon a label and dropped it into a cup. Mr Strickland handed Isaac a small piece of vellum with a diagram depicting the exact dimensions and shape required, which he also placed into the cup.

Mr Strickland continued, "'H' Edward Confessor Sapphire is a 'h' octagonal-shaped, green, rose-cut sapphire of thirty-two carats." Isaac carried out the same ritual for this one, before placing the cup on a wooden tray beside the first, followed by Strickland's technical information on a vellum. The procedure continued all afternoon, whilst we sipped tea and nibbled cinnamon biscuits. Our pile of gems had soon been reduced, and the cups' contents had grown.

"Black Prince Ruby," Mr Strickland called out, "polished, 'oval-shaped, red ruby with one hole drilled from front to back, wide enough for a leather strap, to be carried around the neck in battle by the favourite son of Henry III, Edward the Black Prince. Irregular cabochon of extraordinary clarity, weighing one hundred and seventy carats."

Isaac searched amidst the glistening mound. He looked perplexed, lifted his chin for a moment almost gasping for air then scrambled back through the pile in front of him, he announced, "Not here."

"What?" Dawkins bristled, "There is a ruby right there, at least one hundred and seventy carats. Right there. See it?" he asked, indignantly, his eyes flashing with rage. I don't think I'd ever seen Dawkins more animated.

"No, that's not the one. It is currently the correct size, but it is not clear enough; by the time we have removed such ghosting, it will be too small." Crestfallen, Dawkins slumped back into his chair.

"Just a moment," Isaac said. He walked into the neighbouring room and beckoned the closest apprentice who was at work on an emerald. The young man jumped up from his workplace to join Isaac, and the two of them muttered in Yiddish.

Pia whispered, "He's got something." I had forgotten she was part Jewish. "He's asking for a spinel," she whispered, a semi-precious stone was often mistaken for a ruby.

The young apprentice nodded and set to accomplish Isaac's bidding. Isaac handed him some keys, and the young man scurried away, into an anteroom, where I spied a grand safe, built into the wall. The apprentice soon returned with a new stone and handed it to Isaac without a word, before returning to his scaif to carry on with his work.

There were several other apprentices working at their scaives in the outer office. The scaif at which the apprentice sat consisted of a flat disk, much like a potter's wheel. A film of olive oil, mixed with diamond dust, covered the top surface. A circular frame surrounding the disk caught the oil as it spun off. Hovering just above the disk's surface, a mechanical arm with clamp-like fingers clasped the diamond. It was so finely adjustable that it could move the diamond into the exact position required for polishing each and every facet.

Aside from the pearls—more specifically, four teardrop pearls—we had completed the list by the end of the day, and only a small mound of gems was left on the velvet, including diamonds, sapphires, rubies and emeralds.

"We are short of pearls," I said, at which Pia reluctantly pulled out a drawstring purse from her cleavage. She untied the bag and emptied the contents onto the table. It was virtually her entire retirement fund.

Isaac looked at the pile of pearls, then to Strickland. "She sure has some chutzpah!" he said. "I'm afraid we will need them all, my dear."

Pia shrugged, walked over to another corner of the room, sat down and folded her arms in a sulk. Dawkins followed her and handed her the purse with the remaining, unspoken-for gems.

"Here you go, Pia. You deserve this," he said.

She nodded and sighed with relief before taking his hand in hers and whispering a thank you. Perhaps Jack had a heart after all.

"My entire workshop will now be at your disposal, Mr Strickland," Isaac declared. "I estimate that we could be ready within a few days.

You can pop in and see how we are progressing whenever you like. By the way, given the nature of this extremely sensitive task, we need to discuss the delicate matter of payment."

"Yes, of course, Mr Horowitz," Strickland replied. "Mr Dawkins, the British people thank you and your team for your extraordinary work. Please to retire to the 'hotel named upon this card, hand I will join you in an hour to discuss our future course of action."

We were ushered out of the office without much ado, descended the stairs and were unceremoniously shown, by the guard, through the armoured door. We stepped out onto the dark, wet streets of Antwerp and headed to the Hotel Leopold which was located right by the train station.

We made a daily pilgrimage to the workshop to assess our project's progress, after which we took in the sights of this beautiful city. Pia's favourite was the zoo, especially the brand-new Egyptian house which homed a number of exotic and rare okapi. The following week, we returned to the hotel to find a telegram message in Dawkins' pigeonhole:

DAWKINS I AM REQUIRED TO RETURN TO LONDON STOP. YOU ARE TO COLLECT OUR PROJECT AS SOON AS IT IS COMPLETE AND FOLLOW ME TO LONDON STOP. REPORT TO THIS ADDRESS AND ASK FOR MR THOMAS GIPSON STOP.

The Grapes Ale House

Aldgate

London

TRUST NO ONE STOP

Dawkins committed the address to memory and tore the paper up, placing the pieces in his pocket to be burned later.

On Wednesday, we arrived at Horowitz's workshop and led upstairs, all the stones, finished and labelled with their titles, had been laid out. Isaac was in the process of inspecting one of the green gemstones through an eyeglass, he scrunched up one side of his face to hold the ocular jeweller's device in place.

"Beautiful!" he said. "Such beauty. I never tire of it." He placed the jewel down, turned to his apprentice and congratulated him on his fine workmanship. "Aaron? This is your masterpiece,"

The apprentice beamed, bowed and ran into the workshop, where the other apprentices gathered around him, patting him on the back and shaking his hands. Despite still being in his twenties, Aaron had clearly waited many years for this day.

"We must pack these up safely," Isaac said. "Let us begin."

We spent the next three hours wrapping and labelling, then placed the valuable cargo in my valet bag. With our priceless collection safely packed up, we made our farewells and shook our trusted friend's hand. Several heavily armed apprentices followed us as we left the workshop. We returned to the hotel and threw our luggage together. I didn't take my eyes off that carpet bag—or if I did, then it was not for any longer than a few seconds.

There was a light tap at the door. "It's me," Dawkins whispered through the closed door. "Are you ready?"

"Only my shaving stuff from the bathroom left," I replied. "Hold on."

Dawkins tried the door, but I had locked it. I went into the bathroom to collect my shaving brush and razor. I savoured the lavender scent of the hotel soap. Antwerp's water was softer than London's and my skin was notably changed since bathing in it; like that of a child.

When I emerged from the bathroom, the curtains were blowing into the room, there was a draught from the window which I hadn't noticed before. Strange, I thought. I had closed it.

I pushed down the handle and opened the door, dreading what I expected to find—an empty room no doubt, and confirmation that I had been duped.

A wave of shock swept through my body—I froze on the spot—the bag was gone.

Claggage! I thought. Claggage had tricked me. After all these years, all these trials and tribulations we'd endured together. In my panicked paranoia, my mind raced to various moments I had found peculiar whilst waiting for the jewels to be prepared. It was then that I recalled how Mango had slipped away that night. Where was he now? "Claggage!"

"Yes, Master." He was behind the door and there was the bag.

"Give me that," I scolded and grabbed it from him. "You really are too much."

That night after supper I sent Mango back to the room while I discussed his future with Pia and Dawkins

"I have to send him back to the house when we return to London. He is nothing but trouble."

Dawkins lifted his chin and looked at me with a very grave expression, indeed. "Oliver," he said, "May I ask you a question?"." He didn't smile. "This has been annoying me for some time. I'd like to know why you're always so darned horrible to Mango?"

The leather squeaked beneath my legs as I shifted in my seat, "How so?" I asked.

"I have never seen a master treat their valet in such a despicable way," Pia added.

"It's none of your business, in fact." I turned my face away from them both and feigned to examine the wall display.

"It bloody well is our business!" Pia blurted out. "He saved all our lives, on at least three occasions, and you treat him like a dog."

I shook my head, "I don't want to talk about it."

"You should. It might be good for your soul," said Dawkins.

"Betrayal," I whispered.

"What betrayal?" Pia patted my arm sympathetically.

"When we were in school. He betrayed me back in our school days."

"What do you mean? How?" Pia pushed me a little further.

I sighed. It seemed there was no going back now. "When I first came to Winchester College as an eleven-year-old, there was a bully in the prefects' dormitory by the name of The Honourable Mr Alex Welch. He was terrifying. His father was a Lord and former pupil of the school, a benefactor who donated both generously and consistently every Speech Day, which was why the Trustees tolerated Welch's brutal behaviour.

"Mango and I shared a room. We were firm friends. In fact, we shared everything, including our hobbies, recreation time, Latin, Greek and algebra homework—you name it. We never left one another's sides."

Pia leant forward, curious to know more. "So, what changed?"

"Like all the prefects, Welch had a fag."

"A fag?" Dawkins asked.

"It's a first-year student who cleans the senior's room, washes his clothes and, well, is basically like a slave. Everyone knows they're going to end up being someone's fag in their first year, it was like a rite of passage.

Most of the prefects were reasonably civilised with their wards, but not Welch. He had an extensive list of casualties, prior victims of his sadistic punishments.

Not only did he humiliate us by writing things on our foreheads and beating us but, to make matters worse, he made us do his schoolwork too!"

"So, what happened?" Pia asked.

"Mango and I were conjugating Latin verbs one night, when Welch came bellowing and stomping down the echoey corridor. He was on the hunt for a replacement fag, and since his reputation preceded him, I jumped up and hid under my bed. Mango, however, was too slow, and Welch caught him quivering, in a state of inert panic.

"He yelled out some order or other, but Mango was frozen to the spot. Welch concluded that Mango was not his guy and would never handle being his fag.

"Where is the Twist boy?" Welch asked.

I watched, in horror, as Mango stood stunned and helpless. Before I knew it, some other boy was bursting into the room and though I couldn't make out who it was from where I was hiding, someone in that room gave me away. I'm certain it was Mango, coward that he is—wimp that he's always been. A second later, Welch's sardonic face appeared beneath the bed spars. He reached in to haul me out by my arm.

"Look at the little tiddler I've caught," Welch bellowed, holding me up by the scruff of my collar in a triumphant show of prowess. Strange man—we were the only two left in the room, he was showing his prize off to some imaginary audience!

Pia said, "At least you knew it would be over after couple of terms."

I shook my head. "If only that had been the case. Welch was both a drunk and an idiot. He failed his Finishing Exams at every sitting. The school benefited too much from Lord Welch's donations to let the boy go.

Aside from which, I am certain that he was more than happy to keep his son off the family estate for as long as he could. So, Welch stayed on at school for three extra years, until he finally graduated at the age of twenty-one. Even the college could not countenance another year's extension.

"I was subjected to daily beatings, abuse, humiliation and floggings for three and a half years. That's three years of hell, thanks to Mango.

"In the autumn of that first year, whilst I was preparing Welch's horse for the Winchester Hunt, the horse bucked, just as Mango was passing to prepare another prefect's horse and ended up kicking Mango in the head. Mango was sent to the infirmary, where he stayed for months. His family disowned him, and he was forced to leave the college, as he was deemed utterly unteachable. The headmaster informed Mr Brownlow that I was the one at fault, since I had been in charge of the horse, and the gentleman took Mango in. Mango has been a constant reminder, ever since, of all the hell I went through in those years."

"But wasn't Vladimir at the same college?" Dawkins asked. "Didn't he have to fag for someone?"

"He did but his year was easy. A fellow named Digby Lickfold was Head Boy at the time, and he took a special shine to Vladimir, who wasn't a naturally deft sportsman or huntsman, you see. Lickfold was the one who taught Vladimir to fence and ride. He even taught him to shoot which, given I was almost the victim of his skilfully trained eye, has turned out to be quite ironic."

Pia took both my hands in hers and said, "Look at me, Oliver. Do you know what forgiveness is? Forgiveness is when the terrible thing someone did to you no longer angers you. You've come such a long way, Oliver. Can't you make that last step, and forgive Mango?"

We sat in silence for what seemed an eternity. I felt Dawkins' and Pia's empathetic eyes upon me as I stared at the carpet.

Chapter 22

I dug deep for some form of humility. Perhaps they were right. Hadn't Mango done his time? Something within me shifted. After a good night's rest, I joined the other in the lobby. Dawkins was posing as a priest with Pia, by his side, dressed as a nun. and Mango bounced on the bed behind them, giggling like an annoying child grinning from ear to ear. He handed me a cassock and surplus.

"I was inspired by Father Vincenzo Spano," Dawkins said. "No one questioned him, despite that fact that he obviously wasn't from the clergy."

I was stunned. "Not from the clergy? What on earth do you mean?" I gasped.

Dawkins laughed. "He enjoyed mooching around whilst dressed up as various ranks in the priesthood. It enabled him to access all manner of hospitality and charity, as you, yourself, saw. The British secret service has long been aware of someone travelling around Europe impersonating a priest. I recognised him at once. He fought with Blucher at Waterloo. He's even repatriated bodies from the battlefield. I'd say he saw some terrible things there, which might explain why he's so dotty, but he means no harm."

"What gave him away?" I asked.

"Monks don't wear Cardinal's caps!" Dawkins replied.

We gathered in the foyer dressed as travelling clergy and, I must admit, Pia made a rather ravishing and somewhat seductive nun. We settled our account and left the hotel for the last time. The hotel staff themselves were familiar with couriers employing all manner of disguise, so they barely gave us a second look.

Our Jewish friends had secured us a berth on a barge travelling to the Port of London. Our cover story was that we were returning from a pilgrimage to Lourdes. The journey on the barge was uneventful.

We arrived in the Thames estuary and sailed up the river just as the incoming tide was about to turn. I recognized the familiar smell of sewage. We passed the wharves and the Royal Docks of Tilbury, Limehouse Docks, Canary and Canada Wharfs. We saw the Prospect of Whitby public house in Wapping on our port-side, where chained convicts, fresh from their trials at Clerkenwell Courts, shuffled down gangplanks to their transport ships, urged on by soldiers' rifle butts.

Dawkins said, "That would have been my fate had Sergeant Bibskin not intervened. He took me and saved me. Most of those poor, miserable souls will probably never see Australia. They were more likely to perish of scurvy, typhus or cholera in the fetid hulls."

We slid past St Katherine's Dock and Butler's Wharf, up into the safety of the Pool of London where we moored beside another barge.

All manner of ship lined the wharves; tall ships, carrying wood from Canada, tea clippers from India, screw steamers moving Madeira wine in huge oak casks, hay barges from down river, loaded with horse fodder freshly cut from Essex's lush meadows.

A bunch of beached seals lay on their backs alongside a jetty which jutted out up ahead. From time to time, one would waft its fin through the air and bark, as if giving orders to the workers at the newly built Billingsgate Fish Market. Box-men, anxious to finish their work, dumped the last of their unsold catch across the dock for the greedy seals who lumbered across to profit from the bounty.

A four-master ship named Anastasia was docked to our port-side. She seemed to be transporting trunks, armoured in banded steel, containing gold and silver from Ethiopia. We watched the vast trunks being hoisted by man-operated derricks using hawser-laid ropes. The rope meandered to and fro through block and tackle, aiding the dockers' work one-hundred-fold. The chests were hoisted and swung across to Tower Wharf with ease, where sturdy porters under armed guard transported them unsteadily upon their barrows through the Sally Port.

Several ships lay along the wharf, where dockers shouted instructions to their banksmen who shifted their valuable cargo using a multitude of manual cranes. The Curfew Bell tolled from the Bell Tower of the Tower of London, calling the garrison's soldiers back to camp. A drummer played Tap To. The gates would soon be locked. The Gentleman Porter in the Langthorn Tower was responsible for waving the lantern which reminded captains aboard incoming ships of their responsibility to pay charges to the Constable of the Tower of London before they could enter under the protection of the Tower guns. The captains never failed to pay the necessary dues; paying a crew to man their canons would have been far costlier for them, and the safety of their boats and its cargo was guaranteed under the Tower's watch. They ordered their bosuns to muster men to take a small percentage of their cargo to the Tower gates, along with a note thanking the Constable for his kind charity.

We expressed our gratitude by paying our own captain handsomely and left the barge. There on the quayside was Strickland. He beckoned us to join him, and we walked slowly as he talked.

"Your task has become very much more complicated," he said. "Since we last met, London has been enveloped in a foul temper. Riots spring up at a drop of a hat. Russian agents are sowing the seeds of disquiet. No doubt spurred on by your constant successes over them abroad. As a result, the garrison is on high alert, and everyone is searched going into the Tower. That is why I cannot take the jewels off your hands now. For my reputation, such as it is would be in torn to shreds and I may even face the gallows as a scapegoat."

"What should we do?" I asked

"There is no other course. You will have to break in and deposit the gems for me to set at a later time. I know a man who could help. Wait at your billets. I will send word when all is in place. You should send your manservant back to your house. I have word from my agents that he is needed there."

We walked along the riverbank, past Billingsgate market which was bustling in preparation for the coming night's activities. Fishing skiffs would come and go all night, unloading their catch to be sold at market in the wee hours, much to the raptured applause of the barking seals, of course. At London Bridge we hailed a cab, and I sent Mango off to return to the house in Bayswater. He seemed quite relieved and eagerly climbed aboard. I tossed him a florin to pay the fare.

The George was a bawdy old public house, just off the High Street. Dawkins told me that playwrights, poets, writers and prostitutes frequented the establishment. He often saw 'ne'er-do-wells, popinjays and cutpurses rubbing shoulders with the likes of cabinet members, high-ranking Metropolitan police officers and officers from the Tower garrison. The public house was surrounded by stew houses where the customers of the George could find temporary solace in the company of unreputable ladies. We removed our disguises, for the arrival of three Episcopalians pushed the boundaries somewhat

We ordered a jug of porter from the amply endowed barmaid, just as a drunken soldier was punched and stumbled past me. I pulled the carpetbag, which had never left my sight, to my chest and covered it with my free arm.

Dawkins signalled us to retire upstairs where we could quietly plan our next step. He led us to his balcony overlooking a busy courtyard. The rabble below was a colourful spectacle. Ladies offered their services to gentleman in their gaudy, revealing dresses while boys dressed as women flirted with gentry. It was a seedy scene. We were leaning against the rail, drinks in-hand, when we saw the unmistakable beard and velvet hat of the most famous author in the land step out from a cab. He paid the cabman and entered the inn to great applause from all those assembled. Could it be Mr Charles Dickens. himself!

The next day, I rose to find Dawkins and Pia eating a breakfast of toast and poached eggs.

I joined them, gulping my warm tea and crunching into cold toast when, without so much as a "by your leave", Dawkins announced, "A note arrived last night. Strickland has contacted us. We are going to have to break into the Tower of London."

I was astounded. "Why Jack? My God, we'll be killed!" I clutched my head.

Pia touched my arm and said. "Listen to what he has to say."

"Simply put," Jack continued, "we cannot just walk in. It will arouse too much suspicion from the nosey Beefeaters. We cannot trust a single one of them. At this stage, the only ones in the know are Mr Strickland, the Lord Chamberlain, the Master of the Mint, Mr Thomas Gipson and us!" Then he added in an excited whisper, "We are going to sneak into the very Tower of London itself!" I swear he giggled at the prospect of this deadly plan.

I wanted to argue against it, but I had signed up for all of this. The mission simply had to be completed, come what may.

I slept fitfully that night, and my own nightmarish yelps woke me up several times.

Later that day, we arrived at a tavern with a bunch of grapes painted on the sign swinging over the door. I knew this tavern well, for it was the very place that Dick Turpin had planned his highway robberies many years before.

The beams were exceptionally low, forcing us to stoop as we entered. The bleakness of exposed brick walls was broken by the odd hanging picture but other than that, the place could not have felt any less welcoming. Huddles of whispering conspirators slouched in every dingy, wooden alcove we passed. They silenced one another and threw us furtive glances as if to bid us on our way. We went to the bar and ordered some ale.

"I'll get theirs," someone said, in a deep baritone voice. A stranger reached his hand down the bar in welcome. "I am the Master of the Royal Mint," he announced, chuckling, as if he barely believed it himself. "Mr. Gipson, at your service, how do you do?" The chap had an eager attitude, coupled with an air of superiority and distinction.

Mr Gipson invited us to join him in a secluded, dimly lit booth. He distributed the porter as we introduced ourselves before leaning into our circle, looking about to make sure no one was eavesdropping, and saying, "A secret passage runs from the basement of the Grapes to the New Mint and beyond".

We were speechless, a secret passage! There was no time for us take it all in. Before we knew it, Mr Gipson had downed his porter in one gulp and was beckoning us to follow him. By the time we had struggled to drain our mugs, he was descending a narrow flight of stairs across the other side of the tavern. We rushed after him, down into the basement where he stood waiting, a candle in a brass holder lighting up his face.

The basement was filled with barrels, broken chairs and tables—the usual items you'd expect from a drinking house. Two oak barrels, at least six feet in diameter, lay on their sides, they had been fitted into the walls.

Mr Gipson pointed to a spare candle and said, "Someone should light that," before reaching down and turning the top on the left barrel. A latch clicked and the barrel opened with a groan. "Follow me!" he said, stepping into the open barrel.

Mr Gipson's silhouette led us through the murk of an old, roughly built tunnel. The walls seemed to sway, this way and that, in the unsteady candlelight, throwing my balance on every step. Dawkins scampered up the rear carrying the second candle. I must admit, I felt vaguely claustrophobic and much relieved when, after ten minutes, the tunnel turned right and began to incline towards a faint glow.

All at once, Mr Gipson pulled up with a jerk. "We have arrived!" he announced in a dramatic flourish.

He unlocked a padlock, and, with a click, the door opened, letting a stream of gaslight beam into the tunnel.

We were in the main building. I couldn't believe it. We climbed up a sweeping spiral staircase. Ginormous portraits of previous Masters of The Mint adorned the walls, including, to my surprise, Sir Isaac Newton. We reached the second floor, and headed into a vast office whose door was painted with gold calligraphy reading:

THOMAS GIPSON

MASTER OF THE MINT

The office was immaculate. Even the paper trays on the mahogany table in the centre of the room were lined up just-so. The wooden frames lining the walls encased notes and coins dating back through the ages. The views through the bay windows, which loomed from floor to ceiling, looked towards the White Tower. Mr Gipson closed the door, locked it and drew the blinds. He turned to address us.

"On my desk, I have a map of the Tower with its various, secret entry tunnels. The best and most important route of entry for you, runs from this building, beneath the moat, under the new Waterloo block and in through the basement of the White Tower. From there, you need to exit the Tower and cross to the Waterloo block, where the Crown Jeweller will be waiting for you. He has already begun moving the important pieces into the cellar of the Waterloo block in preparation. Remember, this remains a fully manned garrison, so you may meet soldiers along the way. They must never find out why you are there. Take the map and wait in my anteroom. I will have refreshments sent up to you, but don't come out until I tell you to. I will lead you down to the basement of the Mint, to the entrance of the Tower when the time is nigh." At that, he rolled up the map and took a short length of red ribbon from his drawer and tied it in a bow around it.

I paced around the anteroom staring at the exhibits without taking in a single thing.

I must have walked that room three times and stared at the same item on display three times without seeing it once.

After all, we were only hours away from the end of our adventure. Once all was said and done, I would be heading home.

I had to force these emotions away and refocus on the task at hand. I sat down in a leather chesterfield across from where Dawkins sat with Pia beside him, a little too close, if you ask me—but you didn't, so I shall keep my thoughts to myself.

"I think I can," I finally whispered. Another long painful silence followed. I hadn't eaten in hours, and my head was aching. I stood up to grab an apple from the fruit bowl the very instant the door opened, and Mr Strickland walked in.

"Something wrong, gentlemen, lady?" he enquired. This man made my skin crawl.

"No," I replied, "We're just tying up a few loose ends."

"Excellent." He pushed one hand deep into his tweed coat pocket. "Here are the keys I had made for you. Please destroy them as soon as you have used them. They cannot fall into the wrong hands. I will be waiting for you in my workshop. The guards are on high alert. There have been several attempts to enter the Tower of London these last few days. In fact, last night we captured a Russian within the Inner Ward." Strickland gave Pia a disdainful look, pointing his twig of a finger. "And what will your task be in all this?"

Pia bristled, but Dawkins pressed his hand into her leg before she could arm herself with some damaging riposte. "We have each been charged with our tasks," he replied. "The requirements have been explained in detail. Pia, I will have you know, is a fully trained Secret Service operative. She has been integral to our mission."

Chapter 24

Once the last of the workers had left for the day and the Mint's Grenadier Guards were stationed at their posts, patrols began roving the building non-stop. Mr Gipson led us quietly, in the pitch black, down into the very depths of the Mint. He was familiar with the patrol's schedule and, from time to time, he glanced at his pocket watch, knowing the precise moments when we needed to hide in some corner out of view of the patrolmen.

Mr Gipson paused at a locked, oak door and drew a mortice key from his waistcoat pocket. He slid the key into the keyhole and turned. The lock was released with a clunk, and the door opened inwards. Mr Gipson's lantern illuminated a narrow storeroom with a wood-panelled set of shelves stacked at one end with rolled-up parchments. He crossed to the shelf and swept aside a selection of parchments before reaching into a secret compartment to release a catch. With a click, the entire parchment case flicked forward, revealing a dark tunnel. Mr Gipson pointed to a hurricane lamp sitting in one corner of the room which he must have planted for us earlier.

"You are going to need this," he said, handing it to me. He then gave Dawkins his lantern.

Gangly strands of moss hung from the low brick above our heads and a constant; dripping plink echoed off the walls. The bricks had deteriorated to such an extent that the external water table had begun pouring in through holes in the walls. If I'd known this would be the case, I would have consulted the tide table before we descended. I had no idea if the tide was ebbing or flowing; if we were going to have to head back this way then there was a chance that, on a full tide, the entire tunnel could fill up. I chased the fear from my mind at once, in the hope that Mr Gipson had taken such contingent factors into account.

We sloshed through the foul river water which had collected on the ground, along with all manner of putrid matter as it swilled about our ankles.

We tripped over rubble and slipped along the slimy floor in an effort to side-step the rats which scuttled into the crevices between rotten chunks of broken brick, squeaking out their warning alarms to their friends. Would this never end?

Our splashes echoed along the chamber walls and the yellow light danced along the walls, accentuating Pia strident shadow, making her seem like a goddess of might, perseverance and stamina.

A door! At long last. In their eagerness to avoid our blinding light, piles of rats had gathered in the far corner.

If we opened the door into the White Tower, we'd let in a thousand rats and in doing so, give ourselves away. We sidled up against one wall to give them an escape route back from where we had come, and they duly obliged. I wondered how many kings and queens had escaped through this tunnel during the medieval wars.

Pia stepped forward to unlock the ancient oak door with the key Mr Strickland had provided.

She turned the lock and pushed with the flat of her hand, but it barely opened a wink. She tried again, with two arms this time. Nothing, it hardly budged. Dawkins and I then put our shoulders against it and the door sprang open violently, knocking over a suit of armour which had been strategically placed in that spot to hide the doorway. What a catastrophe. The clamour of the hollow cuirass, the helmet, bevor and greaves plates as they cascaded over the wooden floor was deafening, and sure to herald our arrival all over London. One piece—the breastplate—spun for what seemed forever, as loudly as a cymbal clash.

It wasn't until we were all in the chamber and I had hidden our lamp behind the open door, that we noticed the glow of an oil lamp over on the opposite wall. We froze on the spot, readying ourselves for a potential attack.

As our eyes grew accustomed to the dimly lit space we gazed around at an enormous collection of partisans, halberds and armour, and, a dozing Beefeater, passed out on his watchman's chair, despite the expressly designed discomfort of the slanted, un-upholstered seat which should have made sleep impossible. Still, there he was, he hadn't fallen to the ground the instant he dozed off as one would expect. His chubby cheeks billowed in and out and his nose twitched from side to side. The clatter had barely roused him—or anyone from what we could tell— though his white beard and moustache did bristle slightly, and he murmured something to the effect of: "Who's there?" But soon enough, he was back in the land of nod. The empty bottle of port by his side explained a few things. As did the pewter mug in his right hand, which was tilted at a jaunty angle and dripped red liquid into a puddle upon the floorboards. Dawkins signalled to us to remove our wet shoes to stop us leaving footprints across the wooden floor.

We closed the oak door, stood the fallen mannequin up into position and tiptoed across the chamber to a set of stairs. At the top of the stairs, we were confronted by a massive exhibition of battle weaponry. Walking past all that armour, most especially past the infamous Giant of Hanover, I couldn't help imagining their obscured eyes behind those visors, following us. A haunting moment indeed. The elephant's armour was particularly impressive.

Once we reached the door to the north of the White Tower, Pia stepped forward with her master key.

A cold mist was descending, merging with the city smoke, haunting the Broad Walk beneath a translucent half-moon; I could barely discern the outline of Sir Arthur Wellesley's statue. Lamps lit with whale oil gave the walls an orange glow. A leaky drainpipe plopped into a puddle like the pulse of the Tower's heartbeat. The place seemed empty.

At this point we had come to a stalemate. We had to get into the Wakefield Tower to deposit the jewels. I had just started to cross the Broad Walk when a soldier's voice called out.

I couldn't see him, but I could tell he was close by.

"Halt!" he bellowed.

Pia and Dawkins retreated silently into the shadows. I did as he ordered.

"Who comes there?"

I had to think quickly. "Surgeon Twist," I replied, hopefully.

"Advance one and be recognised!" the sentry ordered.

It wasn't until I had stepped forward, out of the gloom that I could see the sentry was not alone; he was accompanied by an officer.

"My God! Hello, Oliver. Thank God, you are here." An oil lamp illuminated none other than the cheeky grin of my old friend, Merrick-Jones.

"Merrick-Jones! My dear man." I heaved a sigh. "What a relief. So good to see you. You're back on duty, though, and so soon?"

"I'm glad you are here," he replied, just as relieved as I, it seemed. "The Colonel is ill, and the regimental doctor is out of the Tower. Please, would you follow me?" Of course, I had to follow, it was the most sensible thing to do. Pia and Dawkins remained silent and invisible.

We walked a few yards across the Broad Walk to the main door of the Waterloo block and pulled on the bell.

A soldier opened the door and ushered me in. "Are you the surgeon?" he asked.

"Yes," I said. "Where is the patient?"

We were bustled down to the end of a corridor and into an office where, Colonel Merrick-Jones, the Lieutenant's father lay prostrate on the couch.

The Colonel was sweating and breathing very heavily. Lieutenant Merrick-Jones turned to the other soldier and ordered him to fetch a glass of water. The soldier saluted and ran out, slamming the door behind him.

The instant we were alone, the Colonel recovered at once and stretched across to bang his cane on an adjacent door. A few seconds later, Mr Strickland cautiously appeared at the door. Mr Strickland nodded to the Colonel who nodded back, and Strickland slipped back through the door.

On hearing a knock, the Colonel repositioned himself and beckoned me over. Of course, I had worked out what was going on by now, and postured tending to the Colonel as the soldier entered with his glass of water.

Lieutenant Merrick-Jones addressed the soldier. "Thank you, carry on with your duties."

In the minutes that I had been with the Colonel I wondered how Pia and Dawkins, still carrying the bag full of jewels, were working out how to deliver them to Mr Strickland without being caught.

However, I was swiftly led down into the cellars of the Waterloo block and made my way to Strickland's workshop. Various crowns, orbs, sceptres and swords were laid out on display. Several glass cases were empty as they awaited the authentic articles. I noticed that someone had already extracted a number of paste stones and collected the fakes into a pile.

Strickland entered the room with a bag exactly like the one Dawkins was carrying.

"Your Colleague, Pia, is quite remarkable," he said. "She is like a cat. She clambered along the narrow wall and climbed down behind the Wakefield Tower where I was waiting at the bottom. She shimmied down a drainpipe and delivered the bag.

And then straight back up the pipe in an instant and over Salvin's bridge and that was the last I saw of her."

He emptied the contents of the bag on the table and started to take out each jewel from its individual package. Quickly he matched the gems to the relevant crowns. I watched, marvelling at his diligence and skill whilst he went about his business; my respect for his talent and passion was almost begrudged.

He completed the first crown and sat back in smug satisfaction, admiring his own work. "You can keep those if you want," he said with disdain, flicking his hand toward the discarded pile of fakes and instinctively I scooped up the lot. Strickland thanked me and asked me to pass on my thanks to Pia and Dawkins, wherever they were.

Now that I had my medical alibi, leaving the Tower was a lot simpler than it had been to get in. I strolled out of the Waterloo block and down the Broad Walk steps. Yeoman Warder Woolnough was the Watchman on duty. He agreed to release me, though most reluctantly.

"In all my years… never seen anything like it in my life…" he muttered, jingling his keys. He had not seen us enter in the first place, and he was clearly befuddled by this. He shrugged it off, in any case, slamming the picket gate shut behind us, with more disgruntled muttering, as we strode the fifty yards to the Middle Tower.

The Corporal of the Guard of the Middle Tower saluted me and opened the second picket gate.

"Terribly sorry. Terribly sorry to unduly delay your exit," he said, beads of sweat appearing on his brow. "Please, excuse me, this must be the one. Yes!"

The small picket gate sighed open, at long last, and I bid the Tower of London farewell, relieved to be living another day, limbs intact, head attached and free to enjoy my liberty.

"Oliver," hissed a voice I recognised, and Dawkins emerged from behind a London plain tree. "Is it done?"

"Yes, but how did you get out?"

"Once Merrick Jones had found you we stayed in the shadows and quickly realised we had to complete the mission and slipped back up the stairs. I picked the lock that led out on to the ruins of the Coldharbour Tower. Pia did the rest; she has the skills to navigate the Tower at height while I worked on an escape plan."

"Strickland told me how you delivered the Jewels but how did you both escape?" I asked.

"While Pia was climbing, I slipped out and around to the Watergate and there was a boat tied up. The guards are trying to keep people out; they were not expecting anyone to escape. After all, there are no prisoners here at the moment. I untied the boat and picked the padlock to the gate. Pia arrived and we rowed up to Sugar Keys and tied up, simple."

Dawkins suggested we hail a cab from Fenchurch Street. I was aware that this would mean trudging an extra two hundred yards, but I trusted his local knowledge, as he had regularly walked this area.

Chapter 25

It was about ten-thirty at night. Black plumes of smoke belched from thousands of chimneys, intermingling with thick fog and cloaking the city under a leaden blanket, matched only by the weight of my heart which sank deeper and deeper in anticipation of our clan's imminent parting, for we were like family by now.

I hailed down a hansom cab. "Take us to the corner of Pye Alley and Cock Lane, please," Dawkins said.

"Just by the Fortune of War tavern," Pia added.

After everything we'd been through, it felt odd to be seeing London through the window of a cab once again. After a brief ride, we halted before a statue of a golden boy which was mounted on the corner of the tavern. This was where Dawkins and Pia now lived.

I descended the carriage before the others and bid them farewell. Pia held me in a long embrace, and I shut my eyes to take in the caramel scent of her, a moment which would last forever. Dawkins clutched my hands in his.

"We'll be in touch very soon," he said in a deep voice, and he seemed genuinely sorry to be saying goodbye. Astonishingly, he tossed me a black velvet pouch secured with a drawstring. I caught it in one hand.

As they walked towards the tavern, I noticed two men approach them from a side alley. The four of them began chatting in a friendly enough manner and I paid them no mind.

I couldn't wait to open the mysterious sack. Inside it was a fortune worth of diamonds, rubies and two magnificent Russian emeralds. I had heard that the City of London Corporation had begun widening certain streets and wanted to see if they had finally knocked down those horrendous buildings in the slums of Holborn. I climbed back into the cab and told him to take me home via Holborn.

I had spent many a horrific year during my childhood in the notorious Tyndale buildings and, much to my disappointment (and surprise), they were still standing and, to my mind, in even worse disrepair than they had been some twenty years hence. The City of London Corporation had not destroyed a single one of the twenty-two buildings surrounding that small, squalid central courtyard. "Dreary" would be an understatement to describe this uninhabitable quagmire.

I knew from my regular visits with Anna and my own early life that the basements had been turned into a stench-ridden refuse tip and, at times, they even dug their own cesspits there which were infested with all manner of vermin. The stairs and bannisters were battered and unstable, the ceiling plaster was crumbling, mouldy wallpaper peeled off the walls like flaking dead skin. Despite the late hour, lice-ridden children frolicked in the grubby corridors. Both men and women defecated in hapless corners of the yard.

The public privy, it seemed, had not been emptied in quite some time. The very same hole in the roof that Mrs Barthelemy had fallen through whilst trying to escape her furious husband two years before, had still not been repaired. The water in the yard-well was fetid and black as pitch. Unspeakable filth seeped in through its sidewalls, brewing up a toxic stew of cholera, typhoid and every other waterborne disease known to man and beast. Several houses were made up of only two rooms, with several families therein, and no ventilation. What with the foul ditches, open sewers and broken drains, the stink almost had me dry retching, it was so offensive. That is saying something, given that I had spent so much time on the battlefield and surmounted all the hardship I had. Some chemical reaction between the hydrogen sulphide gas in the sewer and the lead from the flaking paint on the window frames must have taken place. They had turned a brown in colour, not unlike the hue of faeces.

The human faces which stared out at me from this world had sunken eyes, shrivelled, papery skin and little to no hope in their souls by the looks of them.

Most of the adults' only escape was to sink into a drunken, gin-soaked mire—a habit which only prostitution could underwrite. It was evident that scabies, lice, filth and venereal disease were part of their quotidian existence, as was infant mortality. In fact, it was likely that some of these poor souls stooped so low as to kill their own babies to sell the clothes off their backs in order to afford the solace of their temporary utopia. Life was cheap here—as cheap as gin.

As I squeezed the velvet bag in my pocket and felt the reassuring hard points of the diamonds Dawkins had given me, I resolved, right then and there, to do something about this squalor—the very same squalor that had killed my beautiful wife.

My heart leapt as I entered Bayswater Road and saw the home I had left two years before. I paid the cabbie handsomely and, as I crossed the street, I stooped to pick up a child's black, woollen mitten from the pavement. I placed it carefully upon the spear-like railings which fenced my house. Satisfied it was secured; I climbed the steps to my front door.

The light was on in the drawing room, and a plume of welcoming smoke rose from my chimney. Oh good, it'll be nice and warm, I thought.

It was eight thirty in the evening and the chilly bite of spring nipped the air. Despite this, the curtains were not yet drawn. Even more alarmingly, the sash windows had been left wide open. My mouth went dry. I swallowed. I fumbled for my key and went to unlock the door—it was already unlocked. I scurried into my dimly lit hall with a ghastly sense of foreboding.

It may have been beeswax or cedar. Perhaps it was sandalwood. Whatever the smell was, it represented cleanliness and care, the familiar scent of a well-run house.

I reached into my inside breast pocket and clutched at my pistol. I drew it out and pulled back the hammer which locked into position with a quiet click. I pulled a percussion cap out of my waistcoat and slid it over the tube protruding from the top of the barrel.

I slipped my shoes off and tiptoed past the portraits of my late benefactor and my dearly departed wife.

Their soulful eyes followed all the way down the hall. The door to the drawing room was ajar. I stopped to peer through the gap between the door and the hinge on the frame. Mrs McNeil was seated on the drawing room chair in dim lamplight, rocking and murmuring to herself,

Then I saw it. The end of a pistol barrel, pointing at Mrs McNeil!

"Come in, Oliver," came a familiar Russian voice.

I entered; my pistol aimed directly at the left temple of my father-in-law.

"Give it up, Sawinov," I said. "The game is done. The jewels are back where they belong, and the war is over. There is no need for any more bloodshed now." Mrs McNeil let out a sob.

Sawinov never looked at me. "Hand over the emeralds which accompany this," he said. He reached into his pocket and drew out the pendant with the emerald. From the shadows behind me came a loud click, the sound of a pistol hammer being drawn back and engaging in its lock, right beside my head.

"This is not about the game, Oliver. It's about revenge." Vladimir stepped into the warm lamplight glow, and I begrudgingly lowered my weapon.

My left hand was by my left coat pocket. I reached in, pulled out a handful of the paste stones and asked, "Do you mean these?" In a flash, I tossed the stones in a loop over the Count's head. His eyes followed the stones, hoping to catch his quarry. They landed with a whiz and a crack, and Sawinov lurched forward, slumped to his knees, and tumbled prostrate onto the carpet. A hole the size of a crown appeared in his forehead. It pumped one glug of blood, then two until after just a few seconds, it flowed like a torrent, announcing the Count's death.

His eyes stared vacant, and soul-less at the fire.

I turned ninety degrees to face Vladimir. The pistol in his right hand was aimed at me, but he was staring at the dead Count as if he had never before seen a dead man.

I grabbed the opportunity to reach out and twist the pistol away. As I turned, Mrs McNeil threw back the swaddling clothes to reveal a sawn-off shotgun. She fired directly at him, a shot whizzed by but firing a gun covered with a blanket is no precise art and the main blast missed its target. Vladimir pushed past me. He must have been grazed by the bullet for he clutched at a bleeding ear. As he turned to run, he was blocked by two burly policeman who charged through the doorway. Quick as a rat, he about-faced and scampered up the stairs.

Mrs McNeil stood up, and I marvelled at how a little taller she was than I recalled. I was stupefied to watch her throw the bundle, onto the floor, and almost reached down to rescue it. But then she ripped off her mop of false hair, removed her teeth and began stripping off her oversized clothes, revealing none other than Mango!

Dawkins emerged from behind the two policemen, holding a sharpshooter rifle.

"Is everyone alright?" he cried.

"Not everyone," I replied, pointing to the old man on the floor.

Dawkins turned to the policemen. "Check the body and collect all evidence for the coroner's court statements," he ordered. "Here's the rifle that killed him," he added, handing the weapon over.

"He went up the stairs," I shouted. "Follow me."

Pia and Dawkins flashed the policemen their warrant cards and followed me. Mango huffled and puffled up the stairs behind us, struggling under the awkward weight of Mrs McNeil's bulky petticoats.

Now the fog had cleared, the bloody trail of Vladimir's wounds was easy to follow; the eager messenger led us through every room, all the way up to Mango's quarters on the very top floor. Mango's door was ajar, and the only light penetrating the room came from the ambient glow of London through an open dormer window. Clothes had been tossed hither and thither. A smear on the architrave around the hinges of the window indicated that Vladimir had fled through the window.

I was the first to nervously peer out. Even in that half-light, I could spot the glimmer of fresh blood trickling along the slate tiles of the roof. My eyes followed the stream to a chimney, where Vladimir's swaying silhouette was bent over double. He was still trying to stem the blood and clutching at the house lightning-rod with his free hand. He seemed barely conscious, due to blood loss no doubt.

"There's something you should know, Oliver," he murmured.

I climbed out after him and crawled across towards him.

"All this time… you thought Mango had… given you away…" he was slurring his words now. "It wasn't him. It was me who ran into Welch that night in Winchester School House. It was me who saw your feet under the bed. And it was me who gave you away."

He threw his head back and laughed, but the motion unbalanced him completely and he lost hold of the rod. He fell with a crash onto the roof before sliding down the blood-greased slate tiles. Desperate to find a finger-hole to prevent his slow slide, he panicked, but this only increased the speed of his descent.

I surged forward to try to help him, but Dawkins grabbed me. Pia, in turn, grabbed Dawkins by the waist. Mango too, hauled himself through the window frame, to join us as we witnessed the pathetic spectacle of this doomed man.

"Help me, for God's sake!" he screamed. His legs were over the edge, sliding toward his abyss. "Help me! Where's your compassion?"

His body stopped sliding. He was almost completely over the side of the roof, hanging from the gutter with both hands, blood pouring down the right side of his face.

We gingerly crossed the slanted roof to stand over him. Peering five floors down I spied the spearheaded, black-iron railings which were bared like a row of deadly fangs.

We stared at the terrified Vladimir as he hung helplessly at the end of his desperate life.

A huddle of bystanders had gathered below. They pointed up, aghast at the scene. A policeman pushed them back.

I am almost certain that I saw one man pass another some money.

"Please, Oliver, please!" Vladimir cried.

By now, Mango had secured himself to the chimney and he had a strong grip on my belt. I stood motionless, calculating my next action as I looked deep into his pleading eyes. I recalled the good times. It was in that moment, with his eyes wide open in anguish, in agony.

As I edged forward and reached down to grasp Vladimir's hand, a boot flashed out and kicked Vladimir's fingers from their grip. He plummeted from the house, to be impaled on my beloved railings, lanced through the abdomen and chest.

His body stood upright. He resembled some ghoulish waxwork. His mouth opened and shut a few times. His head moved mechanically, from left to right, like an automaton or a puppet, and then slumped over like Pulcinella without his hand operator.

A gentle breeze was blowing the fog down my street, and I noticed the glove on the railing was waving. We stared, in shock and immobile for several moments before climbing, in silence, back through the window.

Back in the drawing room, I was shaking, I poured myself and Dawkins a stiff drink and Pia a sherry. I was still in a dilemma. My former best friend turned nemesis was dead. Murdered by one of our own. But why? On seeing how perplexed I was, Dawkins pulled me aside to explain how this entire event had come to unfold.

"Oliver, when you dropped us home, a messenger was waiting. He told me that when our telegram arrived from Antwerp, agents were assigned to track Count Sawinov's every move. The agents got wind of his plan to take Mrs McNeil hostage in order to force you to give up the Russian emeralds. We simply had to step in. Some of my men followed you when you detoured to the Tyndale slum, and so we raced here during that time to exchange Mrs McNeil with Mango and the shotgun bundle."

Pia came over and put her hand on my shoulder.

"Mango had been impersonating Mrs McNeil for years," she added. "He was brilliant, wouldn't you say? Even you couldn't tell the difference from behind in the half-light." She beamed with pride, which gave me the impression that Mango's involvement may have been her idea. "I'll be back in a moment," Pia said, before slipping out the door.

Dawkins continued, "After we had prepared the room, Pia and I observed the house from across the street, on the roof of Crystal Palace's forecourt." Suddenly, a Metropolitan Police inspector marched into the room. All the policemen acknowledged him with a salute.

"Good evening, I am Inspector Fowler," he said, and immediately took charge, delegating duties and sending errand runners about.

He began taking statements. I must say, he seemed sceptical from the outset. And rightly so, for it was an outlandish story.

Even I will attest to how preposterous the scene seemed on the surface of things but as they say, the truth is stranger than fiction. In any case, as soon as Dawkins showed his warrant badge, the inspector about turned. "I am satisfied with the statements," he announced,

Epilogue

Several weeks later, Dawkins, Pia, and I were invited to Buckingham Palace to receive personal thanks from Her Majesty, Queen Victoria, and His Royal Highness, Prince Albert. Even Dawkins, "the unflappable" sweated and fidgeted as he paced up and down the lavish corridor, mumbling incoherently to himself.

"What on earth is the matter with you?" I asked.

"I'm really nervous," he confided with a heavy sigh. "I've never been in the company of royalty. I'm afraid of making a fool of myself."

A footman entered, carrying a silver salver with a teapot, sugar bowl, and milk jug upon it. He bowed to Dawkins and asked, "Earl Grey?"

Startled, Dawkins replied with a deep bow, "Sergeant Jack Dawkins, actually."

Mrs McNeil, wearing a new dress and hat, put on airs the likes of which I had never seen. Lt. Merrick-Jones seemed utterly overawed by the event, whereas Mr Gipson, who had commissioned a florin with a new type of crown as a subtle nod to our achievements—was the only one who seemed accustomed to such company as this. He held himself with the utmost distinction and poise of a gentleman. As for Mango, he looked simply ridiculous in his ill-fitting suit. My pulse began to race as I looked around at this mixed bag of guests. What a tremendous feat we had achieved.

Another round of high tea appeared, which included sandwiches, dainty cakes and biscuits from the Palace kitchen. Then, the door swung open, and in strutted Prince Albert and his entourage. We were overwhelmed by a barrage of questions, particularly from the prince himself.

We took turns recounting our adventures, and Prince Albert clapped with fierce enthusiasm at certain points in the story.

"My lord!" he exclaimed in his Saxe-Coburg accent. "Bravo!" he declared, slapping his thigh during a more animated turn of events. At other moments, he stared aghast and slack-jawed, moaning, "Noooo!"

After Tea, it was announced to us that we were each awarded the Member of the Victorian Order—a personal gift from the monarch herself. As we left the palace, we were greeted by a cheering crowd, although they would not have had a clue why we were there.

A sergeant bellowed, "Make way for the Queen's guard!" and his small squad of soldiers marched smartly past. At first, the sergeant flicked me an admiring glance, but his admiration changed to confusion when my face struck him as somehow familiar. We climbed into the cab.

"Well done, Oliver," Dawkins said. "You have made quite a journey, and no mistake. It's good to have you back."

"For a while there," Pia added, "I thought we had lost you to the poppies."

Of course, she was right, beyond the thousands of miles we had travelled, the great dangers we had faced, the barriers we had broken down, the conundrums we had solved by sheer force of ingenuity, it was the distance within my very soul that which had withstood the greatest challenges and seemingly insurmountable obstacles.

For that, I owed Dawkins and Pia my life. I had forgiven Mango, and, in doing so, my pessimistic outlook had softened. A sense of humility, a quality I had long been blind to, had replaced my singular solipsism and selfishness. Even my former cowardice, made evident by those pathetic addictions where I hid my true potential, had been usurped by the virtue of faith—an inner force and mystical power no man can truly name, but which I will call God.

Other transformations took place in my life. My newfound wealth enabled a more philanthropic outlook and inspired me to take active steps towards rehousing the tenants of the Tyndale slum.

I had it knocked down. And new apartments built to last for years were put up in its place.

A few months later, on a warm summer morning, I was preparing for an outing to view the progress of my new building on the old Tyndale slum site. Mango had recently been promoted to Head Footman. He was instructing our new Junior Footman, Bibskin, on his duties when the front doorbell rang, and a nervous Bibskin answered the door.

A tall man in a smart morning dress handed Bibskin his very shiny top hat and grey gloves, along with a card. Bibskin placed the hat and gloves on the hall table and the card on a silver salver.

"The doctor is in. Would you kindly follow me," he said. He then turned and led the tall man into the reception room. "Dr Twist, sir, you have a visitor," he announced, handing me the silver plate.

I picked up the card, which read:

Inspector J.P. Dawkins,

Special Intelligence Agency

I smiled as I looked over the top of my newspaper to the place where Dawkins now stood.

"Hello, Oliver," he said. "Are you ready for another adventure?"

———————————————

Printed in Dunstable, United Kingdom

71028963R00147